THE
DUKE'S SHADOW

LOUISE CHARLES

ACKNOWLEDGEMENTS

I would first like to thank all members of my online writing group, Writers Abroad, for their commitment in critiquing and shaping my debut novel. They are all without doubt, writers in their own right. I hope our journey together goes on and on.

Secondly thanks to Maureen who edited the final version and for picking up all the errors I left behind, any that remain are purely down to me.

Finally to my family for their encouragement and to my friends who were critical in making the final decisions on the cover. I do hope you enjoy the read!

Front cover credits: Sophia Feddersen and GraphicPA stock

To my darling, Simon for your unfaltering belief, love and support.

I could not have done this without you.

CHAPTER ONE

As he rode around the vast estate, William Rupert Leopold Kenilworth recalled the words of his grandmother, long departed – *the worth of a thing is best known by the want of it*. There were definite benefits to being the second son of a Duke; one rarely was in want of anything. Why was it then that he struggled to find a purpose and make the most of his privileged background? He was not unhappy – how could he be? But he was unfulfilled, and the older he became, the more important it was to make his mark, however small.

William's heart skipped a beat as he recalled the plans he had made to go travelling to his younger sister as they rode out together. However, he had not bargained on the tenacity of Lottie who spurred on her mount to catch up with him.

'But, William! Why do you have to go to America? It's such a long way and so dangerous. I may never see you again.'

William brought Autumn Star to a standstill. She was his favourite and he stroked the gleaming coat of conker brown. The horse turned her neck and nuzzled his hand, she was not as tame with any other and he valued her loyalty. He sat back up in his saddle surveying the grounds of Clomber Abbey which spread as far as the eye could see. They were splendid even in late winter, with the trees bare and skeletal, the ground hard beneath the early morning frost still twinkling on the grass.

The plans for the development of the estate were complete. He and his brother, Henry, worked well together but they were different. Henry was loud and confident, William preferred to sit back and observe. And, with Henry preparing to take on the Dukedom, their father had made it known that William was a distraction he could do without. Now William was free to do what he wanted.

'And what about Henry and the racing partnership?' Lottie cried as she slowed her horse and stopped beside him. Her large brown eyes searched his face.

William had given a lot of thought to the racing partnership know as Mr Lyons. Racing gave him such a thrill and he enjoyed watching their fine thoroughbreds race unchallenged for the past three years. It was one of the things he would miss most, but he was using his portion of the growing purse to fund his travels. He wanted to be independent from his family's money so he considered himself free to go where he liked.

'Stop fussing so, Lottie. Henry and I have had our fun. He needs to give his attention to taking over from Father when he—'

'But that's years away! Papa is as fit as a fiddle.'

'Yes, I know, but Henry needs to concentrate on his future and his role in parliament without me sitting on his shirt tails, begging him to come racing. It's time for Henry to settle down to his duties and for me to try something different.'

'But, it's not fair,' sulked Lottie, squirming in her side saddle. Her horse lowered its head to graze, bored with the conversation. 'I shall be left alone with Mother and no-one else who cares!'

'Oh, Lottie. How can you say that? Your season is all mapped out in London. All those exciting balls to go to and young suitors to meet. Just think of all the gowns you will need. You will be shopping until your feet are sore!'

'But why America?' Lottie ignored his platitudes. 'I swear you are trying to get as far away from me as possible. We've always done everything together. You don't understand how much the thought of you going away pains me.'

William smiled at his young sister. It was true they were close. But he wanted more than his rudimentary position within his family. He wanted to experience how other people lived, far away. He wanted to understand a little more about what went on in the rest of the world.

'Well, because I want to see the colonies and meet some fellow architects. They are doing some wonderful things over there, Lottie and an influential and gifted engineer has invited me – he has a project which he wants my opinion on.' William pressed his heels into Autumn Star's soft belly to move on.

'Mother says that they are an uncouth lot,' Lottie said trotting behind him. 'I do wish I could ride astride like you men, sitting side saddle is so unnatural. I'm sure I will never get used to it, no matter how long I ride.'

'Speaking of uncouth, young lady.' William chuckled. 'I've spent most of my life doing nothing and there is so much to see, Lottie. We take our privileged background for granted more often than not and we have plenty of money; it's difficult to find something that one lacks. But to go to America, well who knows what will happen?'

'But you hate meeting new people. You are as shy as a coconut waiting to be knocked off its stand.'

William shifted in his saddle. 'That's not quite true, Lottie. I can hold myself in public as well as any other.' He had fought hard to overcome his boyhood shyness and this would be a great test for him.

'Though I must admit,' William sighed. 'I shall miss Clomber Abbey and being part of the plans to rebuild the stables.'

Lottie pulled her horse still in front of William and fixed him with a stare.

'And what about me? Or is it only your precious nags you fear leaving behind? You shan't miss me at all?' William noticed the small grin tugging at her lips.

'No, I shan't miss you a bit.'

'You scoundrel! I don't believe you. Come on, race you to the duck pond.'

As they spurred their horses on, a young boy stepped out from amongst the large oak trees and stood in their path, sobbing. William and Lottie pulled to a stop and jumped down. Lottie smoothed down the creases of her riding skirt.

'What the devil...' William removed his hat and crouched down in front of the quivering boy. 'Now, calm down. What on earth has happened, young man?'

The boy wiped his snotty nose along his sleeve; Lottie grimaced and pulled a lace handkerchief from her pocket.

'It's me friend, sir.' The boy's bottom lip trembled and huge tears skittered down his dirty face. 'Mister, sir, your Lordship... oh, blimey – she's going to die!' The boy started to howl again. Lottie offered him the cloth, but he stared blankly and shook his head.

'Don't worry about that, where is your friend? Tell us what the matter is and we can help you. I promise.' William spoke in a soft, calming tone.

'It's Sarah Nuttall, we were playing by the pond. We weren't meant to; our mams will thrash us, so they will. But she fell in, sir, and I can't get her out. She can't swim and neither can I!' The boy's voice rose to a crescendo again.

'William, look!' Lottie pointed towards the pond. William could make out two skinny arms waving around and heard a faint shout.

'That's Sarah, she's going to drown!' the boy sobbed and fell to his knees.

William started to run, ripping off his jacket and cravat, then pulling at one boot and the next. Lottie had picked up her skirts and started to follow him.

'Stay with the boy,' William shouted to her.

As he approached the edge of the lake, he could see the young girl was beginning to tire. Her arms were barely keeping her head above water and she was swallowing large mouthfuls. William knew that the lake wasn't deep even at the centre. He waded through the tall bulrushes, stifling a gasp at the icy cold water lapping around his calves.

'Now, keep calm,' William spoke gently but with a firm tone. 'Miss Nuttall, isn't it? You will be all right, I promise.'

He continued to paddle towards her, his toes sinking into the muddy bottom. He focused on the young, spluttering girl until he could stretch out his hand and grabbed her tunic as she began to sink. William pulled her towards him and gathered her small skinny body into his arms. When he returned to the bank, Lottie and the young boy were waiting.

'Oh, my god, she's dead!' sobbed the boy.

'Now don't be hasty,' said William, turning the girl on her side as Lottie knelt to rub her back. 'She's just swallowed a bit of water, that's all.'

He gave Lottie a hasty look and silently sent a quick prayer for her recovery. Seconds later the young girl spluttered and coughed, leaning her head into the grassy bank.

'Thank the Lord!' said the young boy. 'You won't tell, will you?' His face now flushed with fear. 'We're sorry we got into trouble.'

William put his hands on the young boy's shoulders. 'Look, I promise you won't get into any trouble. You did well, getting help when you did. You saved Sarah's life.' The boy's chest puffed out like a proud pigeon. 'Now, you have to take me to Sarah's house, she will need to be checked over.'

Sarah sat up, leaning against Lottie, soaking her riding habit.

'Oh, sir,' she gasped. 'Me dad can't afford the doctor. I'll be all right. Honest, sir.' She tried to scrabble to her feet but her legs buckled. The patched canvas dress that clung to her scrawny body emphasised her tiny stature. Her hair, interspersed with duck weed, resembled ribbons which fell onto her shoulders. William took his jacket and wrapped it around her, then gathered her up into his arms again.

'Nonsense, you are in shock and wet and cold. I'll take you home and explain to your father what happened. There is no need to worry – all will be taken care off. Now, Lottie,' William turned to his sister, 'you take yourself back to the house and change before you catch a chill. Leave my horse tethered here. And, young man, you take me to Mr Nuttall's house.'

The young boy bowed his head and set off in the direction of the workers' cottages at the bottom of the estate.

*

William returned to the main house, feeling a little more than responsible for the very near disaster. He had promised Sarah's father that the fence surrounding the pond would be repaired, though poor Sarah received a smack on the head for her foolishness. Mr Nuttall was one of the men working on reopening the underground tunnels that ran like a warren through the estate and he needed the work with a sixth child on the way. William had assured him that his job was not at risk. As he stood dripping all over their dirt kitchen floor, several pairs of eyes took him in from behind a curtain, which he presumed was the family's sleeping quarters. He made a mental note to speak to Henry about improvements to the workers' cottages.

'William! Oh, William, thank goodness you are back.' Lottie came running through the hall, her skirts gathered in her hands. She had changed from her riding habit but her hair was dishevelled and her face pale and drawn.

'My goodness, Lottie, the young girl is not dead. Just a little shaken. Dr Morris came promptly and gave her something to help her sleep and she's all dry and tucked up in bed.'

'No, William. Something dreadful has happened while we were out riding.' Lottie stuffed her fist into her mouth as tears poured through her fingers.

'But what's happened, what on earth could be so awful—'

'It's H…He…Henry,' Lottie spluttered. 'He's dead!'

*

William waited and watched as his father tried to contain his grief. The old Duke was trying hard not to crumple in front of his son, though the pain was etched into his face. His father was a big man, but to William he seemed to have shrunken overnight. As a child William had sought his comfort without success and he accepted that Henry had been the focus as heir. William had been nothing more than a spare. Their father had spent a large part of his life grooming Henry for his place and now that he had gone, William was left to fill the empty space.

'Father, I know this is difficult.' William concentrated hard, not wanting his stammer to create a greater wedge between them. His father could not bear signs of weakness but the more he tried to drive out William's stutter, the more William struggled to get the words out. He took a deep breath, determined to show that he was strong.

'You know nothing, quite frankly,' his father whispered so that William had to lean in to hear him.

The Duke placed an arm on the fireplace; the other hand shoved deep inside his trouser pocket, and stared deeply into the unlit dark recesses of the hearth. William shivered and wondered why the fire had not been lit.

'Your brother is dead; there is nothing I can do about that. All that work, all that time, spent preparing him… for nothing.' His father choked on his words and brought a hand up to his mouth.

'Henry would have made a great Duke,' William mused aloud and then wished he could swallow his words.

His father looked at him sharply.

'Yes he would have, William. Henry was committed to his legacy, to his inheritance, to this family. It pains me that his loyalty has disappeared along with him. And now I have to start all over again, with you.'

His father searched his face but William could not hold his gaze and could not give him the answers he wanted. William looked at a point on the floor, a Persian carpet with swirling reds, purples and blues, like a large bruise. They stood, father and son, in the silence that stretched between them, two men grieving for different things. William for a life that he had not sought and his father for a son and his successor.

'Your mother,' his father straightened up and walked over to the window. 'The Duchess does not think that you are prepared to commit to the Dukedom, that you are more interested in your horses, the projects here at Clomber and now travelling. Is this true?'

William coughed and stared around the room at the opulent wall hangings, tapestries and portraits of generations of their family. Sour-looking men with stern faces and high foreheads, stiff and unforgiving and women in silk dresses and creamy breasts that he could not tear his gaze from.

'Without doubt, women cannot be relied upon to assess such situations. They are guided by their emotions and their heart.' His father stood tall and erect, his hands clasped behind his back.

William knew that was not what guided his mother, but bit his tongue. He ran a finger round the edge of his shirt collar and dabbed at the beads of sweat that appeared on his forehead.

'Of course I am committed—'

'I don't need words. I need actions. You are far too personable with everyone on the estate. The workers refer to you by first name, dammit! You need to earn respect and others need to learn it and if that means the toe of your boot, then so be it.'

His father was well known for his acerbic words. The servants, particularly the maids, made themselves scarce when he came to the

Abbey, which was infrequent. And his arrogance included his behaviour towards animals, especially horses, which William could not accept. William despised everything his father represented, yet yearned for his approval.

'Henry had a presence, not only here at Clomber Abbey and at Kenilworth House but also in parliament. In the corridors of power, he was well-respected for his views on how our country should be run and what his place was in making sure that those of us more able be given the freedom to make difficult decisions. When was the last time you encountered any such debates?'

William loathed politics – full of stuffy old, self-righteous, pious men with nothing better to do with their time and their holier-than-thou attitudes. He had listened to Henry's views, though. His brother had been an intelligent and passionate man, and had loved the sound of his own voice. William, on the other hand, was not a good public speaker.

William shook his head. 'I haven't, as you know, had the experience that Henry had, but if it is considered part of the Dukedom, then I suppose I will have to learn. I am not stupid, Father, or indeed without views. But, as you know, up until now it has not been required of me. I can hardly be chastised for something I have not been expected to do.' It was the longest speech he had made to his father and William began to regret his loose tongue.

His father stared through him for what seemed like an eternity, yet his face was like a mask. William shuddered as he realised what his father was thinking. That it was William who was dead and Henry was still alive. His father's eyes narrowed as he made no attempt to deny his thoughts. His thick brush moustache twitched with annoyance.

'People like us don't have choices, we have to rise to the legacy that the Kenilworth family have fought for on the battlefields and protect, not only our present but our future too. The Dukedom not only affects the household, but a whole population around us – the workers who depend on us for employment and expect us to provide it always, and more. You are now in charge of that future. You are now their only hope.'

'Yes, Father. I understand. I'm sure once I return from—'

William checked himself as he saw his father raise an eyebrow, sensing the heat of his anger.

'Do you really believe you can continue with your plans to travel? Pah!' His father sneered and marched over to him, his face so close to William's he could feel the spittle on his face as he spoke.

'You are now the future Duke of Romsey and you will start acting like one.

CHAPTER TWO

William paced the room, his eyes fixed on the tips of his polished boots. Kenilworth House in London was the family's city residence. The drawing room was small and dark, unlike the huge space at their estate at Clomber Abbey. The smaller spaces and lower ceiling always gave him a sense of being trapped with little hope for escape. William strode over to the window, opened it wide and breathed in deeply. He had received a summons from his mother, the Duchess, to discuss the future. It had been six months to the day since a riding accident had changed his life and the funeral still burned fresh in William's mind.

A cough interrupted his thoughts. He looked up to see Mabbot, his valet, standing at the doorway.

'Yes, what is it?'

Mabbot stood as still as a stork. 'Your mother wishes to see you in the library, m'lord.'

'Oh, must I?' William muttered and began to pace again.

'It might be for the best, sir. Sooner done, the better.' Mabbot lowered his voice and his gaze.

'Yes, of course, you are right. But first, pour me a brandy.'

Mabbot hovered across the room like a spectre and stopped at a small walnut table. He poured a small measure of the rich amber liquid into a large snifter and handed it to William. The young master thanked him, swirled the contents around the large glass with a deft flick of his hand and drank it in one gulp. William winced.

'Best not keep the Duchess waiting much longer, sir.'

'Another minute won't hurt, Mabbot.' William combed his hand through the thick silver-white streak in his otherwise raven dark hair and checked his appearance in the large gilt-edged mirror above the fireplace. He looked tired and his right eyelid drooped even more than usual. The damaged muscle had never recovered after his difficult entry into the world. He ran a finger along the starched collar of his linen shirt and brushed at some imaginary dust on the shoulders of his black frock coat.

Mabbot bowed and left the room, leaving the door slightly ajar.

Audiences with his mother, the Duchess of Romsey had been very rare all through his childhood. He had been more than happy with the company of Nanny Simpkins and her welcoming arms and soft ample bosom. Since he had grown up, his two passions – attending the opera and running his horse racing partnership with Henry – meant he had little time for family gatherings.

William stared at a portrait of his brother, completed the previous year. The bite of the brandy settled at the base of his throat.

'Goddamn you, Henry!' he muttered. 'How inconsiderate of you to leave…'

Mabbot appeared in the doorway and tapped on the door.

'Yes, Mabbot, I am on my way.'

'Her Grace is here.' Mabbot neatly stepped aside as a swish of full black silk skirts brushed the top of his shoes.

'Thank you, Mabbot. You may leave us.'

The Duchess regarded her second son with steel grey eyes. Her hair was pinned back in a severe chignon, the skin pulled taut around her face.

'You've been drinking.' She swept past him and poured herself a small sherry.

'Only a brandy, I have had an upset stomach.'

'You are still grieving?' His mother arched an eyebrow.

'Well of course I am, Mother. Henry was my brother and his loss has been hard to understand.'

'The consequences are more far-reaching than your distress. As you have known for the last six months, you now have to take your responsibilities seriously.'

'I think I have.' William kicked at the fringe of a Persian rug. Why did she always make him feel so small? 'But the role of Duke was always Henry's. It's not something I was ever meant to be. I'm picking things up and spending times with Father, when he is able.'

'To be fair, William, you have always avoided your responsibilities and relied on your so-called – delicate – nature, and your sister, to get you out of trouble. Things are not moving quickly enough. You need to be making much more progress.' She sat down in a large wing chair and indicated with her hand that he should sit opposite her. William closed his eyes, breathed in and swallowed the retort he would like to make.

'Mother, I am sure we have plenty of time to talk about—'

'There is no time like the present,' she snapped. 'And anyway, I do not want you scurrying back to Clomber Abbey and your precious horses before I have had chance to talk to you.'

William flicked up the tails of his frock coat before sitting. 'No, Mother, of course.' It was pointless arguing, the sooner he listened to what she had to say, the sooner he could escape.

The Duchess nodded. 'Your father has taken it all rather badly. But I am sure now that the funeral and all the legal arrangements are over, things will get back to normal.'

William stared at the lace antimacassar behind his mother's head. Did she feel nothing about the death of her eldest son, heir to the Dukedom? What would ever be normal again?

'For you,' she said as if reading his mind, 'nothing will ever be the same again. Nevertheless, it is now your destiny to be the heir. You must get on with the tasks in hand and give your family the attention that it deserves. Your father and I expect no less.'

'But, Mother, Henry has… had been prepared for this role from the day he was born! It is such a responsibility and I do want to do it right.' If William were honest he wasn't ready for such ties on his time. He had set his heart on travelling and not only was he grieving for his brother but also for the experience of a lifetime he would probably never see.

'Do you think you are alone in your anxieties, or that there is only yourself to think of? Your precious riding stud and the opera have been your 'responsibilities' up until now. And your plans to travel were decadent and foolish. On the death of your father…' his mother looked at him without a flicker of emotion. 'You will become the fifth Duke of Romsey, whether you like it or not.'

She stood up. William sighed and stood up to face her.

'Really, William, it is time you settled down and took your life seriously. As future Duke you have many responsibilities; the running of the estate and the welfare of the workers, not to mention your role as a figurehead in society. You are thirty-four years of age and have very little to show for it. Your father needs assurances that you will embrace your new position in this family and make sure that you carry out your duties as expected.' She mentioned nothing of his time served in the army. It was as if he had not existed until now.

'Yes, Mother. Father can rely on me.'

'And the first thing we must do, William, is to secure you a suitable wife.'

The Duchess gathered her skirt in one hand and swept out of the room.

William smiled. A wife – maybe now was the right time to make that proposal. It was fortunate he had tickets for the opera on Friday evening.

*

William sat in their family box, with a perfect view of the stage. He was dressed in full evening attire, persuaded by Charlotte, his adventurous young sister, to try a more modern cut. He preferred his tall hat and his breeches and was not at all sure he liked the shorter jacket, tapered trousers and a hat that looked as if someone had sat on it. A silver cane stood against the back of his chair and he held out the hat and gloves to Mabbot.

'Lady Charlotte is on her way up, sir,' Mabbot whispered. William waved a hand in acknowledgement. William had refused the usual companion of a footman. Mabbot was used to his ways and tonight was important. The orchestra was warming up, a cacophony of strings, brass and percussion filled the air with a raw, uncoordinated sound. He scanned the theatre, and a low mumble of excited conversation rumbled beneath the squeaks from the music pit. A bell sounded once amidst the continued mumbling of the audience. William's heart pounded like a drum in his chest and he willed everyone to be silent but knew such was not the way of the opera.

He leant forward, his chin resting lightly on the pyramid made by his hands, and concentrated on centre stage.

'Psst! Dear, William. Apologies, I am late.' William stood and guided his youngest sister into the seat next to him. Barely a year separated them. Her pale skin burnished with excitement and her golden locks of hair fell like corkscrews on her long neck. William was reminded of one of the china dolls she kept in her cabinet. But to him, she was his confidante and best friend. They had grown up together, lost in the vast corridors of Clomber Abbey where their status in the family ranking had been unimportant, until now.

'I met a dear friend from finishing school, you remember that dreadful place?' She pulled a face. 'No, of course you don't, no-one visited me, despite my squeals for help! Well, she didn't stop talking.' William handed her a champagne flute from a small table by his chair. Lottie leaned towards the balcony edge. 'She's with her beau.' She surveyed the auditorium, pointing with her glass. 'Somewhere down there, a rather dashing young gentleman from Somerset, of all places. I must introduce you in the interval.'

'For heaven's sake, Lottie, do be quiet.' William grasped her arm. 'It is about to start.'

Fanny Kendrick stepped out onto centre stage, dressed as Aeolia, the mountain sylph with magical powers. She waved a tiny wand in one hand and transfixed William in an instant. Golden harps, the instruments of seduction, adorned her head, securing her hair away from her face. William stared spellbound at the image in front of him as the first aria took flight. Her dark coal eyes gave her a cunning feline look and long eyelashes fluttered like excited butterflies. Her full lips were painted cherry red, a stark contrast against the pale face makeup. The sylph sang and sang, her strong voice pushing its way through the confines of the tight bodice, which William imagined hid the beauty mark. The tiny heart shaped beauty mark, which rose and fell at every breath.

When Fanny was off stage, William gazed around the large auditorium decorated in lush gold and burgundy coloured flock wallpaper. The huge arched ceiling above the gallery rose skywards, fading into darkness; it was impossible to see the top. The dim gaslights, which burned throughout the performance, gave off a stuffy, stale smell, but tonight William did not object. The flat scene, painted on a stretched canvass behind the performers, provided a mountain backdrop with a Wedgewood blue sky and a small stream tumbling its way across a line of stones. As Act One approached its crescendo, Fanny appeared back on stage to spirit away the shepherd Aeolia loves, on the day of his wedding to another. Her soprano voice at the top of its range filled the theatre with such power that the notes bounced around William's head as he imagined her declaring that love for him alone.

A commotion in the stalls interrupted William's desires and he glared into the crowds below. A group of latecomers, in keeping with fashionable opera behaviour, pushed and shoved their way through to a line of empty seats. William resisted the urge to shout at them to be quiet; he had often been late, but never, ever, to one of Fanny's performances. As they settled down, William returned his attention to Act Two.

After the final note and a happy ending, the audience was on its feet, with deafening applause and shouts of bravo. William tried to catch the attention of Fanny who curtsied to the crowd. Flowers thrown from the audience lay scattered at her feet and then as the heavy folds of red velvet began to fall, she turned to his box and blew him a kiss. William breathed a sigh of relief. He straightened his cuffs, tightened the silk cravat around his neck and smoothed the creases in his trousers.

Mabbot lingered in the back. 'Lady Charlotte says she will meet you in the foyer.' William hadn't noticed her departure.

'Mabbot, you are dismissed. Tell Lady Charlotte I have business to attend to and take her home. I shall see her in the morning.'

'Certainly, sir. Do you wish me to return for you? Or should I send the driver—'

'No, Mabbot. I am perfectly capable of finding my own way.'

The audience began to leave, weaving their way through the seats. Laughter and chatter trickled away until the theatre fell into a graveyard silence. William stared into the inky darkness of the theatre, trying to calm the flutters in his stomach. He pulled out a small dark blue velvet box from his top pocket and opened the lid, then ran the tip of his finger around the contours of a large diamond. It was a family heirloom which had been waiting in the vaults of their jewellers for decades, for this very moment

No time like the present. Indeed, Mother, he thought as he followed the stairs down into the dark recesses of the back stage. He paused outside the dressing room of Miss Fanny Kendrick, her name etched on a small wooden plaque. He tapped twice with his stick before entering.

As William closed the door, a figure appeared from the shadows in the corridor. The Duchess of Romsey smiled wryly and turned to leave.

CHAPTER THREE

Fanny returned to her dressing room grateful for the hour she had until the reception. The exhilaration following a performance gave her the butterflies for some time after, her blood running hot and passionate. As her dresser fussed around her, uncoupling buttons and hanging her costume, Fanny relived the evening. She had not expected to see William in his family's box tonight but then she never did know when he would appear. Thank goodness she had not made arrangements with anyone else. William could be a little possessive and, if she were honest, she liked the attention from one of such standing. With that in mind, she dismissed her dresser insisting that she could manage, and started to loosen the pins in her hair.

A few moments later the door swung open and Fanny swivelled round, a broad smile to welcome William.

'Miss Kendrick?' A woman stepped into the room wrinkling her nose as if there was a bad smell. Dressed from head to toe in expensive black silk, she carried a black frilled umbrella. She lifted the veil covering her face, and displayed a strong aquiline nose and small, beady eyes, which together gave the expression of an irate mother eagle.

'Well, that depends on who is asking.' Fanny stood in her chemise, bone stays and a pair of cream leather button up boots. Her semi-nakedness did not embarrass her. The unannounced visitor stifled a gasp and narrowed her eyes but did not look away.

'Oh, I'm sorry. I don't mean to offend you but if you go barging through dressing room doors, you never know what you may find. Excuse me.' She grabbed a dusty pink silk robe and threw it about her shoulders taking a sly look at the caller whilst pretending to fix her hair.

A look of contempt puckered at the corners of the woman's mouth, forming tiny lines from her lips to her nose. She had a face bred for aristocracy, but her bloodless lips seemed harsh and cruel.

Fanny bristled and straightened her back.

'Yes, I am Miss Kendrick, Fanny Kendrick.'

'The Duchess of Romsey.' She thrust out a gloved hand and touched the tips of Fanny's fingers before withdrawing it as if she had been burnt.

'Oh!' Fanny's hand flew to her mouth. 'I'm so sorry, I didn't mean... people such as yourself, well, they don't visit that often.' The Duchess continued to stare coldly at her and Fanny pulled the robe tighter around her. 'Yes, well, pleased to meet you, your Grace.' Fanny swallowed. She bobbed her head and curtsied. 'I hope you enjoyed the performance, your Grace.'

'The performance was of no consequence. I'm sure it was quite adequate.'

'Thank you.' Fanny lowered her voice. Why was William's mother here, at the opera? Two hot spots burned her cheeks.

'I am not accustomed to talking to one with... talents such as yours,' continued the Duchess. 'There is no need to take offence; I do not have the time to enjoy the opera and I did not watch the spectacle. I hear that you are a popular performer on the stage, neither your performance nor the opera is of interest to me. However, I am sure that what I have to say will be to you, Miss Kendrick.'

Fanny nodded, intrigued by what a woman of such standing could have of interest to her, a mere performer on the stage. She poured a small sherry into a tiny stemmed goblet and offered the glass. The Duchess shook her head.

'This won't take long, Miss Kendrick. I have a proposition for you but I do not have much time.' The Duchess paused but Fanny did not reply. 'I assure you, you will be interested in what I have to say.'

'If I may be so bold, your Grace, but I've never met you before in my life, how can you know what I will or will not be interested in?' Fanny played with the silk tie of the robe and hoped she hadn't gone too far.

'Indeed you are bold. Rather refreshing, I must admit. I admire your belief in yourself. And that is because you have ambition. It is much to be desired, especially for those who are less fortunate or lacking the access to opportunity.' The Duchess narrowed her eyes and straightened her back. 'And I can help you.'

'And in return?' Fanny had not seen her aristocratic lover, Lord Romsey in some time. He was an arduous admirer who tried his hardest to please her and she enjoyed the attention. She lapped at the sweet sherry, allowing the smooth, soft liquid to sooth her tired throat. This was going to be about William, she knew it.

'In return? Why, of course. You will promise to reject any further advances made by my son.'

Fanny stepped back spilling some sherry on her hand. 'Your son?' She sucked at her fingers.

'Do not act so surprised. I am aware he has been pursuing you for some time.'

Fanny laughed at her directness; it was so like William's own. She walked over to the vase of roses, stroking the soft velvet petals. 'Oh, yes. Dear William. He does follow me around like a little lap dog.' Fanny caught the cold look on the Duchess's face. 'I'm sorry I did not mean to sound over familiar, your Grace. William has been very generous to me. And he loves my singing.'

'Generous with his money as well as his time.' The Duchess sniffed.

Fanny reddened. 'I have never asked for money. The gifts were his idea.'

The Duchess tapped her umbrella on the floor. 'I am not interested in the how and why. It is no matter to me how my son chooses to spend his time and his money. Well, I should say, it didn't matter.'

'I'm not sure what you mean.' Fanny put a hand to her head; an ache was forming across her temple. 'I'm tired after the performance, I need to change for the—'

'This won't take much longer, Miss Kendrick, only a few more thoughts. Of course this is a private conversation. I would appreciate you keeping it between ourselves. I am only here because I am concerned about William, recent circumstances have had a profound effect on him.'

'Of course, please continue, your Grace.' The sooner this woman left, the better. Fanny was tired of the conversation and knew she was being impolite.

'I'm not sure when you last saw William, but his circumstances have changed very recently. His elder brother died.' The Duchess did not display any sign of emotion.

Fanny bowed her head. 'Yes, I heard, although not from William. I am very sorry. Please,' Fanny indicated to her chair in front of her dressing mirror, 'are you sure you wouldn't like to sit down? It must be terrible for you, the death of a son.'

'Indeed not, I do not dwell on the death. It has happened, and there has been much to do since the funeral. I'm more concerned with William, and the position this has put him in.'

'Indeed,' mused Fanny unfazed by her cold approach, supposing women like the Duchess could not afford much time for emotions.

'For William, this means his future is now very different, and there are some things that cannot be allowed to continue.'

Fanny bristled but the Duchess continued. 'By that I mean not everyone involved with William would want the life he now has to follow. His elder brother was due to inherit the Dukedom of Romsey.'

Fanny straightened making herself taller but still could not match the stature of the Duchess. 'And that means that William will—'

The Duchess nodded, a grave look on her face. 'Yes, William will inherit the title, and he needs to make preparations, without distraction. We have some time, the current Duke is well...' the Duchess looked away for a moment. 'However, it means that the choices William makes could well affect this responsibility of the future.'

Fanny paused and looked at the dusty floor, realising that William would no longer have time for her. 'I'm sorry, I am still not sure how all this involves me, your Grace.'

'I believe that William is about to propose marriage to you, Miss Kendrick.'

'He is?' Fanny tried not to blink. He could not possibly be thinking of proposing. The thought was impossible. He must know that. Why would he be testing his mother so, and now at this time of mourning?

'Yes and whilst I have no doubt about your capabilities regarding your... career.' The Duchess smiled wryly.

'You doubt me as a suitable wife?' Fanny raised an eyebrow despite knowing that it would never be an eligible match.

'No, not at all, I'm not in any position to comment on your abilities in the home. However, as a wife of a future Duke, you would have to forfeit your ambition, your singing. Being a Duchess is a full time job in itself; staff to organise, functions to plan, charities to represent, two large homes to run. One's life is not one's own and we have a duty to those less fortunate than ourselves. Performing on stage would not be considered as...' The Duchess closed her eyes for a second, '...oh, how would one put it? Appropriate. William has always had this independent streak, which may well have suited his lifestyle before, but things have now changed.'

Fanny's head began to spin. How clever, this woman was. Fanny knew that she would never be accepted as wife to William, whatever the circumstances, but the woman was obviously convinced of her son's intentions. She had come here to offer her an alternative in exchange for her silence.

'I know that this may come as a bit of a shock, Miss Kendrick. But, as William's mother and the present Duchess of the estate, I do have a certain duty to be apprised of all things that affect our family. And, I do have your interests at heart, as well as William's. I'm sure we can come to some suitable arrangement.'

'And your proposition is what exactly?'

'I believe there is one place, one theatre that you have wished to perform at for some time now. Unfortunately, that opportunity has never been afforded to you. I am told this experience is the ultimate for someone in your position and at this stage of your career.'

For someone who claimed to have no knowledge of the stage, Fanny thought, she knew more than she was letting on. Her heart missed a beat.

'You do?'

'Yes, La Scala in Milan. I am known to a gentleman there, a singer like you, who has agreed to grant you an audience.'

Fanny's heart raced. La Scala was the most famous opera house in Italy. Composers and singers yearned for a chance to perform there. For once, she was at a loss for words.

The Duchess reached into her purse and pulled out a piece of paper.

'I have taken the liberty of booking you and a travelling companion of your choice, a passage, first class. It sails this Friday to Naples and then a carriage to Genoa.'

Fanny hesitated. What if this was a trick to get her out of the way? She took the tickets and scanned the details. She imagined the roar of applause as the curtains parted to reveal her, Fanny Kendrick, performing at La Scala.

'I have also arranged accommodation for five nights and an audience with a Signor Patrizi. He will contact you regarding a convenient time.'

Fanny flushed with excitement and anticipation. A revered tenor, Eduardo Patrizi could introduce her to the best there was. She held the tickets to her chest worried that the Duchess might take them back.

'Now, do we have a mutual understanding, Miss Kendrick? Are you clear about the conditions of this contract?'

Fanny nodded and turned away, unable to speak.

'And, not a word to William, about our little chat?'

Fanny bit her lip and turned back. But the Duchess had already left.

*

William strode into Fanny's dressing room, his head held high, determined to secure a wife of his choosing, even if the rest of his life was no longer his to do as he wished. He knew his mother would do everything in her power to prevent it. He needed to anticipate her moves. And what better time than now.

'It is I, William, at your service.' He removed his hat, bowed deeply, and swept it across his feet.

Fanny stood sipping her sherry. She wore a gown with full bell shaped sleeves, and in a shade of deep plum that reflected her pearlescent skin. Her golden hair had been brushed until it shimmered and was pinned loosely so that it fell in coils around her long swan-like neck. She wore only a little face powder, but her cheeks shone like two polished apples. William sensed tenseness about her, but thought she had never looked as beautiful.

'My dear William, or should it be your Grace?' she asked.

'No please, William will do fine, my dear Fanny. I have to tell you that your performance was exquisite. I don't know quite how you do it, my dear, but for me only you could portray the Mountain Sylph in all her glory.'

Fanny dipped her head, then straightened her shoulders and gazed at him. William wished he could sink into the entrancing indigo pools that formed her eyes.

'I know but it is such hard work perfecting my interpretation, William. I know you understand what a difficult thing it is to perform.'

'I only wish that I did.' William bit at his lip. 'Then perhaps I would be better placed to meet these expectations of being a Duke.'

Fanny blushed, her gaze falling to the floor in between them. She walked towards him and took his hand. William felt his heart twist. He knew he could make her happy.

'William, please do forgive me, I don't know what has come over me. My sincere condolences.'

His hand trembled within hers and he inhaled her scent of heady rose water.

'Your apology is not required, my dear. It is a sad state of affairs. He was racing, like the fools we are, and his horse startled. It was all so sudden. They carried him to the Lodge but nothing could be done. Poor Henry, he broke his neck instantly. My father has taken it worst; after all, Henry was the heir. Now he has to make do with the spare. A poor second, I fear.'

Fanny squeezed his hand, bringing it up to her chest. William's heart began to race and he wiped away a tear that had fallen on her cheek.

'Please, don't. I can't bear to see you upset.' He shook a silk handkerchief from his pocket. 'Here, take this.'

'Oh, William, please don't do yourself an injustice. It is most unbecoming in a man of your stature and your standing. It was such a terrible accident, and how horrid for you to have lost your dear brother, I do know how much he meant to you.'

The gap that Henry's death had left widened by the hour. The moment he learned his elder brother, who had taught him everything he knew about life in general, was dead, he had wept for a friend as well as a brother.

A sharp rap at the door broke the silence between them. Fanny rushed forward and opened the door a fraction.

'Yes, what is it?' she demanded. A whispered conversation followed and William took a deep breath. He had not come here for pity. He loved this woman, and could care less whether she was a suitable wife in the eyes of his mother. He knew that he could continue his relationship with Fanny and meet his mother's expectations for a 'suitable' wife. But it was Fanny he loved and if she agreed to their joining, then he could face the future and the challenges that awaited him. She had as much class as any other woman he knew, all she lacked was the right of birth. Surely he could be granted one thing that would bring him happiness? Despite his desire, his head told him that the happiness he wanted would not be easy to attain.

'Forgive me, William, it's always so frantic after a performance. They are demanding my attention at the reception. Perhaps you would like to accompany me?'

'It would be my pleasure, Madam.' William bowed. 'But I need to keep you to myself for a little while longer, if I may.' He stepped forward, closed the door and leaned back against it, taking in the contours of Fanny's figure, shaped like an hourglass.

'I would follow you to the ends of the earth if I had to. I adore hearing you sing and watching you perform. But I fear that it is no longer enough.'

Fanny's smile dropped and her hand hovered over her creamy cleavage. William fought hard to tear his gaze away.

'Have I done something to displease you, William? Or am I not worthy enough to be known now?' She looked hurt, and her eyes shone again with tears.

'No! It is exactly the opposite. It is my turn for an apology for I am not making myself clear. You see, this is very new to me, not something I am familiar with… nor asked before. Although I knew what I was going to say before I came in here.' William's mother had paraded many a young lady in front of him in the past and had always been disappointed at his lack of proposal. He laughed nervously as he pictured her reaction if his mother were here now.

Fanny sniffed and dabbed the handkerchief at her face.

'I know you would do me no harm,' she whispered. 'But I'm afraid I have been unkind and unthinking.'

William shook his head, fumbled in his inside pocket and brought out the box clasped in his fist. He bent down on one knee and took a deep breath.

'Miss Kemble. It would do me a great pleasure if you would agree to be my wife and the future Duchess of Romsey.' Opening the box with shaky hands, he thrust it towards her, the diamond twinkling in the candlelight.

The silence stretched between them as she stared at the jewel before her, not daring to breath. She swallowed hard, closed her eyes and put her hand to her forehead.

'You do not like it?' William asked, confused by her reaction. 'I'm sure we can find something more suitable if you do not take a fancy to this one. It is a family heirloom, been handed down for generations. Perhaps you would prefer something more personal?'

Fanny bit at her knuckles, and William wondered if she felt unwell. His knee resting on the stone floor ached but he dare not rise until he heard her acceptance.

'Oh, my dear William, it is beautiful. But, I cannot take it from you. I just cannot.'

'You are worth a thousand diamonds, my love.'

'You don't understand, William, and please don't call me your love for I am not, and have never agreed to be.'

She paced the room.

'Do please get up, William, please let us forget about this.'

'Fanny, I have asked you to be my wife. I do not want to forget about it. Surely, you must have known how I felt about you. And we have spent many times together. Are we not lovers?' His head pounded and his legs trembled as he stood.

'That may well be, William. But I cannot marry you and more to the point, I do not wish to marry you.'

'But why not? What better offer of marriage could you possibly have? I am offering you not only my companionship and love, which will be attentive to your every need, but Clomber Abbey and eventually, the title of Duchess.'

Fanny twisted her hands together before moving towards the door. 'That I don't believe is within your gift. And even if it was, I do not want your companionship, nor a large house in the country, William. Being a Duchess is not the move I had in mind. I have my work to do, and several theatre companies would love me to sing in their productions. A man of your standing cannot surely be serious about a marriage with someone like me.'

'Damn convention, Fanny. I do not care about such divisions. I thought you would be delighted with my proposal, I can offer you security and you will never be in need of anything. Surely that is more important than your career.' As he watched her face harden, he wished he could bite back his last comment. Of course she was upset at the thought of having to give up her career. How short sighted he had been. He should have prepared his proposal more carefully. 'I'm sorry, I have made assumptions. I am sure you will be able to perform at some of our functions, indeed it would make such a refreshing change!'

'William, I cannot marry you, please do not make me refuse you again.'

'But, my dear, I cannot understand why not.'

Fanny sighed heavily, and William searched for meaning in her face. But it had set in a sad pose, lips together, chin dipped, eyes lowered.

'I cannot marry you, Lord Romsey, because…' William closed his eyes, half wanting to hear the reason. Fanny crossed her fingers behind her back. '…because I am already betrothed.'

*

It was a well-known fact that masters could be and often were, wrong. However, it was not a butler's place to inform them of such. And mistresses, Mabbot added to his father's sound and sombre advice given many years ago.

The Duchess appeared outside the theatre as he had been about to accompany Lady Charlotte home, as requested by William. Not his place to question her presence, but shocking all the same, after all, she was still in mourning. Once they arrived at their London home at Kenilworth House, she insisted that Mabbot return to collect William, despite his clear order not to. His services as a valet to the Romsey family were more peculiar than most but his father's words rang loud and true.

Something must have gone wrong with William's audience with Miss Kendrick, Mabbot thought. But what, he did not know. Only that William and Lady Charlotte had been whispering in dark corners since William's audience with the Duchess. Lady Charlotte had made sure that he had been kept out of it. Mabbot did not mind, but she wasn't around now to mop up the mess was she? It was fine to be a member of the ruling class and be able to buy and have what you want, when you wanted it, but idle minds made work for the Devil and it was Devil's play that had been going on tonight.

Lord William almost fell through the back stage door, his face twisted and his hat hanging between his hands. Mabbot coughed discreetly.

'What are you—'

'I thought the weather was about to turn, my Lord.' Mabbot looked up into the inky darkness. 'It felt like rain, and I thought it might be best.'

'Did you now, Mabbot?' William walked towards him. 'Sometimes I think you have a sixth sense.' William turned back towards the theatre and sighed heavily.

'Ride in the carriage with me, Mabbot, would you?' William shivered.

Mabbot raised his eyebrows; usually he took his place alongside the driver.

'Certainly, sir, shall I fetch a blanket? It's a cold night.'

'Whatever you see fit, Mabbot. I really have no care.'

Mabbot was not shocked by the change in his master's mood. As a child, William had been prone to fits of sadness and melancholy. At first, he had felt sorry for the small boy, who needed attention and reassurance about his appearance. The injury to his eye, which William had suffered at birth, seemed to bother him as he grew more aware of his appearance. As he had become a young man, the moods had ceased a little in their frequency but possibly because William made himself absent, even from Mabbot.

'Kenilworth House?' Mabbot enquired.

'Well it's too damn late to go to Clomber.' William snapped. Mabbot nodded and tapped once on the ceiling of the cab. The carriage jolted into action and Mabbot placed a blanket across his master's knees and sat opposite but slightly to the left. The carriage made for a snug ride but for master and servant was a little restrictive. William fumbled in his jacket and produced a small blue box.

'Please return this tomorrow to the vault.'

Mabbot stared at the box then took it. Faded gold leaf lettering had been embossed into the velvet.

'Of course, my Lord,' Mabbot raised and shut the lid. 'A ring, sir. A diamond ring. Quite a gift I should imagine.'

'Yes, but a redundant proposal I'm afraid.'

Mabbot stared at the thin line of his master's mouth, but betrayed no emotion.

'The lady refused?' He lowered his voice a little aware that he stated the obvious.

'Yes damn it all.' William thumped the seat beside him. 'I've made a proper fool of myself tonight, and Lady Charlotte will have something to answer for in the morning.'

Ah, thought Mabbot, so that is what they have been scheming. A marriage and a bargain probably made without the full knowledge of the Duchess. This proposal was preposterous.

'I'm sure things will look different in the morning, my Lord. When you have had time to think about things. And maybe the lady in question might have had time to think also. Women do have a habit of…' Mabbot coughed once, 'of changing their minds. I do believe it is quite common.'

'Well that might be the case, Mabbot but I do not think Miss Kendrick will be changing her mind. She had already made it up long before tonight. And maybe things will look different in the morning. Maybe I'll just disappear, away from everyone I disappoint, and then that shall be the end of it.'

CHAPTER FOUR

'William!' Lottie shouted through the door. 'Don't keep Mother waiting; you know how it vexes her so.' She waited for a second before removing a key from inside her sleeve, opening the door and breezing in.

'Lottie, for heaven's sake!' William boomed. 'Can a man not be guaranteed any privacy?'

'But you're not dressed! Why do you always have to make things so difficult for yourself?'

Although Lady Charlotte was younger than William was, she had taken charge from the time she could talk and walk. William had been besotted with her doll-like features and enjoyed being the elder brother. He spent all the time he could in the nursery, making her laugh, listening to her constant chatter and she loved to boss him around. She was known to everyone, apart from her mother, as the *Little Duchess*.

'I'm not making things difficult for myself as you well know.' William stared moodily out of the window. Cavendish Square was awash with water, rain gushing from the drainpipes and bouncing in the puddles. 'I'm returning to Clomber Abbey this morning. I cannot stand being in London one moment longer.'

'William, you know Mother has arranged a visit from Alice Gantry. She's expecting to see you. It will take your mind off things.' She ignored the sharp look he sent and opened a large oak wardrobe and stepped back. 'Now you must look smart, William. Otherwise, that will be another black mark from Mother. You need to play her game a little, then she'll relax and you can get back to normal.'

She peered into the dark depths of William's closet it didn't offer much choice. He liked continuity and disliked change, rows of long tailed coats with high collars, pure linen shirts and piles of neatly folded cream breaches filled the space. William preferred to dress in the style of the last century, which gave him an eccentric air. Lottie had long ago stopped nagging him to adopt a more fashionable look – he was not a vain man and rather shy but often this was misinterpreted by others as being curt and aloof. She found his demeanour refreshing and more honest to most of the men she mixed with. William treated her like an individual; as far as she was concerned, he could wear what he liked.

'Well at least that's one decision made… first a shave.' Lottie rolled her sleeves up to her elbow. At least she had persuaded him to tame the mutton chops he used to sport, now he favoured more tailored sideburns.

'Don't, Lottie. Mabbot will do that.' William put a hand on hers.

'Oh don't you worry about Mabbot, I dismissed him with some errands for me this morning. Can't bear having him hanging about, like a corpse that has come back to haunt us. You don't mind do you, William? I don't think he was too happy though.'

'I shouldn't imagine he was. Still, there are worse things than upsetting my manservant.' William managed a smile.

'Come on then,' said Lottie picking up the double-edged razor and running it across the leather strop. 'Look sharp!'

'Can't you tell Mother I'm ill or called away on business? Do I have to go through this sham?'

'You know very well that you can't, William. I've told you – let her think that she's in control, she has to. That way you will have more opportunity to do as you want.'

'It doesn't feel like that at all,' grumbled William, tilting his head back.

'Of course it doesn't, silly, because you're doing what you always do, fighting back without an army or without reason. Come on, William you're strong – I know it and you can get through this. You know that it is one of Mother's roles to find you a future wife. You just have to accept it.'

'I jolly well don't. I would like to choose a wife of my own. In fact I already had.'

'If you mean Fanny, then it was never going to happen. She wouldn't want to be trapped in this gilded cage; can you imagine the two of you confined together? You'd be miserable and murderous. It was never going to happen and I think you know that.'

'So why did you let me go and make a fool of myself then?'

'Would you have listened to me? William, you were intent on proposing to Fanny. Nothing I could have said would have changed your mind.' Lottie stood behind him, putting her hands on his shoulders.

'No, I wouldn't have listened to you. And more to the case in point, I will not have you shave me, Lottie. It is not a job for a woman and hard enough for Mabbot to complete without injury. Now please, ring for Mabbot.'

Lottie hesitated for a second before pulling the cord beside the fire place. Within minutes, there was a light tap at the door. 'I swear that man hangs around, just waiting…' she muttered to William who laughed.

'Of course, dear Lottie, that is his job.'

Lottie watched Mabbot as he dipped the badger hair brush into the cold water on the washstand and then rubbed it on the tablet of shaving soap. He applied the suds to William's cheeks and chin. He had a strong face with a long nose and despite the lack of symmetry of his eyes; they were what drew one in. Lottie knew her brother had hidden depths and a passionate soul.

Ladies were not expected to carry out such personal tasks. Lottie did not care for such conventions, however, if it were up to her she would do a number of things not considered fit for a lady, after all, it was only a matter of application as she saw it. She knew her attitude vexed her father, whose generation demanded the current female etiquette and did not understand her at all. Her mother tolerated her behaviour only because her place in the family was not that important.

Lottie loved William and hated seeing him depressed. She had never been as close to her elder brother Henry as he had been a good ten years older and had always seemed distant. She didn't fully understand his fight against the demands of their position; despite her independent nature, Lottie did like the trappings that came with her family's status and knew one day she would have to compromise. Therefore, she would do what she could to help him. That is how it had always been between the two of them.

Mabbot expertly wiped the sharp blade across the white creamy chin, leaving behind a smooth line of skin.

'So you think you could really learn to shave a man?' William asked.

'Oh, it's not difficult at all, I've watched Mabbot do it and I've accompanied you to the barbers when I was younger. Anything is possible, William if one wants it enough. Now keep still, or the blade will slip.'

Mabbot, expressionless, wiped the razor on a cloth. It was as if he wasn't listening, but Lottie knew full well that he didn't miss a thing. Still, William seemed to trust him.

'What would make you really happy right now?' Lottie asked. 'I mean if you could have anything, be anything. What would it be?'

'You've always wanted to be a fairy godmother.' William spoke tightly, his eyes shut.

'Anything?' He asked after a short while.

'Yes, anything. Come on, William – let your imagination run wild.'

'To experience the life of an ordinary man, I suppose. Neither the future Duke of Romsey nor the brother of the dead one. Where I earn an honest living and where I could perhaps find love without fear of them being afraid of or overly excited about what I – well my status – can offer them. I want someone to love me for me. A little like you do, but less sisterly, of course. I know Mother doesn't agree with these notions but I want to care for a woman. I thought Fanny loved me, though I could not understand why, she had the pick of many admirers. I can't believe how stupid I was.'

Mabbot wiped half of his face with a small towel.

'To be fair, William, I don't think Fanny ever encouraged you to think that way, she is a very ambitious and independent woman.'

'No, she did not discourage me either. I would have been happy for her to continue her singing, in fact I would have supported her ambitions financially.'

'Yes, well I don't think Mother saw it that way.' Lottie murmured. William grabbed her wrist, stood, and turned to face her. Mabbot busied himself around the washstand.

'What do you mean? Mother has never met Fanny, she did not know how I felt.'

'William, please that hurts. Let go. I didn't mean to say anything. Ignore me, it was nothing, I meant nothing.' William released his grip.

'I'm sorry, I didn't mean to hurt you, but it damn well wasn't nothing. Did Mother go and see Fanny?'

Lottie looked at the floor and bit her lip, then raised her head.

'I hadn't meant to let it slip out. And I didn't tell Mother, I promise. I thought I could trust Nellie—'

'You told Mother's maid? Of course she would go back and tell her! Lottie, sometimes I despair of your eagerness to gossip.'

'I am sorry, William. However, it has happened and there is nothing you can do about it. Mother merely arranged for Fanny to have an audience at La Scala. The rest happened by itself.'

'An audience?' William laughed harshly, stalked over behind the dressing screen, and began to pull on the clothes that Lottie had selected for him. 'So not a husband then, perhaps she thought she was trying to spare my feelings. At least I could fight a rival admirer. How ironic that I am now to be auditioned by someone considered more suitable for the role of my wife?'

'William, you know that this isn't within your gift, she has a job to do as the mother of the future Duke. It was the same with Henry – his love interests were very closely vetted and he accepted it.'

'Fine words from you, Lottie. You can't have it all, you know.'

'Well, William, without changing your identity I don't think there is a jot you can do about it.' She watched William stride over to the door.

'Just watch me.' As he disappeared, Lottie stared at Mabbot and realised that he had only shaved one side of her brother's face.

*

William stood in front of the large oak entrance to the library, his previous confidence evaporating like a morning mist. He ran a finger along his collar and pushed open the doors.

'William, at long last – we have been waiting…'

His mother paused in mid-sentence staring at his face. He rubbed his hand over the half stubble and reddened. Damn, how reckless of him, but what was the use now? With a sense of resignation, he returned his mother's stare.

'I'm sorry I am late, Mother.' He bowed his head and turned to the woman sitting beside the Duchess.

'Miss Gantry has been kept waiting, which is most rude of you, William, It is to her that you should make your apologies.' His mother spoke harshly with a tight, thin smile.

The young woman stood up and took a step towards William, holding out one hand, a pair of gloves in the other. William appraised the small waist accentuated by the nip of her powder blue dress, tiny ears with a pearl stud in each and a slightly upturned nose. Her eyes were a bright but cold blue, complementing the shade of her dress. William supposed she was pretty, but he didn't want pretty, he wanted a proper woman, like Fanny.

He clicked his heels together, took her hand, kissed it and then bowed extravagantly.

'I apologise, Miss Gantry and for the unfinished business of my appearance.' He ran a hand over his stubble and smiled. 'But I was under the impression that your audience was with my Mother, not me.'

He watched the young face flush with embarrassment and felt her pull her hand away so he held tighter.

'There is no need to apologise, Lord—'

'Oh, please call him William.' His mother stood and walked over to him. 'You should only address a gentleman who deserves his title and gentlemen are never late.' She forced a smile. 'I shall arrange for tea, William, whilst you make amends to Miss Gantry.'

The Duchess swept out of the room with a flourish and William wondered why she hadn't summoned a servant. A silence as wide as a chasm filled the room and he was unsure of how to fill it.

'So, Miss Gantry. How are you acquainted with my mother?'

Her features relaxed a little. 'Oh, her Grace is an old friend of my family. We used to visit Kenilworth House often when I was a child.'

'You did? How long since then? Your childhood, I mean – how old are you?'

'I shall be twenty at my next birthday, in June.'

'Twenty? And what have you been doing? What pleases you?' William walked around the room picking up familiar objects as if it were the first time he had seen them.

'Well, I've been learning French, embroidery and I play a little tennis.' Miss Gantry tried to smile but failed, the corners of her mouth fell like that of a sad clown.

William played with the stopper of a crystal brandy decanter; a tot of which he felt would go down very well at this moment. He knew he was making her feel uncomfortable and he didn't like it but he felt such an anger within. The glass plug spun around tinkling with temptation.

'And do you read, Miss Gantry?' he asked without turning to her, his mind now fixed on the brandy.

'Please, call me Alice,' she paused, her brow creased, '… and read, Lord Romsey?'

'Yes, read,' he said slowly. 'Miss, I'm sorry, Alice. What books, novels have you read?'

'My father is of the view that reading is not an appropriate pastime for young ladies,' she replied primly, her lips pursed. 'I have read some French to help with my language development and a little poetry.'

'Poetry?' William sneered then, seeing her startled look, regretted his retort. He swallowed hard; it wasn't Alice he was angry at. 'Have you read none of the novels that are abound? My sister Lottie is practically fanatical about them.'

Alice eyes widened and she shook her head.

'Poetry is fickle, in my view. I suppose for ladies like you, Alice, it is considered the correct form of education.'

To his surprise, she stood her ground. 'Well, you are well entitled to your opinion, William. However, I shall not be persuaded otherwise.' William raised an eyebrow at her bravery.

'And what about riding, Miss Gantry. I presume you have a horse?'

She stared back at him, her defiance burning behind her eyes.

'Miss Gantry?' William pressed.

'I know that you are very fond of your horses and racing.' Two bright spots of red sat high on her cheeks. 'Though I could never condone gambling, I do believe you have quite a gift for it.'

'All that might be true,' William replied. 'But it really does not answer my question, Miss Gantry. You are avoiding it.'

She bit her lip and then said quietly. 'I do not have a horse nor do I ride a horse or have not done so for a very long while.'

William nodded, encouraging her to continue.

'I was thrown when I was a young girl and have nurtured a fear of them ever since.' Her voice wobbled. 'I have tried, but it's impossible, the more afraid I am the more skittish the horse becomes.'

'You're afraid of horses?' William said. 'What a pity.'

'It is not an activity I miss, I can assure you.'

William smiled, encouraged by her boldness for a moment. Then he remembered his mother's real intentions behind the audience. 'Well, tell me, why are you here today, Miss Gantry? What brings you here to my home at the behest of my mother? As I said earlier, I thought your audience was with the Duchess.'

She breathed in deeply. 'I think you know the answer to that, William. We have met several times recently at the functions your mother has hosted. Indeed, the last time you asked me to dance. It was a waltz I believe.'

'Really?' William had genuinely forgotten – he was usually a little tipsy at his mother's social evenings; it was the only way to endure them. He disliked having to entertain. 'I'm afraid I don't recall our encounters. I do have a terrible head for names and faces… unless, of course, they belong to a horse.'

Miss Gantry stood and straightened her shoulders making herself taller. Her eyes sparkled like ice. William could feel a warm blush rising from his neck and wished he could bite back his silly words.

'Indeed, Lord Romsey, you surprise me. I was invited here to take tea with your mother and yourself. However, it appears that you would prefer to be elsewhere and I shall not waste any more of your precious time. I would like to say it has been a pleasure meeting you this morning but frankly, I don't care to ever meet with you again let alone dance with you. I do hope you find what you are looking for. And please accept my condolences regarding your brother, he was a true gentleman and a model character, one I trust that you are able to reflect in the duties you have inherited from him. Good day, Lord Romsey.'

William watched her disappear in a cloud of crinoline, then crossed the room and poured himself three fingers of brandy. He held the glass to his lips and only hesitated for a second before downing the fiery liquid. A little like Miss Gantry when provoked he thought – hot and passionate – and he respected her retaliation to his jibes. He deserved everything she had said. He had no regrets. He and Miss Gantry were not a match, he would in the end destroy her confidence and he couldn't live with that. He needed someone who could control and dilute his bitterness. And his mother would have to get used to that.

*

Lady Charlotte joined her mother and William in the library thirty minutes later. The air was thick with a strained silence and there was no sign of Alice Gantry. Lottie frowned at William who did not return her gaze, but looked out into the gardens, hands clasped behind his back. Mabbot was pouring tea, in his usual slow and laborious style while her mother stood stiffly, like a volcano readying to explode.

'Thank you, Mabbot. I'll finish that.' Lottie dismissed him swiftly, taking the teapot. He straightened his back, his arms rigid by his sides and his face a mask.

'As you wish, Lady Charlotte.' Mabbot stepped away and walked towards the door.

'Mabbot,' William interrupted. He turned and nodded. 'Please make ready for my return to Clomber Abbey at once.'

'Before lunch, sir?'

'Yes, Mabbot. I shan't be long.'

'Certainly, my Lord.'

Mabbot left the room and the Duchess sniffed.

'And Miss Gantry?' Lottie enquired while she finished pouring the tea.

'Your brother has done his best to disgrace this family yet again I'm afraid, Charlotte. I cannot say I am surprised. I half expected it and wonder why I bother at all!'

'Mother! It is no wonder why William fights against you. You don't mean those things, I know. Give him some time, please.'

The Duchess took the cup offered to her and sipped at the tea.

'I am here you know. You don't have to talk about me as if I wasn't,' said William.

'You might as well not be here,' snapped the Duchess. 'How could you treat Miss Gantry so badly that she left before tea? I found her in the hallway muttering something about books and horses and most determined to leave. And I have known her mother for a long time; the poor wretched girl will probably go back with all kinds of gossip.'

Lottie watched the hurt expression flash across her brother's face and willed him to be strong but sensible. He sensed her thoughts because he smiled at her, a short smile that did not quite reach his eyes.

'Miss Gantry and I had a chat, Mother, as requested by you. The girl cannot ride nor is interested in reading. I can hardly find companionship with one who doesn't share my likes and neither would she be happy with me. However, she stood up well to my scrutiny; in fact, she matched my interrogation and questioning rather well I thought. She was in control when she left here, I can assure you. She will make a fine wife for the right man.'

'It wasn't an interview for a rider for one of your horses, William! I have taught you better manners than to interrogate a young and gifted woman who is fluent in French and can read the most beautiful poetry without prompt! And happiness? Who said marriage is made of happiness.' The Duchess shot a sharp glance at Lottie. 'I blame you partly for this, Charlotte,' she took another small sip from the cup, her little finger extended.

'Fine, Mother. I do believe Alice's appearance is deceptive. She can stand up for herself and I'm sure she did as William said.'

'Yes, never mind all that.' The Duchess put her cup down with a bang. 'But William's expectations of a future wife are obviously modelled on you. You know full well I disapprove of young ladies like yourself riding and reading those ghastly novels. They fill your head with such nonsense.'

Charlotte sighed but did not respond. It was a useless argument and she didn't want to inflame the situation further.

'Miss Gantry has been training to be a lady since her birth and her mother has done a fine job. She would make a perfect wife and Duchess. She is healthy and would produce some fine heirs.'

'Really, Mother. Do you have to be so cold about all this? Marriage is surely not about training to be a wife and producing children. Women are individuals with characters of their own and not just the chattels of her husband. You have such old fashioned views—'

The Duchess silenced her with a stony stare. 'Well, young lady, I hope you are able to find a suitor who would take on such a wayward wife, and a lady, it seems, who would prefer to enjoy more gentlemanly activities. We are the fairer sex, Charlotte, and our duties are very clear. You would do well if you came to your senses about this or you may well find yourself a spinster, God forbid. Then William would have to look after you.'

'Please, Charlotte is not at fault. She had nothing to do with my behaviour at all.' William stood before his mother. 'I'm sorry if I've offended anyone but I am sure it is for the best.'

'And be thankful I shall not be informing your father about this incident. He has too much on his mind now. Fear not, William, you will be expected to marry; however, I am prepared to wait until you accept the responsibility. I do not want any more disappointments.'

She glanced at Lottie as she left. 'And Charlotte, if you want to be of any help to your brother, you will encourage him to accept the way things are. At least I know he might listen to you. Please talk some sense into him and convince him I am only trying to do the best for him.'

After the door had closed, William sank into a large leather wing backed chair.

'You look exhausted,' said Lottie filling his cup and adding two lumps of sugar. 'Here take this, it will help. I don't suppose you made it to breakfast.' William shook his head. 'Come on, drink up. What a sight you must have looked to poor Alice. She is a bit deceptive though; I hope you weren't too wicked to her.'

William tried to smile but a dark shadow crossed his face. Lottie knew their mother was trying to toughen William up – and she was afraid the opposite would happen and somehow he would shatter into a thousand pieces. Lottie clenched her fists; she would have to help William's dream of experiencing life as someone else, perhaps once he got it out of his system, he would be more accepting of his position.

CHAPTER FIVE

William stared through the library window. It was October and the leaves were about to turn. Hues of gold, amber and yellow floated from the trees and lay like discarded pieces of torn paper on the ground beneath. Several gardeners were at work, tidying and sorting the kitchen allotment, picking cabbages and digging over the patches ready to lie low for winter. Although the days were short and the light wanting on many occasions, he warmed to the idea of hibernation, of preparing for a long sleep. He loved this time of the year at Clomber Abbey, the family's main seat. The large estate, once a monastery in medieval times, had been granted to his ancestors following the Dissolution. It had been handed down, from generation to generation, whose portraits hung in the hall overseeing the changes of time.

He squinted as he saw a movement at the edge of the woods, which extended for thousands of acres. He smiled as he saw the branch-like antlers of a large deer who stared cautiously across the expanse of land towards the window. Thank goodness his father was not out hunting today and the stag would be safe to roam, unheeded.

'William, I thought I might find you hiding in here. I won't allow it to continue.' Lottie's voice lightened the room. The confidence with which she spoke reminded him of their mother and he allowed himself a little smile.

'Why not? Can I not do as I please as the future Duke?'

'Of course you can, silly. But, William, sometimes I worry about you.'

'Only sometimes?' he teased. 'There really is no need. I am capable of worry all by myself. I am sorry I have been such a cad. I must make amends with Mother, and I will write and apologise to Miss Gantry. I'm a fool.'

'No need to apologise to me, though I think it might help smooth the water a little. I'm sure Alice would appreciate your explanation, but she's not easily fooled you know. And she never forgives. It's not in her nature. For what it's worth, I don't think you two would make a good match anyway. She's far too bossy.'

William laughed deep from inside. Lottie always managed to bring him out of a dark mood. She paced the room, her full skirts rocking backwards and forwards as she walked. She was tall, like William but her delicate looks belied the strong woman underneath. He admired her and would like to meet the man who would take on his feisty sister. Many suitors came calling, and more often were sent off unable to match Lottie's expectations of a male equivalent. She was a woman born out of her time and it annoyed their father immensely. Lottie enjoyed being centre of attention but she would never entertain the thought of marriage until she had met her match. Which may, William thought, be quite impossible.

'Look, I understand how you feel. Honestly, I do.' Lottie's face darkened a little until William smiled. 'You must trust me, or tell me to go away. I have plenty of other activities I could be spending my time on, I assure you.'

William nodded. 'You know I trust you more than I trust anybody. Surely you don't need my assurance about that?'

There was a swoosh of crinoline as Lottie swept towards him and took his hands in hers. 'William, I know you are finding it difficult to adjust to your new responsibilities. But what if you could also get a little of what you do want?'

'Lottie, my dear girl, you do talk in riddles and honestly, right now is not the time—'

'No, this isn't a riddle. It makes perfect sense and I know we can do it. I just know it.'

Her face flushed with excitement.

'Lottie, please——'

'What is it you said you wanted more than anything in the world?'

William paced the floor now, as he pondered the question. He had decided, after a sleepless night, that he was being selfish. He had more money than he could spend; a stable full of fine horses who were the envy of the racing community and his family owned lands that were fruitful and extensive. The estate itself provided jobs for a large number of local families and he felt a personal responsibility for the roofs over their heads. What more could a man possibly desire?

Alas, everything came with a price.

'I know I said I wished to be someone else… it is just a silly dream.'

'William, I knew that was exactly what you would say. Now I shall go about proving you very wrong.'

*

Lottie noted the confusion steal across her brother's face.

'I don't know what you mean. My head is beginning to pound with your conversation.' William slumped in the chair and rubbed his chin.

Lottie grinned, her brother was the eccentric one but she had a far more creative mind. She believed in the principle that anything can happen and if one willed it enough, it would.

'I know I'm being a bit vague,' she said. 'Do forgive me, I haven't worked out all the fine details.'

'Details?' William gazed at her through veiled lids.

'Yes, details. Don't you worry. Leave that to me.' She fiddled with a lock of hair, a faraway look in her eyes. 'But you need to be serious about this, William. You have to be committed. Otherwise it won't work.'

'I may be a little odd, but I feel a bit stupid, Lottie. I'm not altogether sure what you are talking about?'

'Of course you're not stupid, perhaps a little obstinate?' She paused.

'Obstinate? Me? I can't recall a time when…' He put up a hand to silence her as she started to quote examples. 'All right, maybe a little – determined – some of the time. But that's beside the point when we're talking about taking part in one of your little schemes. I remember the time you convinced me to speak to Father about allowing a new friend into the nursery. A friend, who turned out to be one of the servants children! You'd already asked Mother who had refused point blank, but with Father you left out some of the more critical details. So forgive me for being a little wary.'

Lottie laughed, remembering the incident with fondness. Nanny had been called away on an urgent family matter and the Duchess was due to return from a trip to London. Their father was not used to, nor interested in, such requests and waved them off with an order not to disturb him again.

'That was so funny, Mother was particularly offended to find Charlie Parker's son playing with our wooden blocks! She hardly ever visited the nursery – I swear she has a sixth sense.'

'Mmm… and I wonder where you get yours from?' William crossed the room and pulled a silk cord. 'I shall ask Mabbot to organise lunch and then you can tell me more about your little plan.'

Mabbot brought a light chicken salad, freshly baked bread and a carafe of French white wine. He placed the tray on the small reading table before backtracking out of the room without a word.

Lottie picked at a crust. 'Do you trust that man?'

'Why do you ask?' William poured the wine and handed Lottie a glass.

'Well, it could be important.'

'Of course I trust him. He's been with the family for years and years and his father before him. There has never been any trouble. Mabbot is the only person I know who seems to care little about my responsibilities or activities. He has no opinion on matters, unless of course, I ask him.'

Lottie arched her eyebrow.

'Don't you? Trust him, I mean.'

'He's a little creepy… always lurking.' Lottie sipped at the wine.

'Too many novels, I've told you before, they don't replicate real life. On that matter, Mother may be right. And anyway, isn't it part of his job, to lurk, be around when I need him?'

'Yes, perhaps. I do have a bit of a wild imagination but if you value him, then I must try.'

'Well, are you going to tell me or are we going to play cat and mouse all afternoon?' Lottie watched William pick at the salad, chewing carefully and putting down his cutlery after every bite and dabbing at the corner of his mouth with a linen serviette. She had lost her appetite. She pushed her plate away and scratched her neck.

'Well, I think you would benefit from seeing the world through another set of eyes.'

William frowned as though she were talking a different language, but nodded for her to continue. Lottie rose and stood behind him, her corset felt tight, crushing her chest but it was excitement and she could hardly contain herself. She exhaled slowly and rested her hands on the back of William's chair.

'I started to think about how you might do that, and how it would only be possible if you were someone else. Not William, not the future Duke of Romsey, but an ordinary businessman. You would need some standing, it wouldn't work any other way.' She giggled. 'Silly idea, I thought. How on earth could that happen?'

William nodded again. 'A ridiculous idea, I totally agree.'

'But it is done all the time, most of all in the theatre and in your beloved operas. Look how Fanny was transformed into the Mountain Sylph!' She watched William wince at the mention of his ex-love. 'Well,' she rushed on, 'actors take on different characters all the time. We need a bit of preparation, some changes to your appearance – a change of style in clothes and perhaps your voice…'

Lottie was aware she spoke without taking a breath. 'Isn't it exciting?'

*

William stared at his plate for a long time. When Lottie had stopped talking, he had almost laughed aloud at her preposterous suggestions. She removed her hands from his shoulders and the silence burned between them. She found it easy to make up things as she wished and became a little petulant if one did not show as much enthusiasm as she did.

'Come and sit,' he urged, refilling her goblet. 'And do eat something please. I think the lack of nourishment has sent you a little excitable.' He pushed her plate back in front of her. Her face was flushed, two pink patches like ink spots seeped over her cheeks and above her top lip were tiny beads of perspiration which she dabbed at with a serviette. The emerald green silk gown she wore complemented her amber coloured eyes, flecked with gold flashes and fiery with exhilaration. She looked like a gazelle, straight necked and alert.

'I mean it, eat. Then we shall talk more,' William said.

They finished lunch in silence, difficult for Lottie who loved to fill the gaps with chatter and gossip. She was fond of stories and worlds beyond William's imagination. This was another one of her fantasies. His head told him that her little plan would not possibly work for all kinds of reasons, his responsibilities as future Duke, for one. But his heart pounded with an unfamiliar desire, a great need to take up the challenge and create a new him, see the world through the eyes of another and without the shackles of his heritage and obligations.

Lottie finished her lunch and sat demurely looking into her lap.

'I think we should discuss this further on a walk.' William offered his hand. 'Although I know it is very unlikely we will be disturbed, all the same I'd like to be prudent.'

'Of course.' Lottie beamed back at him. 'What about the labyrinth?'

Clomber Abbey had a labyrinth buried underground. It was used by the monks to avoid persecution. When his family had inherited the estate years ago, the tunnels had not been used for some time. His father had started to rediscover them and William had completed the project not long ago. As children, he and Lottie had come across the key, neatly labelled hanging above the locked door. They knew it was out of bounds but had stumbled across the entrance, playing hide and seek, and the temptation had been too great. Lottie had climbed up onto William's shoulders to get the key and they had crept into the maze of tunnels. Then it was dark and dank, lit only by small gas lamps, which threw shadows around the curved walls. The labyrinth soon became a natural hiding place, somewhere to go when one wanted to be out of sight and William now used it regularly to cross the estate when he didn't want to be seen coming or going.

They wandered through the tunnels for two hours as they talked about Lottie's plans, the downfalls, and the risks they would both have to take. William had designed skylights, tiny domed windows, during the reconstruction and extension of the labyrinth and the weak sun warmed the earthen walls. As they wandered down one tunnel wide enough for his carriage, William felt a building sense of possibility, then as the light faded and his hope with it – they reluctantly had to take their leave from the maze.

'Lottie, I do appreciate your efforts, really I do,' William said as they returned to the Abbey. 'But I am no actor, and I find it difficult to believe that my appearance could be changed so much as to fool others. I should just forget all about it.'

Lottie shrugged her shoulders. 'Why don't we wait and see, William.'

*

On the day of All Hallows' Eve, William heard a commotion in the chamber outside his bedroom. He opened the door to find Lottie standing by a large wooden chest.

'Where have you been for the last few days? And what is that?'

Lottie smiled broadly. 'Help me in with it and I'll tell you. I bribed one of the footmen to carry it upstairs. I didn't want Mabbot sticking his nose in where it's not wanted.' Lottie peered into the room 'He's not here is he?'

'No, but I've sent for him.' William scratched his ear. 'I need him to take some correspondence.'

'Quick then! Let's get this in and when he comes tell him you are not to be disturbed all afternoon.'

'Not even for lunch?'

'No, not even for lunch; this is much too important to stop to eat.' Lottie put on her serious face but two dimples remained on her cheeks. His sister infuriated him at times.

'For goodness sake, Lottie! Why does everything have to be surrounded in mystery? You should be on the stage.'

They each took a handle and carried the case into the room. It was surprisingly light.

'You're a fine one to talk,' exclaimed Lottie. 'Look at you doing correspondence and dressed before lunch. Only a matter of days ago—'

'Well, I listened to you for a change, dear sister, you bent my ear. I'm trying to play Mother's game but I'm finding things rather dull.'

'Well!' She giggled and sat on top of the chest. 'William, dearest, that is about to change.'

There was a quiet tap at the door. Lottie brought a finger to her lips. 'Shh… not a word,' she mouthed before disappearing behind the dressing screen.

'Yes enter, Mabbot.' William commanded.

'You called, your Grace, the correspondence?' Mabbot looked at the empty space beyond William.

'Well, yes, that was the reason,' William stammered. 'But now something else needs my attention.' He struggled to find the appropriate lie. He looked around the room desperately until his gaze fell upon the stable plans.

'Yes, of course, the plans for the stable. A problem. Maybe more. I hadn't spotted the errors before. Silly me, and I'm very cross so I need to work it all out. It is very critical to the next stage of the building works. I don't want to be disturbed – for anything.' William was aware he rambled but he never did find lying came naturally, he was always found out. He ran a finger around the collar of his shirt and behind his back crossed another two. Mabbot did not move or acknowledge, standing as still as a garden statue.

'Is that perfectly clear, Mabbot?' William tried to sound curt but he desperately wanted Mabbot to leave. His gaze kept wandering over to the dressing screen and William could see the hem of Lottie's dress to one side.

'Certainly, sir, is there anything else. Tea, some light refreshments?'

No, Mabbot, the instructions include any disturbances by you. I do not wish to be interrupted at all. I will call if I need anything.'

'And lunch?' Mabbot spoke slowly making William more frustrated.

'Cancel lunch for heaven's sake, Mabbot. Do I have to tell you everything?'

'No, sir. I shall go and speak to the cook now, as you wish.'

Mabbot turned and left.

'Well done, William!' exclaimed Lottie skipping out from behind the screen. 'Though I am desperate for a cup of tea, dragging that thing all the way from London.' Lottie sat back down on the chest.

'Well, you'll have to make do with plain water. You wanted it this way – no disturbances. If water is good enough for me, then it is for you. Thank heavens I ate breakfast this morning otherwise I'd starve. Now, come on and put me out of my misery. What is in this damn case?' William prodded his toe at the large container.

Lottie giggled with glee. 'Sit down, William and not a word.'

Lottie laid out all the clothes on William's bed. A pair of modern breeches in taupe, most fitting he thought. A frilly shirt with a silk cravat in mustard and a wool and silk jacket in dove grey, cropped much shorter than William would usually wear. He pulled a face but said nothing. She brought out a flat hat, with a small bowl on top, brushing at it with her hands; a walnut walking stick topped with some kind of figure, which she tapped lightly on the floor before leaning it against a chair; and a pair of dove grey gloves. William's frown deepened.

'Remember, you are not allowed to say a word until I am finished. Promise me, William.'

He nodded. He presumed the clothes were for him in an attempt to modernise him for parliament, one of Henry's duties that he did not relish. Surely, his sister didn't think a few new clothes would suffice to create a new identity?

'Now before you try on the clothes I need to make some adjustments to your appearance. Come here.' She dragged a chair in front of the long picture window. 'Come and sit in the light, facing the window.'

Lottie spent the next hour restyling William's hair, which he enjoyed. He always found grooming to be a relaxing experience. She applied a skin coloured cream to the moles on his neck and temple. Finally, she placed a pair of plain round eyeglasses on his nose, adjusted them slightly and smiled. She handed him a looking glass and stepped back.

'Is it really me?' William asked, his fingers fluttering over his hair. His floppy eye looked back at him, quite symmetrical and the eyeglasses changed the shape of his face dramatically.

'No, it's not you, William. It is Reuben Chambers, a London businessman and he is your alter ego. Don't you look fantastic? Now let's get you dressed and remember, no talking.' William was at a loss for words anyway. Did she really think he could get away with it? No matter what she did to his face or his clothes, he was sure everyone would know it was him.

William followed Lottie's instructions like a young child learning to dress. He stood admiring the image in the long full-length mirror; the cut of cloth gave him a different shape, slightly fuller in the waist and a smaller but more confident demeanour.

He rather liked the look and what was more; he did not feel like William Rupert Leopold Kenilworth any longer.

CHAPTER SIX

Mabbot stood outside William's door for several seconds, listening, but it was impossible to hear anything.

'Damnations,' Mabbot cursed, pulling at his jacket cuffs. He spied a maid scurrying around the corner and gave her such a filthy look that she turned and scurried back again. They should have finished the rooms hours ago and anyway, he did not really want to be caught eavesdropping at William's door.

Mabbot sighed and turned back along the corridor, down the backstairs and headed towards the kitchen. It was unusually quiet. Mrs Campbell, the cook, was lifting a large fruitcake out of the oven, her face red with heat and a young footman sat at the wooden table shining silver.

'Where is everyone, Mrs Campbell? Why is Edwin performing the duties of a housemaid?'

'It's that damn flu,' muttered the cook without looking at him. 'I've got three of 'em in bed burning up and the other two ill at home – they can't travel. I can't risk them in here contaminating the food.'

'Indeed,' agreed Mabbot a little irked that he had not been informed of the staff situation before by the housekeeper; they would have words later.

'Lord Romsey sent for the doctor this mornin',' cook continued as Mabbot's chin dropped in surprise.

'His Lordship knows about this?'

'Oh yes, he sent for that lovely Dr Carter. Such a gentleman. He's given them some potion or another and says it's only a mild case. Hopefully they'll be right as rain by tomorrow. All the same, I'm doing the work of all of 'em.'

'Well,' said Mabbot gaining his composure and brushing aside his irritation. 'His Lordship has given orders, strict orders, not to be disturbed all afternoon. He has some problem with the stable project.' Mabbot, who was a small man, peered down his nose, stretching himself as tall as he could.

Mrs Campbell stood with her hands on slim hips, her lips set in a straight line across a pinched face. Mabbot wondered if she ever ate, as thin as she was. 'And what about lunch?'

'Lunch is cancelled. Surely that will make things better for you?'

Mrs Campbell tapped her foot. 'Well it would have been better to know three hours or more ago. I've just made two fruit pies, a cake and a jugged hare. What am I supposed to do with that lot?'

'If I had known three hours ago believe me, I would have told you. And anyway are you seriously telling me that you won't find a hungry mouth or two for that food?'

The cook's shoulders slumped. 'If I'd known my food was going to be eaten by the workers I'd have finished ages ago. They don't like this fancy stuff. Never mind. I can turn some of it into a broth for them three in bed. Build their strength up, they'll need it tomorrow, you mark my words. And I don't wonder that you wouldn't mind helping dispose of some food now you've been dismissed for the afternoon?' Her eyes narrowed.

Mabbot flinched. 'Of course not, Mrs Campbell I would be delighted to help. Please bring a tray to my room in...' he paused watching her mouth open and shut like a large fish. 'In about ten minutes.' He smiled, turned and left the kitchen. He could feel her glare burning a hole in his back.

A few minutes later, there was a light tap at his door.

Mabbot counted to ten. 'Yes, enter.'

The cook backed in with a large tray, slammed it on the small table by the window and left without saying a word. Well, she didn't need to. Mabbot had the upper hand and that pleased him. Only then, did he remove his jacket, hang it in the closet and scrub his hands for a good five minutes.

He dozed off after his unusually large lunch and woke with a slight indigestion. He frowned and checked his timepiece; he could hear hushed voices outside in the corridor. Those cheeky maids, no doubt shirking their work duties again and with half of them ill in bed. Mabbot

rose and paused until the small tinge of pain in his diaphragm subsided. He reached for his jacket, threaded his arms through the sleeves, and buttoned it up with one hand while he smoothed the creases in his trousers with the other. Mabbot opened his door and peered to the left and right. He saw the back of a young woman in a dusky rose crinoline dress that swayed like a pendulum across the stone floor as she walked. It was none other than Lady Charlotte. It was most unusual to find a member of the family in the servants' quarters. What was she up to?

Mabbot stepped out and coughed lightly.

'Can I be of any assistance, Lady Charlotte?' he asked sweetly. He was aware of her indifference towards him and he could not afford to get on her wrong side. Trouble was she was a wily character, for a woman. Lady Charlotte stopped in her tracks and slowly turned around, her face flushed and a wide grin split her face. There was a gentleman behind her but Mabbot could not make out who it was in the gloom. Damn his eyesight, he thought, it was not as it used to be.

'Oh no, Mabbot. Sorry. We're in a trifle of a hurry. Mr Chambers here has a train to catch but I wanted him to have some of cook's wonderful fruitcake for his journey. With all the maids sick I thought I'd bring him down myself. Sorry to have disturbed you. Now we must dash.' The man raised his hat an inch before replacing it hastily on his head and followed Lady Charlotte out of the corridor.

Mabbot sighed heavily. Lady Charlotte creeping around the corridors without a chaperone? Whatever next?

*

'I can't believe it!' giggled Lottie as they fell back into William's room. 'Mabbot of all people – probably one of the most observant men around. Particularly when it comes to you, William, or should I say, Reuben?'

William strutted around the room, his heart racing, but naturally comfortable in his new identity. It was as he'd imagined; he felt as though he really was Reuben Chambers. He walked differently, using the stick to feign a very slight limp. He talked in a lower tone, pronounced his words more carefully as he'd practised and was more considered in his delivery. However, would he be able to keep it up? Mabbot had not been close and the corridor had been dark. William wasn't sure he could stand closer scrutiny.

'It is amazing, quite amazing. You really are the best sister one could have. I wish I could feel as confident as you sound. This newer style of clothing rather suits me don't you think?' William preened in front of the mirror like a peacock readying to charm its intended mate.

'Oh, the young men have been wearing this fashion all season! You do look so different, I must admit. Not like Lord William Kenilworth, future Duke of Romsey.'

'Indeed, I am not William.' He stretched the lapels on the frock coat, removed his hat and bowed deeply. 'I am Reuben Chambers, local businessman from London and what a pleasure it is to meet you, Lady Charlotte.' His mouth went dry and his heart throbbed in a fit of panic. 'But how on earth would you have met me? And what kind of business am I in? Do you think this will all work?' A hundred doubts flooded his mind.

'Of course it will, my dear William – I mean – Reuben. There are many 'ordinary' people within London. They're not all aristocrats, you silly thing! If you socialised more with humans instead of your beloved horses you would know that. You are going to meet Freddy at the Chelsea Gentleman's Club tonight – I've told him that you are a friend of a friend, who has just returned from travelling in Africa, collecting artefacts and items of interest and that you are looking to set up a business.'

William raised his eyebrows; Freddy was the son of distant family friend, whose sister Lottie corresponded with on a regular basis. And William was not a frequent visitor of gentleman's clubs. 'Goodness, where did you dream all this up?'

Lottie shrugged her shoulders, her crinoline dress swished along the carpet as she paced, creating tiny motes of dust to swirl and dance. 'Oh, I read something, somewhere. Probably in some journal I should not have been reading. I've also told Freddy that you are a little travel weary and that they shouldn't bombard you with too many questions.'

'I'm not sure that I can go through—'

'And we'll have to develop some story about your family.' Lottie interrupted tapping a finger to her lips. 'Probably best not to have any.'

William went cold. 'But, what if they find me out, what if they expose me? I don't want to become a laughing stock amongst the men at the Gentleman's Club!'

Lottie tutted and shook her head. 'Well, if you don't want to go through with it, that's fine.' She took William's hand. 'It was you who said more than anything else in the world that you wanted to be someone else. Someone ordinary, I recall you saying. Now this is your chance. Reuben Chambers is an ordinary man in the purest sense of the word and at the same time the most extraordinary man! Just have some fun. You are really enjoying it I can tell. You've already fooled Mabbot, granted from a distance, but the people you'll be mixing with tonight don't know you as William Kenilworth. And Freddy is as short-sighted as a bat. What do you have to lose? We can pass it off as a big prank if they do, Freddy would be game. But I seriously think they won't have a clue.'

'Well, I suppose you are right and you have gone to an awful lot of trouble. It's a little like performing for nanny when we were young – of course we can do it!'

'Well, it's all in your hands now, Reuben.' She smothered a small smile.

'And?' he prompted.

Lottie clapped her hands excitedly. 'I wasn't going to let on until after tonight but what harm can it do? If we pull this off I've got tickets for myself and one Mr Reuben Chambers for the opera on Friday.'

William narrowed his eyes and his heart started to thud again.

'Yes.' Lottie cantered on hardly drawing a breath, 'and an introduction to the leading lady after the show!' She put a hand over her mouth as William processed the information.

As William, he would without doubt, refuse the invitation. He had no desire to see Fanny and be reminded of his humiliation. Nevertheless, he was intrigued. After all, as Reuben Chambers, he had never met an opera singer before and especially one who had been commissioned to star for a season at La Scala.

Lottie bit at her lip as the silence enveloped them like a morning mist.

It probably wouldn't happen, William thought to himself, after tonight, Lottie would get bored with the whole thing. Why not go along with her, after all, she had put a lot of time and effort into creating Reuben. And it was a great distraction for the time being from his other obligations.

'I'd be delighted to accompany you to the opera, Lady Charlotte.'

∗

Reuben hesitated at the door listening to the buzz of conversation inside the dining room of the Gentleman's Club. The usher opened the door wide for him to enter. Too late now, Reuben thought wryly. He pulled at his lapels, ran a finger along his moustache and stepped inside.

'Ah, good fellow, you must—'

Reuben held his hand out. 'Chambers, Reuben.' His voice cracked a little, he cleared his throat. 'And you must be Freddy?'

'Yes,' Freddy slapped him on the back, 'do come in Mr Chambers. May we call you Reuben? Good… we've not started dinner yet. Let me introduce you.'

Reuben shook hands with four other men before they took their place at the round table, set with silver cutlery and cut glass goblets. They all shook out the linen serviettes and placed them across their laps, as the waiter began to serve the soup. They were a vibrant group, full of tales and business talk and Reuben listened carefully as they ate their way through a three-course meal. They retired to the lounge and Reuben accepted a glass of port and a cigar. At first, the unfamiliar taste of tobacco irritated his throat but he persevered with a strained smile. William had never smoked, detesting the stale smell that followed his father, but now he began to find it most pleasurable.

'I say, Chambers.' One of the men tapped his shoulder, Reuben could not for the life of him remember his name.

'Yes?' The man handed him a card with his name and address in Cavendish Square. 'Yes, Mr Lockhart?' Reuben relaxed and inhaled on his cigar.

'I've been thinking about your business plans. I reckon that artefacts as exotic as the ones you have been talking about would be of interest to many of a certain standing in London.'

Reuben smiled, he'd enjoyed talking about Africa and was thankful for his previous studies and his time in the army. His dinner companions were not worldly travellers and therefore it had been easy for him to adopt a light sense of authority.

'You do? I'm sure you are right. I haven't really had time to look into the details—'

'Well, you'll need somewhere to operate from. As it happens I know of an opportunity, in King Street – central and very fashionable for those with a bit of money. The accommodation is on the ground floor and a reasonable rent. Might be just what you are looking for.'

'Indeed,' Reuben replied slowly, he hadn't anticipated that the evening would bring about further opportunities for him.

Edward Lockhart tapped the card Reuben held. 'Call on me, when you've had time to think about your plans a little more. No time like the present, eh?' He grinned broadly.

'Indeed, not, Mr Lockhart.' Reuben shook his hand. 'I shall certainly take your proposal into consideration.'

*

Later that night as he lay in bed buzzing with the conversation at the Club, William sighed with satisfaction. He fingered the business card thinking, why not? He needed something in which to invest his winnings from the racing partnership. He thought he would never sleep, so fuelled with excitement and anticipation but soon the exhaustion of his second identity overwhelmed him and he fell into the deepest slumber since Henry had died. And he dreamt, Reuben Chambers' dreams. No Dukedom, no parliamentary seat and no plans for him to wed a replica of his mother.

CHAPTER SEVEN

Reuben Chambers arrived at the theatre doors early; he wanted to walk about, taking in the familiar environment in his new skin. He tipped his hat at the young ladies who walked past, and nodded at their chaperones. On his way, he had stopped off at King Street. The Bazaar was in a perfect position, a place that potential buyers would pass through at some time or another. He had thought of little else since the evening at the Gentleman's Club and if tonight deemed to be a success he had decided to proceed with the acquisition. He had debated things in his head many times and then he had thought as Reuben Chambers. Would he ponder? Would he have second thoughts? Of course not, was the conclusion.

As he waited in the foyer his heart fluttered in his chest like a trapped bird, urgent, maybe a tad frightened but determined at the thought of being introduced to Fanny in his alternative identity. He spotted familiar people that he had acquainted on previous visits to the theatre and stared at them directly, challenging them to uncover his real identity. Although they were courteous and acknowledged him – men lifted their hats slightly, ladies smiled – they showed no flicker of recognition. His confidence grew and his anticipation of the night became filled more with wonderment and less of worry. Everything appeared brighter; the rainbow colours of the brocaded wallpaper, the flicker of the gas lamps and the buzz of conversation.

'Reuben, I mean, Mr Chambers! I am awfully sorry I'm late.' Charlotte flashed her brightest smile at Reuben as he took her hand and bowed deeply.

'I'm delighted that you have invited me to join you and your party, Lady Charlotte. And don't apologise, please. I have been taking in this wonderful atmosphere. I can't tell you how excited I am to be here at my first opera performance.'

'But surely, sir, you have seen performances on your travels?' Lady Charlotte asked a little louder than usual.

'Yes, yes of course but not one starring the divine and beautiful Miss Fanny Kendrick. I do believe...' Reuben lowered his voice, 'that she has an opportunity at La Scala?'

'So they say,' Charlotte replied. 'I'm sure she will find what she's looking for.' Reuben smiled tightly as they made their way to the family box.

*

Later, at the reception, Reuben waited patiently in the shadows, making small conversations with the odd stranger and sipping a glass of champagne.

'Ladies and Gentleman, please welcome, Miss Fanny Kendrick,' announced a snooty anonymous voice. The room erupted into a cacophony of applause and Reuben joined in, the resonant tones of his ex-lover filling the room with cries of 'but oh, you are all so kind.' The voice that had once made William tremble with desire, for Reuben had no such effect. He watched Charlotte take Fanny by the arm, guiding her towards him, and then turned his back to them. He could hear them talking as they approached.

'It was such a shame that your dear brother could not attend. I have written to him advising that this would be my last performance before I leave for Italy. I was hoping he would be here.'

'Oh, he would have been here if he hadn't come down with some ghastly bronchitis.' Charlotte lied, almost too easily. 'He is simply not well enough to attend. However, he sends you his very best wishes.'

Letter? What letter, Reuben rubbed his sweaty palms together. The Duchess had been up to her tricks again but it mattered not. He mustn't give things away now. They were almost at his side and Reuben suddenly had a great urge to run. He took a deep breath and turned to greet them.

'Mr Chambers, I am sorry to have abandoned you but here we are now. May I introduce you to Miss Fanny Kendrick?' Charlotte's voice trembled.

'I'd be delighted, Miss Kendrick,' Reuben stared deep into Fanny's eyes for a fleeting second and then broke away to sweep into a bow, his fingertips almost brushing her shoes. 'What a wonderful night and how delightful your performance was! So much more refined than anything I have ever seen.'

Fanny was distracted by several well-wishers, a plastered smile on her face as she shook their hands before returning to Reuben.

'Thank you kind sir,' she beamed, her gaze still scanning the room.

Reuben tapped his stick on the floor, keeping his eyes lowered. 'Lady Charlotte has been most kind in helping me integrate back into the London social life.' He reset the eyeglasses on the bridge of his nose.

'Indeed, Mr Chambers.' A knot furrowed at Fanny's brow and Reuben coughed, twisting his head away. 'I presume you have been introduced to Lord William? He has been a great supporter of mine for many years, a loyal follower. He will be the future Duke of Romsey.' Reuben watched Fanny plump up her shoulders and her breasts threatened to spill from the neckline. Loyal follower indeed, he mused.

Charlotte stepped into the void. 'Oh no, Mr Chambers has not yet had that honour. William has been dreadfully busy with the plans at Clomber Abbey and has not visited London as frequently as he might.

Now he has bronchitis. But there will be an introduction.' Reuben sensed the false smile on her face.

Fanny looked between them. 'And of course all of you, including you, Mr Chambers, have an open invitation to come and visit me in Milan. La Scala is such a wonderful theatre. Though, here,' she drew her arms in front of her. 'Here I shall always consider my home.'

'I am sure I would be delighted to visit you, Miss Kendrick. Now, if you would forgive me, it's been rather a long day and I'm still a little fatigued by the time differences.' Reuben turned to Charlotte and bowed again. 'And thank you for a most entertaining evening, Lady Charlotte. I owe you a debt of thanks. Ladies.' Reuben replaced his hat and began to make his exit.

'What a most endearing gentleman,' he heard Fanny say as he walked away. 'He did remind a little of someone, though I can't quite put my finger on who.'

*

Charlotte returned to Clomber Abbey the morning after the opera still giddy with all the excitement. It had been such fun watching Reuben, particularly with Fanny Kendrick. Her mother appeared at the drawing room door.

'Mother, I thought you were returning to London?'

'I had planned to, yes. Have you seen William?'

Charlotte fingered the lace around the neck of her dress and stroked the pearl necklace at her throat. 'Yes, I mean no, not since…'

'You're not making any sense, dear. Do come in from the draughty hall. I have no idea why William adores this place so. I much prefer London.'

Charlotte followed her mother and took a seat beside her on a large sofa, sinking into the feather cushions. She kicked of her satin covered shoes and watched her mother's silent disapproval then stretched her feet, like a cat on waking. Her silk stockings pulled at her toes.

'You enjoyed the opera, with the Bennets?' The Duchess ran a finger along the mantelpiece and clicked her teeth. 'I really must have a word with the housekeeper. She's new isn't she? Hasn't anyone told her of the standards that need to be maintained?'

'It was divine, Mother. Fanny Kendrick is—'

'Do you think William understands his responsibilities?' her mother interrupted. 'You are closer to him than any of us. I swear I do not understand him, much as I try.'

'Yes, I think he does.' Charlotte observed her mother's lined face, the lips turned downwards. 'But losing Henry and taking his place has been a shock for him, as it has for us all, but his life is going to change the most for it.' Her mother peered at her, unblinking. Charlotte continued. 'Henry was always better at everything because Father naturally spent more time with him. William hasn't had that opportunity and it seems unfair to expect him to fill the empty space immediately. He is mourning – they were very close. And he had made such great plans for travelling to America.'

Charlotte knew that her mother protected herself with a harsh veneer that encased her from head to foot. She was always uptight, like a coiled spring unable to relax. But then she had to keep things together. Papa was good at being a Duke to the outside world but not so good at the family head. Nor as a husband she supposed.

'You always have been too forgiving with William.' Her mother sighed letting her shoulders and her defences droop a little. She wrung her hands together and then shoved them quickly behind her back.

'But you can't deny that Henry had years of getting used to being the heir, in fact from the day he was born he'd been prepared and educated for the role. William is just a little—'

'Different?' Her mother allowed herself a small smile. 'I know you think I am hard on him, Charlotte, but I'm only doing what I think is right. I am his mother and know him best.'

Charlotte, emboldened by the excitement at the opera and the rare moment shared in her mother's confidence, decided she had to protect

William and be seen to support her at the same time. 'Yes of course, and deep down William appreciates that you are doing what is only right and proper. But at this particular moment he's in a hard place, rejected by Fanny and taking up the reins here, you know we all need a little time to adjust to change in life. I do understand how difficult it must be for you.'

'Time is maybe one thing he hasn't got.' The Duchess pinched the tip of her nose and sighed.

'What do you mean? Is Papa ill?'

'No, no. Your father is fine. It's just that, well some things need to be done. You know, William is very like your father, and he has coped. He was never born for the role. It really is no excuse.'

'Yes but Father inherited the responsibility when he was a young boy, it was very different,' Charlotte caught the raised eyebrows and the slight twitch in her mother's cheek. 'I'm sure he'll come round in the end. I can help, if you will allow. As it looks now, it will be a continual battle that neither of you will win.'

'Indeed, Charlotte. You may be right.' For the first time Charlotte noticed how strained her mother looked, the dullness of her skin and the wrinkles around her eyes. 'I'm not sure that your father would approve. You know how he feels about these kinds of things and he cannot understand William, never has. Anyway you will be busy, it is the year for your season, after all.'

Charlotte's heart quivered with injustice. 'I want to help, whatever Papa thinks about my actions. Surely, our family and duty come first. Everything seems to have fallen to pieces since Henry died and I can't believe he's gone and left us.' Charlotte brushed a tear away from her cheek. She didn't want to be paraded around London with all the other debutantes. She disliked their petty obsessions with their looks and eligible suitors. She would much prefer to be reading or out riding.

The Duchess straightened her back, hands clasped in front of her. 'Well, all I'm saying is that life must go on. We can't put things on hold whilst William gets used to it. And—'

'Well, can't we ease William into some of his responsibilities? He can be my chaperone and at the same time meet some suitable companions? Perhaps ones you approve of? Please, Mama, do say yes.'

Her mother searched her face, her features softening. Charlotte could see how pretty she had once been. The moment disappeared as the Duchess's face hardened again.

'Very well. The issue of a wife is not the most pressing, but the wrong one would be irreparable. William will need to provide an heir if the Dukedom is to remain in our family.' Her mother turned away, a slight gasp escaping from her lips as if remembering something. 'And one inside wedlock.'

'Certainly, Mama.' Charlotte stood, picked up her shoes and curtsied. 'And now I'm tired, would you mind if retired to my room before lunch?'

Her mother shrugged and waved a dismissive hand.

*

Mabbot paced the hallway his hands behind his back, counting the footsteps in his head. Now and again, he would stop to straighten a picture frame or reposition an ornament that to his eyes seemed out of place. William had gone missing for the second time that week. Mabbot found some comfort in the pacing and the obsessive attention to detail. It helped him clear his head and think things through.

The Duchess had been furious. She had wanted to discuss an urgent matter with William and had expected Mabbot to produce him. 'What do you mean you don't know where he is?' she had snorted, her nose raised above him.

His fingers twitched with frustration. 'I'm terribly sorry, your Grace but I believed his Lordship was busy with the plans for the stables.' The white lie tripped of his tongue as easily as a child reciting a rhyme.

The Duchess tapped her cane on the tiles. 'Really,' she arched an eyebrow, 'Mabbot, I did think I could rely on you.'

Mabbot's neck burned angrily but he kept his face straight as he recalled the advice his father had given him: 'One never reacts to the accusations or indeed anything thrown our way by the masters and their family. It doesn't matter whether you think you didn't deserve their anger or their malice. You are paid to be discreet and discretion can mean allowing words to pass over you without effect.'

It was hard for Mabbot; deference did not come easily to him, despite his role in life. Nevertheless, he had practiced and practiced in front of a mirror perfecting his facial expressions and switching himself off from the emotional outbursts of others.

'Indeed, your Grace. I apologise.'

After the Duchess had flounced away, Mabbot returned to William's room and used his skeleton key when there had been no answer to his knocking. Mabbot always left the room as he had found it. The plans for the stable covered a small table. Mabbot noticed that the day clothes William had been wearing were strewn across the bed as if taken off in a hurry. Mabbot folded them and put them to one side for the maid to collect for laundering before returning to the hallway.

Sometime after midnight, as Mabbot was retiring to his room, he heard heavy, quick, footsteps above him on the first floor. His ears pricked like an animal sniffing out its prey. Walking very slowly Mabbot found himself again outside William's room listening like a thief in the night. He tapped lightly, one ear close to the door.

'One moment, Mabbot.' William's voice filtered through. 'Right, you can come in now.'

Mabbot opened the door to find William dressed in the clothes that Mabbot had folded two hours earlier.

'I came up earlier this evening, sir. There was no answer and—'

'Oh damn, sorry, Mabbot. I should have told you.' William tucked something into the wooden chest in the corner of the room. 'I had to go down to the stables, check out some changes I'd made. I hadn't realised it was so late.'

'Of course, sir. But the Duchess wanted to speak with you.'

'Oh, dear, I've got you into trouble haven't I?' William stood up and held the door open. 'I'll sort things out with Mother, tomorrow. Goodnight, Mabbot.'

*

The Duchess of Romsey watched her daughter leave the room and rubbed at her temple. Charlotte was turning into a clever woman, one who could gain control of situations, as she once had. Secretly she admired her independent streak.

The Duchess sat in a chair facing an oil portrait of the Duke and herself, commissioned for their wedding nearly thirty years ago. The Duke stood behind her, his face set in pose and his hand on the chair she sat on. He towered over her, protective and possessive. But the husband who had promised her fidelity had betrayed her and now that act of disloyalty was threatening their family's future. She pulled out a folded letter from her sleeve, the seal broken. A single tear fell on to her cheek.

How she resented it here at Clomber Abbey, where she had learnt of her husband's bastard child. Since the day they were married she had known of the expectation to produce an heir and for some time she had worried that she may be barren. There was no-one to share these worries with and she had gone through long periods of greyness where, no doubt, she had been less attentive to her husband's needs. And she was fully aware of the rights that men seemed to take as a natural and obligatory part of their life. That she accepted, as long as she didn't know the details and there weren't any consequences, like children.

The Duchess re-read the letter again and the words blurred into one.

Your Grace, Duke of Romsey

Forgive my temerity at writing to you but I would like to express my condolences at the loss of your son, Henry. I read of his early demise in the newspaper some weeks ago.

However, my purpose for writing is to inform you of a bereavement of my own. My mother, Edith, died twelve months ago. I understand that she was in your employ as a housemaid for some time and left when she became with child. After I was born we came here to Edinburgh. However, I believe that you may know some, if not all, of these details?

I was unaware of my links with your family until only recently when a letter, left by my mother to be opened only on the death of your son, was passed to me. I would like the opportunity for an audience with yourself, to discuss the contents of this letter at your convenience. I can be contacted at the address above.

Edwin Hales

Now the indiscretion was coming back to haunt them. It was only by chance that she had intercepted the letter on the silver correspondence tray left for her husband. He had been too eager to get out hunting and the Scottish return address had caught her eye.

She gripped the arms of the chair until her knuckles went white. Why had the bastard son been allowed to live while Henry had been taken away? She screwed up the letter into a tiny ball and threw it into the fire, watching the edges curl and blacken.

CHAPTER EIGHT

Amelia hesitantly rapped the knocker of number 37 Queens Row. She pulled her shawl around her; the fog had crept up and was enveloping everything in sight. Amelia hated the gloomy mist. It always seemed as sinister as the figures who innocently appeared in front of her without warning. She could hear the shuffle of feet getting closer behind the door. Amelia patted her damp hair and checked her shoes. The door creaked opened and an old lady looked up at her and smiled, the skin around her mouth puckering like the skin of an old apple. A fragrant aroma of lavender wafted in the air between them. Gnarled fingers curled around a walking stick in each hand and Amelia tore her gaze away from them.

'Mrs Lovelady?' Amelia raised her voice a little presuming that she must be hard of hearing.

'Well it depends on who is asking,' the old lady replied firmly. 'And there is no need to shout. I can hear perfectly well.'

'Oh, I am sorry. I meant no disrespect.' Amelia stepped back a little and tried to smile. 'My mother said you might be interested in a lodger – a lady lodger?' Amelia thrust forward a piece of folded paper. She had returned from an interview for the position of a governess to find her mother had left the lodgings they were staying at without explanation. Just the note and the week's rent in arrears.

Her initial reaction of dejection had turned into a small flame of anger in the pit of her stomach as she walked across the city in a daze. Now, it began to drizzle and Amelia was tired and hungry. She knew she had to secure a place to stay before nightfall. If Mrs Lovelady refused her mother's request, Amelia did not quite know what she was going to do.

The old woman looked skywards as if she had not heard but Amelia did not want to offend her again by repeating the statement.

'Come in, child. You will catch your death standing all wet there on the step. You can tell me why you are here once you have warmed up a little. Come, come,' she beckoned with one of her bent fingers and stepped aside to allow Amelia to enter. The damp air in the corridor folded around her like a blanket and Amelia looked upward towards the cavernous ceiling and shivered.

'And your mother is?' asked the old woman who had begun to trace her steps back into the darkness. Amelia could make out a small beam of light from under a door.

'Esme. Esme Banks.' The old woman stopped and Amelia almost ran into her.

'You are Esme's daughter?' Mrs Lovelady coughed. A rough racking cough and it took a good while before she got her breath back.

'Shall I fetch a glass of water, Mrs Lovelady?' Amelia peered into the gloom. 'Or a seat?'

The old woman shook her head, waved a hand and continued her painful shuffle. 'No indeed not. I shall be as fit as a fiddle in just a moment. It will pass.'

They reached a small living room dimly lit by one flickering gas light that threw shadows. Despite the daylight the heavy drapes were drawn.

'The light gives me a headache,' the woman explained indicating again with a bony point of her finger that Amelia should sit. Mrs

Lovelady lowered herself gingerly into a large chair, pulled a woollen shawl around her knees, and balanced the sticks against the armchair.

'Esme Banks. I have not seen your mother since…' she closed her eyes, '…well I cannot remember but long before you were born. How old are you, Miss…?'

'Amelia and I am nineteen years old.'

'Nineteen?' Mrs Lovelady sighed heavily. 'Now, what has your mother been up to?' She slowly unfolded the note, squinted at the writing and then scrabbled in the side of the chair producing a pair of tiny pince-nez glasses which she balanced on the end of her nose. She mouthed the words, her lips moving in silence. Mrs Lovelady folded the paper and placed her hands in her lap.

'So, she's moved on again? I am very fond of your mother, even though I have not seen her for many years. I understand. It is probably a time she would rather forget.'

Amelia's bottom lip trembled. Her mother had left without a word of her intentions. No explanation. No forwarding address. She didn't know what she was going to do.

'I was going to get a post as a governess, to help Mother. However, they gave it to someone more… experienced.'

'Now, don't you fret, my dear. Of course you can stay. I have more than enough room and there is plenty to do to keep you occupied. I hope you don't mind doing a few chores in return for a roof over your head?'

Amelia shook her head and managed a watery smile. 'No of course. I do not expect to stay here rent-free. I shall look for paid work and alternative lodgings. I will not be a burden to you for long.'

'No, I insist, you will not be a burden. Indeed, a bit of company will be most welcome. I do not see many people these days. Apart from next door, she kindly brings some provisions each week. And anyway, I did not charge your mother to stay all those years ago and I will not charge you. I will not change my mind. I do not need your money. Your mother is not without a care, not really, maybe a little impulsive.'

Mrs Lovelady sighed. 'Where are my manners? You will want some refreshments after your journey, not the mutters of an old woman. Would you mind making us a nice warm pot of tea? The parlour is through there.'

She pointed to a door to the right with one of her canes before she leaned back in the chair and closed her eyes.

*

Reuben looked around the Bazaar. His Bazaar. He walked from item to item. A large wooden totem pole dominated one corner, whose ornate carvings and brightly coloured war painted face stared menacingly back. It was his favourite piece and not for sale. A ceremonial sword and shield sparkled on the wall, the light from the gas sconce catching its sharp contours and edges. Several silk paintings and rugs from Persia hung on the walls. Reuben closed his eyes and heard the cry of the warriors and foreign tongues spoken at the looms.

Setting up the Bazaar had not been without problems. Reuben had understood very little about commerce or running a shop, but he had learnt quickly. He had stumbled upon this stock quite by accident and the owner – in some financial difficulty – had welcomed his offer to take it off their hands. He turned to the large window, which bowed out onto King Street. In large white and gold lettering were the words *King Street Bazaar* and above the door a plaque that read '*Sole Proprietor: Mr Reuben Chambers - Established 1844*'.

Today was the first day of public opening but it was far too early for any customers. The event had been mentioned in *The Times* – a small advertisement. The piece had been a great boost for business even before today and some of the items had already been sold at private viewings. His thoughts ran around in his head until he felt giddy. One minute he chided himself for believing he could actually run a business, the next he was filled with sense of excitement at trying something so different. But it mattered not, his journey was too far along the path to turn around.

He took out a large fat cigar from his inside pocket and carefully unwrapped it. Reuben had grown accustomed to the odd cigar since his first venture to the Gentleman's Club. He carefully snipped off the end with a silver cigar blade then wet the tobacco with his tongue and reached for a box of matches. He puffed until the end glowed red and then sat, enjoying the heady feeling and the smoke wafting around his head.

One hour later and the shop teemed with ladies and gentlemen browsing around the goods, a glass of champagne in one hand and a catalogue in the other. Reuben recounted his tales of trips to Africa and the Far East and Egypt many times. Many of his customers had never been outside London, never mind England, so he allowed himself to embellish his tales of travels and far off cultures and wallowed in the awe of the customers' questions. The questions and comments developed into a warm and pleasant crescendo that soothed his head and brought him great joy.

By lunchtime, the customers were still coming and his order book was more than half-full. A light buffet of canapés had appeared, with the compliments of Lady Charlotte, who apologised for not being able to attend but wished Mr Reuben Chambers the best of luck in his new venture.

At 2pm he clapped his hands.

'Ladies and Gentlemen, thank you for showing your support to the King Street Bazaar. I am most grateful. But now I'm afraid I must close.' He waved the full order book in front of him. 'I must take stock and set about obtaining your requests. I look forward to supplying you with a little hint of the exotic. Until then, I bid you good day.' Reuben bowed and a small ripple of applause rang around the room. He had refused to take payment on anything until collection, more than a little worried about the safety of his coffers after such a successful opening.

Satisfied with his morning's work he turned the large key in the door, locking out any further intrusions and sat down with his orders. It did not take long to dawn on him that he was going to need some help with the finances and accounts. He drafted a handwritten notice in large letters asking for an assistant who was familiar with *accounting and fulfilment* and in smaller letters, *a little light cleaning, to apply within*, and stuck the notice in the window then locked up and left.

*

Amelia enjoyed living with Mrs Lovelady in return for some cleaning, meal preparation, and her company. Every morning, after breakfast, they would sit together in the sitting room, Amelia with some embroidery she had found started and forgotten long ago by Mrs Lovelady. Amelia listened intently as the old lonely woman recounted her life, transporting her to a different century. Mrs Lovelady also talked about Amelia's mother.

'Esme, your mother, lived with her parents next door.' Mrs Lovelady wrinkled her brow as she recalled the memory. 'They were good people but both fell ill with consumption and within weeks, she was an orphan. I could not let her go to the poor house – she would never have survived and she was a good girl. I took her in, sold the house and put the money away for her.'

'She must have been very grateful for your kindness.' Amelia put down the sheet she had been darning.

'Well, she was at first. And I enjoyed her company, like I do yours, dear. But the day she came of age, she took the money I had saved and then disappeared.'

Amelia took in a sharp intake of breath, the anger at her mother's departure returning like a bad smell.

'Your mother has always been able to charm the gentlemen.' The old woman smiled fondly. 'I wouldn't be surprised if she was too embarrassed to come home. She need not have been. I will always have a soft spot for Esme, she was like the daughter I never had.'

Mrs Lovelady stared at a portrait that hung on the wall. A young soldier in full uniform stood erect and proud, a bayonet in one hand and the other leant on a chair. His eyes, as black as coal, appeared to stare right back at the old lady.

'Archibald was sent off to fight in the Napoleonic War six months after we were married.' Mrs Lovelady sighed. 'I received news of his death on our first anniversary. Now I just have my memories for company. If I could do anything in the world, it would be to bring my Archie home. I still miss him, maybe more now.' Rheumy eyes blinked at the picture and Amelia swallowed back her tears. She focused on the gnarled fingers lying in the old woman's lap, skin like tissue paper. Amelia realised that she could not take advantage of Mrs Lovelady as her mother had. She had to secure herself a future – and that meant a husband or a job.

'And I am sure your Archie thought of nothing else but getting back to you.' Amelia wondered if she would find such companionship, as the old woman closed her eyes, escaping into her dreams.

Some moments later, Mrs Lovelady sat up, eyes open wide and bright.

'You will find someone,' she said, her chin set and determined. 'But make sure whoever he is can provide for you first. Now I have some correspondence I must see to.' She straightened out the fingers on her right hand with her left. 'I can just about manage it, but it takes me a long time. Before you go out on your errands, could you arrange my writing desk? That would be most helpful.'

Amelia stood. 'I can write the letters for you if you wish. It is something my mother did make sure I could do, read and write.

'Thank you, my dear, that is very kind but this I must see to myself. And the exercise does help a little. And don't worry, you mark my words. Everything will turn out right.'

Amelia arranged the writing desk, laid out some vellum, a quill and made sure that the inkwell was full. She helped Mrs Lovelady to the chair and placed her sticks close by.

As Amelia turned to leave, the old woman pressed half a crown into her hands. 'Please treat yourself. Buy a hat, a nice hat. A young woman should be dressed well at times.'

'Oh, but I could not—'

'I insist. I will be insulted if you refuse.' Mrs Lovelady removed her hand.

'Well, thank you, it is most kind of you. It is such a long time since I had a new hat. I shall not be long.'

'And do not hurry, take your time, you cannot rush these kind of decisions. Go to Mrs Smith's haberdashery, just off King Street. She will see you right.' The old woman picked up the quill. 'And anyway, this shall take me the best part of this morning to finish.'

*

Reuben opened up the Bazaar, surprised and a little dismayed that he had not had any applicants for the position of assistant since he'd put up the notice two weeks previously. He expected a flood of enquiries from young gentlemen eager for the experience of helping to run a small and intriguing business. He walked through the showroom and into a small parlour at the back where he could make refreshments and hang his outdoor clothing. Maybe he should put in a word at the Gentleman's Club. He could not manage to deliver much longer and the last thing he wanted was to annoy potential customers. Not good for business at all.

At that moment the front door bell rang as someone entered the shop. He counted to sixty, not wanting to appear too eager. He believed it was better if he allowed customers some time to take in the marvels inside the Bazaar. Then he straightened his jacket, ran a finger over his moustache and stepped out into the showroom.

'Good morning, ma'am.' He could only see the back of the woman who was peering at a silk painting from Japan. She wore a long powder blue coat and had a pretty hat in grey and pink secured firmly on her head. He observed a nest of sandy brown curls in the nape of her neck. She had appeared not to hear him, her concentration focused on the picture.

Reuben cleared his throat. 'It is a fine piece of art, from the early sixteenth century I believe.' The customer jumped back and nearly ended up in his arms.

'Oh! I am sorry, sir. Do forgive me.' The young woman stepped back once she regained her balance and Reuben found himself staring at a pale, thin face, eyes hidden by a gilded cage of gauze. She stood erect, her back stiff and she fiddled with the fingers of her gloved hand.

'I apologise if I startled you, Miss.' She looked as if she could do with a good meal and some sunshine, he thought as he brushed past her, rather than a silk painting. 'I like to allow customers to browse alone before I make contact.' The woman continued to straighten her gloves and he sensed she wanted to say something but either could not or would not.

'Do you have a particular acquisition in mind?' he asked pointing back at the painting. 'This is a particularly pretty piece, from Japan as I mentioned and hand painted, many years ago. They have been very popular.' He turned back and found that she had lifted the veil. He stared into the palest blue eyes he had ever seen. Her face broke into a shy smile, which lit up the space between them.

'Oh, no, I am sorry if I have given the wrong impression, Mr Chambers. I am not here to buy.' She continued, 'I am here for the position that you have advertised in your window.'

CHAPTER NINE

Amelia hurried down the road, her skirts soaking up the early morning rain. She waited to cross the street as a carriage thundered past and the large wooden wheels thrust through a puddle, soaking her coat.

'Oh, no!' She brushed away the dirty water. A flower seller behind her chuckled. 'Fancy a bunch to cheer you up, ma'am?' She held out a limp bunch of mixed flowers of undeterminable origin. Amelia shook her head. 'No, no thank you.' She spied some roses behind the seller, 'but those, are they for sale?'

The woman grinned showing a mouth full of half rotten teeth. 'Everythin' for sale – for a price.' After a moment of banter between the two women they agreed on a price and Amelia clutched a bunch of pale apricot rose buds to her chest. She was a little nervous about her first day, particularly as Mr Chambers had sent a note and keys with a messenger earlier that morning saying he had been called away on urgent business and could she please open up. At first she was offended he would abandon her on her first day but realised that he must trust her with his precious business.

Amelia fumbled with the keys until she found the right combination. What the smaller key was for, she didn't know, it didn't fit either lock on the door. She pulled and pushed at the door until it opened with a whoosh and she fell inside. She turned the card hanging on the glass partition from *shut* to *open* and started to remove her gloves. Threads of hazy sunlight filtered through the front window and picked out the layers of dust on the tops of everything.

'That will never do,' she muttered, removing her coat and hat and hanging them on the stand next to the door. She fumbled in a large bag. As it was her first day, she hadn't known what to bring. Mr Chambers had not left any instructions. She had packed a feather duster, some soft cloths, a writing pad and a pencil. She was looking forward to meeting the charming Mr Chambers again. Mrs Lovelady had mentioned at breakfast that Amelia hadn't stopped talking about him since the day they met. Amelia fingered the cameo brooch at her neck, the only possession her mother had left behind. She had dressed carefully, in her favourite, and admittedly her only, Sunday best dress in turquoise. Her shoes could do with new soles, she thought as the damp soaked through her stockings. Perhaps when she received her first stipend she would treat herself to new pair.

She began to dust, humming a tune as she went and soon started to arrange items into particular sections. There was such an array of stock she thought it must be difficult for customers to see what was what and she experimented placing items that complimented one another and which might encourage more than one purchase. She didn't hear the doorbell ring as she concentrated on moving the smaller pieces like the Chinese fans and silks, the Italian oil paintings and the Greek stone figurines and stood back to admire her arrangements. A deep cough interrupted her thoughts and she stumbled backwards.

'I'm sorry, sir. I didn't hear—'

'Never mind all that,' a large, rather rotund, gentleman boomed, his voice resonating around the room. His stomach wobbled as he spoke and he pinned a monocle to one eye which gave him the air of a mythical monster. 'Is that Chambers fellah around?'

'No, sir, sorry, sir. He was supposed to be but he left word—'

'Stop blathering, girl and just tell me what I want to know.'

Amelia took a deep breath. She wasn't going to be bullied by anyone, not on her first day.

'Well, maybe if you could give me a little more information I could help with your query?'

'The order I placed with Chambers. When will it be delivered? He said four weeks and it's been five. My wife is planning a dinner and the ivory mask has to be in place by then. It will be the talk of the evening.'

'Oh, I see. Well I'm not familiar with the orders, it's my first—'

'You are the cleaner, then?' The man eyed the duster in her hand.

'Well, yes and—'

'No good to me. Why have you wasted my time, damnation!' His face turned puce and he almost stamped his foot. 'Tell Chambers I want that mask and I want it soon!' He turned and strode out of the shop, slamming the door behind him.

*

Reuben stood outside the Gentleman's Club and hailed a carriage.

'King Street, as fast as you can,' he ordered the driver. He was eager to see Amelia, feeling such a cad for leaving her alone on her first day. He hadn't expected to be delayed long, but his duties as William sometimes meant he had to drop everything and do his mother's bidding. She was becoming increasingly agitated but had yet to tell him exactly what the cause of her concern was. He'd managed to escape by inventing a business meeting regarding the Abbey's renovation plans at which he had to be present.

He tipped the driver generously, walked into the Bazaar with a light step and stood absorbed by the transformation. A small but beautiful arrangement of pale orange roses stood in the window. The whole place sparkled and most of the smaller items had been arranged in an artful manner. Only the larger items like the totem pole remained where they had been. He smiled broadly and strode towards the back room. Amelia stood in front of a mirror arranging her hat and wielding a rather long hat pin, turned suddenly.

'Miss Gray, I am sorry—'

'No need to apologise,' Amelia responded stabbing the pin into the fabric on her head. Reuben wondered how she missed her head. She pulled on her coat and began to fasten the buttons. 'I cleaned through and made an inventory.' Amelia handed him a list. 'Now, I have to go, Mr Chambers. I have errands to run.' A clock chimed four. 'I do believe we agreed my day would end at four?'

'Yes, indeed. Those were the arrangements and I'm very happy with them. But I feel awful, leaving you here to fend for yourself. However, you do appear to have occupied yourself in a most admirable way.'

Amelia shook her head. 'It has been quiet,' she admitted. 'That is why I managed to get things done. If you don't like what I have done I can put things back where they were?' She started for the door.

'Miss Gray, please one moment.' Reuben stepped in front of her. 'I am very grateful for what you have achieved. It looks first-rate, absolutely. The customers, I am sure, will see much more now with your gifted approach to arranging things. I cannot thank you enough. I do appreciate it.' He looked out of the window and then back to Amelia. Her gaze was firm though her lips trembled. 'I do hope my absence has not offended you and that you still want the post?'

'No, no, Mr Chambers, I am not offended in the least.' Amelia swallowed a sob. 'But I fear I may have let you down. And I really need this job. If not I fear I may end up in the poor house.'

Reuben's heart contracted as he watched two fat tears slide down Amelia's cheeks and he scrabbled in his pocket for his handkerchief and offered it to her. Amelia took it and dabbed at her nose.

'Surely things cannot be all that bad, Miss Gray? The poor house, surely not, you are far too...' Reuben bit back the desire to say beautiful. 'Far too refined and of good standing, surely?'

'It matters not,' Amelia sniffed. 'Mrs Lovelady is most kind offering me rent at a very reasonable price, though I had to insist I pay something and I don't have any other means of support. If I can't pay Mrs Lovelady, or God forbid something happens to her I have no means of support and the only option would be—'

'No!' Reuben asserted. 'I assure you that will not happen, not if I've anything to do with it. Now, tell me what has happened to think such thoughts.' He guided Amelia to a high backed chair, his hand touching her arm with the lightest of touches which sent a thrill down his spine.

'Well, this morning, a gentleman did come in demanding where his order was. Said it was due some weeks ago and you promised it would be here on time and that you should contact him right away.' Amelia took a deep breath and started to pull on her gloves. 'He was very upset. He mentioned a dinner his wife was hosting and an ivory mask.'

'And his name?' Reuben prompted.

'Well, that's just it. He didn't leave a name. He was very cross that I couldn't help him. He shouted and stormed out. It wasn't until after that I realised I had forgotten to take his details. I am very sorry, Mr Chambers.'

Reuben tried to look serious to emulate Amelia's worry, but her beauty made him smile. 'Don't worry, tell me what he looked like.'

'A big man, dressed like any gentleman but he wore an eyeglass, only one.'

'Ah, I know who you mean. Mr Carmichael. His bark is worse than his bite, I can promise you.' Reuben leaned in a little and whispered. 'It's said his wife has a very sharp tongue, so he takes it out on others.' Amelia's eyelashes fluttered and her face lit up with a smile. 'Don't concern yourself about it, I'll sort it out. His order has been here a week and I've been meaning to contact him. Now you understand how much I need your help?'

Amelia nodded. 'Yes, Mr Chambers, only if you are sure. I will see you Wednesday as arranged.'

'Splendid!' Reuben squeezed her hand and then withdrew smartly horrified at his presumption. 'Wednesday it will be and I promise to be here.'

*

'Mr Chambers is here?' Amelia gasped. She had spent the last three months working at the Bazaar and there had been no more incidents with disgruntled customers. Could she have done something wrong?

'Yes, my dear, he is. Most charming.'

'But it's Sunday!'

'Does that matter? He's your employer is he not? I think I'll go for my afternoon nap early.' Mrs Lovelady said with a knowing smile. 'You go and see to your guest, I trust you will be all right without me as chaperone? I left him in the dining room.'

'Oh, yes. Of course. Mr Chambers is a gentleman and we do work with each other in the course of the day.' Amelia stood in front of the mantelpiece rearranging the ornaments and winding the carriage clock. 'I am sure I don't know what he wants! Maybe he no longer wishes to employ me. Oh dear, how dreadful.'

'You have been working there this past few months without a worry. In fact I think you have blossomed since you've been there.' The old lady smiled a secretive smile. 'Don't you think that you would have known before now if it wasn't working out?'

'Yes, but he said it was a temporary arrangement in the beginning. To see if we, well, to see if we understood one another and apart from the awful first day, it has worked out very well.'

Mrs Lovelady patted Amelia's hand. 'Don't fret, my dear. Go and find out what Mr Chambers wants. I told him you would bring him some tea, the water has almost boiled.' The old lady shuffled off into her bedroom across the hallway.

As Amelia prepared the tea she ran possible scenarios through her mind. The book keeping was in order; in fact after expenditures and outgoings, the Bazaar was in a handsome profit. She had been proud to hand him the end of month accounts, neatly prepared. He had been most complementary. She had continued with rearranging the shop, drawing the eye of the customer through the use of colour and mirrors, on a tour of their making. Almost every visitor commented on the charming nature of the shop and how they felt transported to a different country. It was as if they were creating tiny dreams for them to escape into, taking them to places they may well never see.

She had relaxed in his company since those early days and they seemed to converse very easily. However, she realised, recently he had been withdrawn and absent from the shop more often, not that she minded now she knew the drill. He appeared to be a solitary man, never talked about his family, if indeed he had any. And of course she would not dream of prying into his personal life. Still she found herself wanting to know more.

She warmed the pot and swirled the water before adding three large spoons of Souchong tea that Mrs Lovelady kept for special occasions – Mr Chambers liked his tea strong and sweet. She placed the sugar bowl, two china cups and saucers on a tray, straightened her back and walked to the dining room.

'Miss Gray, I apologise if I have disturbed your day. I didn't want to interrupt if you were resting but your landlady was most insistent it would be in order?'

Amelia smiled broadly at him before setting the tray on a small table between two chairs. 'Not at all, Mr Chambers, it is a delight to receive you. Mrs Lovelady sends her apologies, it is time for her afternoon nap.'

'Not at all, and you shouldn't have gone to the trouble of tea.'

'No trouble, please do take a seat, Mr Chambers.'

Reuben placed his gloves and hat on a sideboard and walked around the room.

'What a pleasant room, and these,' he indicated the wall hangings. 'Are these not the ones you purchased from the Bazaar?'

'Indeed they are, Mr Chambers. The colours are most bright and fanciful I thought they would suit this room, lighten it up a bit. Of course Mrs Lovelady cannot see well, but she can make out these in a fashion. You don't think them too crude in here?' Amelia bit at her lip.

'They look perfect and as you say they brighten the room considerably. They are of Indian origin, I believe, most vibrant. Your landlady seems a most endearing woman; she did say you had very few visitors.'

'She has been on her own for a long time, Mr Chambers. Very independent and many of her friends have passed on…' Amelia tailed off, shocked by her indiscretion. 'Sorry, I shouldn't, I spoke out of order.' She concentrated on the tea pot, stirring in a brisk fashion and rattling the cups.

'Well, I did mean that you had few visitors, Miss Gray. Anyway, I won't tell, if you don't – now how about tea?' Reuben sat opposite and extended a hand.

Amelia nodded, feeling rather foolish and handed him a cup.

'Mr Chambers, if I've done something wrong, I'd rather know straight away. I mean if I've made a mistake with the accounts or upset a customer, I'm sorry but I'm willing—'

'My dear,' Reuben looked shocked and put his cup down and stood up, pacing the room his hands behind his back. 'I didn't intend my sudden visit to unsettle you. I assure you there is not a thing wrong, on the contrary, they have never been better! Even Mr Carmichael has returned to purchase more goods. No, you are doing all the right things. I came because I…'

Amelia stood to face him, wringing her hands, her heart beating like the wings of a trapped bird.

'You see, I've found myself thinking… about you and your predicament. I can't bear the fact that you have no-one in the world to protect you. And it's not only that, I have feelings. Oh, this is so difficult!' Reuben adjusted the glasses on his nose and took a deep breath. 'I did have my speech all planned out but now I'm blabbering like a court fool. What I want to say, I mean ask is… Miss Gray, Amelia, would you be willing to become my wife?'

Amelia's head span giddy for a moment and she watched him pat at his forehead with a handkerchief that he withdrew from his top pocket. She steadied herself on the arm of the chair.

'I mean, I'm more than willing to ask the permission of your family. Are you sure that there is no-one? I don't mean to pry, but...' Reuben carried on, a rush of words, his face flushed and his eyes shining.

'No, I mean I don't—' Amelia saw his features crumple as he thought she was rejecting him. 'Oh, I don't mean,' she flustered, feeling a hot flush up her neck. 'I mean to say. I don't know who my father is and my mother... well she abandoned me some long months ago. I have no idea where she is I'm afraid. So, no, I don't have anyone.' And I'm under the age of consent, she thought, but only a year, and if Mother cares little about me to leave me. Amelia realised that she was considering Mr Chamber's offer with some sense of seriousness and why not? She had become accustomed to his company, enjoyed his considered but not overly talkative nature and he had an air of goodness about him. A husband would secure her future. She unconsciously chewed at her knuckle as the thoughts tumbled through her head.

'Oh, I see. Yes of course. Well, I suppose my question still stands, Miss Gray. Will you do the honour of becoming my wife?'

Tears sprung behind Amelia's eyes. Her head was full of doubt and yet she desperately wanted to shout out, 'yes'!

'I'm not—' her voice cracked as she reconsidered telling him about her age. 'I need a little time to think?'

*

Reuben returned to the Bazaar deep in thought. He wasn't surprised Amelia wanted time to think. Following his first arrogant proposal to Fanny, he had learnt to temper his expectations. He stopped outside a small jewellery shop and surveyed the rings in the window. He had thought long and hard about asking Amelia to be his wife. He knew he was taking a risk but having succeeded in managing his two identities well so far, the thrill of taking it one step further filled him with new desires.

His feelings for Amelia had shocked him at first – nothing could have been further from his mind – but she had made such a difference to the Bazaar and business had grown well in such a few weeks. She made it easy for him to slip from one life into another and therefore his life as William was not the chore it had been. In fact he was rather enjoying the plans at Clomber Abbey and watching them come to fruition. And the thought of her entering a poor house had eaten away at his conscious until he could no longer bear to think about it.

He decided to return to the jewellers with Amelia when she could choose a ring of her liking. After all, ladies have certain ideas regarding these things. To him it seemed less important than having Amelia on his arm as his wife. The next thing he had to worry about was lodgings, but time enough for that; once Amelia had accepted his proposal of course, he realised with a heavy heart.

A familiar figure paced outside the Bazaar window, skirts swishing at the pavement. It was Lottie. What on earth was she doing here?

'Lady Charlotte,' Reuben doffed his cap and looked around him. He opened the door and made way for her to enter. 'I do hope you haven't been waiting for long.'

'Not at all.' Lottie took the keys and locked the door. 'William! I've not seen you for absolute ages. I must say you do look rather dashing as Mr Chambers.' She started to remove her gloves. 'Mother thinks I am visiting a friend, it's not a lie, I'm actually on my way, so thought I'd pop in.'

'It's delightful to see you, my dear Lottie. I've been busy, as both chaps.' Reuben chuckled deeply. 'And how is Mother?'

'Still fraught as you well know, William. I don't understand what is going on. I thought things would get better with time, but she's still as agitated as ever. You haven't done anything to upset her, have you?'

'Of course not, she has a lot to think on and doesn't want to upset Father. I believe she is happy with the plans for the Abbey, though I must admit I try not to involve her too much.'

'Indeed.' Lottie smirked from under the brim of her hat. She walked slowly through the shop, picking up things now and again. 'It looks fabulous, absolutely wonderful. How clever of you, of course. Are sales going well?'

'Extremely well, in fact this month we made a considerable profit after our outgoings.'

'We? Our?' Lottie raised a questioning eyebrow. He hadn't told her that he had employed Amelia and he hadn't planned to tell her of his proposal.

'Oh, I mean the business—'

Lottie disappeared behind the larger items at the back of the shop, as Amelia burst through the door using her own set of keys.

'Oh, Mr Chambers, I hoped I would catch you here,' she panted. Reuben looked around alarmed.

'Miss Gray, how lovely. But this is not a good time—'

'Oh, I shan't be long, I wanted... well, it was after you had gone, I realised I didn't need any more time to think. Not long I know but I was so very surprised when you asked me that I couldn't think straight all. I wanted to say that, well, if your proposal still stands, I would be honoured to be your wife.' Her cheeks flushed with a burnished shine.

Light footsteps crept up behind them and Amelia's hand flew to her mouth.

'Indeed, Mr Chambers,' Lottie said slowly walking around him to stand between them. 'A proposal of all things?' She glared at Reuben unsmiling. 'Well, Mr Chambers, are you going to introduce me?'

CHAPTER TEN

Amelia was shocked to discover Reuben had acquaintances within the aristocracy. Lady Charlotte had been very sweet about their news and it appeared that they had known each other for some time. However, Reuben insisted that Lady Charlotte had been about to leave and bustled her out of the Bazaar and requested that he find time to speak to her later regarding an important 'business matter'. When Amelia questioned him about his knowledge of Lady Charlotte he would not been drawn on the issue and insisted that they obtain a marriage licence there and then.

Within minutes, they were at Doctors' Commons. When the clerk asked if Amelia was old enough to consent, she had felt sick, she wasn't yet twenty-one but she was determined that nothing would hold her back. She added an extra year to her birthdate and looked the weasel-faced old man straight in the eye.

'Very well,' the clerk whined in a nasal voice. 'The licence must be used within three months.' Reuben nodded enthusiastically and pulled out his wallet. 'The cheapest form of marriage,' the man looked at Amelia with a raised eyebrow. 'That will be ten shillings plus two shillings and sixpence for the certificate.'

Amelia smiled and put her hand on Reuben's arm. He turned to the clerk, 'Thank you, but cost is not an issue, I can assure you.'

Amelia and Reuben married a fortnight later in the registrar's office only streets away from the Bazaar. Amelia wore a simple dress of cream linen, with a high lace neck, tiny buttons that ran along her spine and long sleeves that tailed off into a point over her fingers. It had been the cheapest she could find at such short notice, but she adored it. Mrs Lovelady pressed a lace hankie embroidered in blue into her hand along with a sixpence before she had left.

Reuben looked like he always did, in a dove grey frock coat, a matching waistcoat and gloves and smart beige breeches. The only difference to his attire was an ornamental tie, which on Reuben looked a little extravagant. He handed her a small nosegay of orange blossom as they turned to the registrar. The ceremony was brief and despite the dry delivery of the blessing, Amelia's heart soared as they left the building as man and wife.

'Now, Mrs Chambers, I think some refreshment is in order? I took the liberty of reserving a quiet corner in a small tavern.' He pointed up the street and then turned back to her, his face grim and his brow furrowed.

'Whatever is it, Reuben?' Amelia said, worried that already she had done something to offend him.

'You don't mind that this hasn't been a bigger affair? I am very aware that marriage should be such a grand occasion and I fear I have failed you.' He bowed his head and tapped his stick on the pavement.

Amelia refrained from smiling, though relief swept through her. 'Of course not, it has been quite perfect and I couldn't be happier. I wouldn't lie to you, Reuben, I promise as solemnly as I promised my vows.' The worried expression evaporated from Reuben's face and he began to whistle quietly as they walked down the road, arm in arm.

'Well, I suppose I will have to start looking for a replacement assistant now.' Reuben guided her through the smoky tavern to a table set for two by the fire.

'What do you mean?' asked Amelia removing her gloves.

'Well, I cannot have my wife working and certainly not for me. Surely it is not the done thing.'

'But I don't want to give up my job.' Amelia lowered her eyes. 'Not yet anyway.' Amelia knew that opposing Reuben was not the way to retain her position. Who knows what the future held, they hadn't discussed having children, but it was something she desired from the centre of her soul. She was determined to become a mother who deserved a child's love. 'And we will need the money to pay lodgings to Mrs Lovelady, after all she has offered us the larger part of the house to live in until we find something suitable.' Amelia searched Reuben's face as he fidgeted with the cutlery, his mouth set straight, neither smiling nor scowling. 'And you are regularly away on business, we need someone who is familiar with the Bazaar to keep everything on the straight and narrow.' She lifted her chin in determination.

'And that someone is you?'

'Naturally, husband dear, who else?' She grabbed his hand. 'Please, Reuben, let's see how things work out. I do not want to be stuck in the house with very little to do while you are away. It would drive me mad. Then if my – if our circumstances change – we can think about getting someone else in.'

A shadow crossed Reuben's face and he looked away from her, as though he wanted to say something and then changed his mind. Perhaps she had gone too far, after all, they had only been married all of an hour and already she was defying him.

'I'm sorry, Reuben. I did not mean—'

'No, of course, you are right.' Reuben returned to face her with a forced smile. 'The extra money will come in handy as you say, well…until the next accounts are settled. But I do want to do right by you, Amelia. We will discuss it again, no need to make rash decisions?' Reuben took out his pocket watch and signalled for the taverner. 'Time for our wedding breakfast. How does chops and a glass of ale sound?'

Amelia nodded in agreement but she sensed the tension that pulled between them and that Reuben was not being totally honest about changing his mind.

*

Reuben stared out of the carriage window as they approached the long tunnel, which led to Clomber Abbey. He had been loathed to leave Amelia so soon after their marriage but there were matters which needed his attention, as William, at the estate. Her face had fallen but she was also distracted by her concern for Mrs Lovelady who had taken to her bed two days ago.

'Call for the doctor, Amelia. Perhaps he can prescribe something?' Reuben suggested as he pulled on his coat. Amelia brushed at his collar and tightened his tie.

'I'm not sure, she doesn't want any fuss. It is almost as if she's given up. She won't even take a cup of tea!'

'She is old, Amelia. You must prepare yourself.' Amelia gasped and her fist flew to her mouth. Reuben scalded himself for his lack of thought. Mrs Lovelady was the only family Amelia had. 'Oh, I'm sorry I did not mean to upset you. I hate going away and leaving you like this.'

'No, don't worry, I'll be fine. I'll call for the doctor as you suggest. Maybe a tonic or something.'

Reuben planted a small kiss on her damp cheek and offered her his handkerchief. 'I promise to be back as soon as I can. Two, maybe three days.'

As the carriage began to slow, he braced himself. He found it harder and harder to pick up his life as William and he was not looking forward to seeing Lottie. He knew she worried for his welfare but since she had discovered that he had proposed to Amelia she had begun to have second thoughts about his double life. She even suggested that it wasn't too late to put a stop to it and that it had all been a bit of a 'game'. He breathed in deeply, it had stopped being just a bit of fun the day he had fallen in love with Amelia and he wasn't prepared to leave it all behind now. He would have to face her wrath for now. She would have to accept that there were consequences to their little game, as she termed it, and he for one was taking it seriously.

He avoided her for most of the day, but she finally discovered him in the stables. William without waiting, admitted that his relationship with Amelia had been blessed by the marriage vows. Lottie's mouth dropped open like a fish gasping for air. For once, she was stunned for words.

'William, have you gone completely mad?'

William increased his long strides around the huge empty carcass of stables, which were being built for his precious racehorses. He'd dismissed the workmen whilst he worked out a few issues with the plans, nothing too difficult but he didn't want the men carrying out work whilst he sorted things out.

'Well, rumour has it, Lottie, that I always have been a little on the mad side.' He had always been aware that the estate workers talked about him as the 'odd' one of the family. He didn't treat them like everyone else did, that was all, and if that made him different, so be it.

Lottie ran to keep up with him. 'What rumour? And you know jolly well what I mean. When we started this little experiment, I never dreamed that you would take it this far. This is just too much, William.'

William stopped in his tracks and turned to face her. She had returned from a ride and wore full riding gear. She snapped a whip to her side. Her frustration with him was evident in her burnished cheeks, but he could not give her the answers she wanted.

'Oh, Lottie, this is no longer an experiment. I must agree I never thought it would work, but thanks to you and that wonderful creative mind of yours, it did and it has been one of the best things I ever did.'

'But to get married? I am sure you must have broken the law, William. I mean we never used to have secrets. If I hadn't met Miss

Gray in the Bazaar, well I don't believe you would have told me at all. Are you sure she is old enough?'

'Old enough? Of course she is, she would have said. I asked about her family and she has no-one, well a mother somewhere... anyway I shall not justify my actions. Amelia is a wonderful—'

'Oh, I don't doubt the qualities of Miss Gray—'

'Mrs Reuben Chambers, actually.' William grabbed Lottie's hands in his. 'I don't mean to upset you – it's the last thing I want. I knew you would try to talk me out of it, just as you are doing right now. Believe me I did have doubts, as William, but in the end Reuben made the decision.'

'But Reuben isn't real, William! Surely you can see that this all has got out of control and now you've gone and involved someone else. This could be a disaster. It was never meant to become part of real life. How could you be as stupid as to think so?'

William dropped her hands as if they were as hot as coal. Lottie bit her lip but he didn't want to hear her apology.

'Oh, but it is true life, Charlotte. Perhaps more than any other time in my life. I, or rather Reuben, is very much in love with Amelia and she will make a fine wife.'

'I don't doubt she would,' said Lottie in a more calm and soothing voice. 'But what if she finds out? How are you to keep up the facade? It is one thing fooling a group of people who hardly know you, but a wife? It's a much more intimate relationship. People are beginning to talk, William!'

'Who is talking about what?' William pushed his frustrations down, trying to douse the flames of his sister's worry.

'On the estate, the workers, the staff. How you sneak in and out through those tunnels. I am sure Mabbot has a hand in the rumours. You know what he's like, snooping around, questioning the maids—'

'Mabbot is doing his job,' William said with a sarcastic tone. He realised he had offended Mabbot by not taking him on his frequent trips and William spent more time away from his manservant's keen eye.

'And your obligations here at Clomber, they are going to pull on your time and to marry a woman who is not—'

'Not what exactly?' William's voice was brittle and hard. 'Reuben Chambers does not need to explain his choice of a wife to anyone. It makes no matter where she came from, she could be a whore for all he cares. The only thing that matters is that he loves her.'

Lottie stepped back, shaking her head. 'I'm sorry, I did not mean to cast aspersions. I am worried, William. I had no idea you felt so strongly. I fear that you will be hurt and I would be responsible for that hurt. I couldn't bear it.'

William grabbed her hand and squeezed. 'Lottie, do not worry. Please. I am more than grateful for all your help and support. I, William Kenilworth, am not married to anyone, I am still a single man. As for Reuben Chambers, his life is for him to decide.' But the niggling demon in the back of William's mind wondered if his sister's concern was bathed in more than a little of the truth.

*

Mrs Lovelady fell into her final sleep three weeks later. The doctor visited as Reuben suggested but there was nothing he could do. Amelia sat with her day and night, reading quietly from a book until the old lady opened her eyes for the last time and sighed happily. Amelia told herself she could not be sad for long because all Mrs Lovelady wanted was to be reunited with her Archibald. She received notice of Mrs Lovelady's last will and testament and no-one had been more surprised than Amelia to learn she had inherited 37 Queens Row as a gift for her company.

Three months had passed since she and Reuben had wed and it was ideal for a family Amelia thought, placing a gentle hand on her stomach. It was meant to be filled with the sounds of children and family life, like Mrs Lovelady had dreamt of. She knew she would approve. The doorbell chimed and Amelia frowned. She wasn't expecting Reuben for some time and anyway, he had a key.

Amelia opened the door. Her mother stood unsmiling on the doorstep. She was smaller than Amelia remembered and her auburn hair was tinged with grey. Her dress, in a rich, burgundy velvet, warmed her sharp features.

'Aren't you going to invite me in?' her mother asked, unblinking.

Amelia wondered why she was not more surprised at her unexpected appearance. 'Do I have much of a choice?' She stepped aside to allow her mother through.

Esme went straight to the sitting room. Amelia had opened up the whole house after the funeral, all three floors were bathed in daylight and Reuben had paid for a full redecoration, in fact he insisted. Amelia looked around with a sigh of approval; Mrs Lovelady's presence still lingered.

'It all looks so different. Nothing like I remember at all!' her mother exclaimed looking around. 'The place was always pitiful; drab and dreary, as though in continual mourning. You have made a lovely home, Amelia.'

'Yes I have, Mother, and now just what is it that you want?' Amelia, irritated by her mother's degrading reference, felt tense and uptight. She did not like her past revisiting her and was aware Reuben would be returning home for lunch soon. Her mother shot her a shrewd glance. 'There is no need to be curt with me, Amelia. I am still your mother.'

Amelia raised an eyebrow. 'Really? I assumed you forfeited that position on the day you threw me out onto the streets.'

'I did not throw you out; you would not be here if that were the case. Anyway, it hardly looks as if you suffered. Seems to me like I did you a good turn.'

Amelia knew there was no use confronting her mother. She was a simple woman in thought and emotion. She believed she had truly done no wrong and Amelia was not in the frame of mind to convince her otherwise. What was the point?

'Would you like some tea?' Amelia lowered her voice as her mother sat down and placed her gloves in her lap, a smile of pleasure plastered across her face.

'That would be most welcome, it has taken me a while to get here. I'm quite parched.'

'I shan't be a moment,' said Amelia turning towards the kitchen door.

'You don't have servants?' her mother enquired, her voice laced with sarcasm.

Amelia whirled back, her skirts twitching with the sudden movement.

'Indeed no, what on earth would I do with servants? Reuben would never allow it. He despises all that aristocratic nonsense. I am more than capable of running my own home. And anyway, we couldn't afford staff, not even with my wage.' Amelia flushed with irritation.

Her mother looked at her with wide eyes. 'Wage? My dear, do not tell me that your husband is unable to keep you as his wife?'

Amelia bristled again, clenching her fists, her fingernails digging into her palms. 'Indeed he is, Mother. I choose to work and wouldn't have it any other way. I work in his Bazaar on King Street. What may I ask; would you know about being a wife?'

'Ah, so you work for him. Well, that is a little different.' Her mother ignored her barbed comment about her unmarried status. 'Mr Reuben Chambers sounds like a clever gentleman indeed. I am hurt you did not deem fit to invite me to the wedding. Who gave consent? You are not yet twenty-one.'

Amelia knew her mother was playing with her. Something she had done since she could remember, making her feel awkward and small, but not now. Not in her own house. It seemed Amelia had done better for herself than her mother ever could. Amelia believed her mother would not expose her indiscretion regarding her age, she didn't like to bring attention to herself with the authorities.

'Reuben wanted to invite you but I refused to consider the notion. Even Mrs Lovelady could not persuade me I'm afraid. And I didn't know where you were! It was a small private affair and I absolutely refuse to discuss my decision. Now, I shan't be a moment.'

When Amelia returned with a tray and the cake she had made that morning, her mother was reading a letter.

Amelia poured the tea while she observed her mother. She had aged in the time since she had seen her. Lines framed her pale blue eyes, the corner of her mouth turned downwards, her brows knitted as if in pain, and the grey tinge in her hair extended further than she first noticed. She handed her mother a cup and saucer, took a slice of cake and sat opposite her.

'From Mrs Lovelady.' Her mother waved the letter at Amelia; she could make out the spidery painful writing. 'Her solicitor passed it on to me after her death, on her instructions. I saw a notice in the paper.' Her mother spoke as if no-one else was in the room and Amelia realised that she must have thought the old lady had left her something.

'Oh?' Amelia shook her head, what business of it was hers? 'It was painful for her to write, her hands were in a terrible state. She must have wanted to say something important to make the effort.' Amelia took a small bite out of her cake and chewed slowly.

'Oh, yes, she wanted to chide me for my treatment towards my only daughter. She thought very highly of you.' Her mother looked down into her lap. 'I do regret not seeing her before she died – she was once like a mother to me.'

'Yes and you abandoned her too, seems like you have a habit of leaving those around you.' She watched her mother's face crumple for a second before she managed to regain her composure.

'I do what I think is right at the time. It might not work out that way, I agree, but I did do everything with the right intentions. When I left her all those years ago, I was with child.' The silence stretched between them as Esme pulled a laced handkerchief from her sleeve and dabbed either side of her nose. 'The father, your father—'

Amelia put her cup down and waited for her to continue. Her mother never talked of her father.

'I left because I didn't want to bring shame on the old lady and expect her to support us both. No sign or chance of a husband in sight. Your father was not the marrying kind. Well, in fact he happened to be married to someone else, though I swear I did not know that at the time.' Her mother sat forward, her face searched Amelia's. Her mother sighed and continued, stirring her tea vigorously. 'Mrs Lovelady never had much money, only a small widow's pension and I knew she would insist on trying to support us. I could not take advantage of her since she had been most kind to me after my parents died. It just seemed the easiest thing to do, I knew she wouldn't follow me and try and make me change my mind.' Her mother leaned in towards her again. 'I tried very hard to be a good mother to you, Amelia. I am sorry if I let you down.'

Amelia wished her heart would soften at her mother's sudden and rare emotional admission but still she couldn't help feeling what her ulterior motives were. She stood up and crossed the room.

'The letter, from Mrs Lovelady, what did she say?'

Her mother held it out. 'Here, you can read for yourself.'

Amelia shook her head. 'Look, why are you here? Why are you telling me all this now?'

Her mother stood up and walked over to her side. 'Mrs Lovelady's letter was a good telling off, she wanted me to know that you would be all alone after her death, she said it was never too late. I don't know, she made me think—'

'Well, as you have discovered, I am not alone. What is it you want from me?' Amelia did not believe her mother wanted to be reunited without other motivation.

'No! I do not want anything from you for heavens' sake, Amelia. What do you want me to do? Beg for your forgiveness? The letter made me realise how much I missed you. I wanted to make amends, say I am sorry. I'm not getting any younger and—'

'Enough, Mother, I don't need to hear any more.' Amelia stood for several seconds rooted to the spot as her mother pulled on her gloves and buttoned her coat.

'You are right, I probably should not have come.'

Amelia reached out and put a hand on her mother's arm.

'No, don't go. Not just yet. I'm not sure about your abilities as a mother, but I do know life is too short for quarrels. Whilst I do understand some of your actions, Mother, it doesn't mean I agree with them.'

Her mother nodded and blinked and Amelia realised, for the first time, her mother was being genuine with her.

'Well, I am glad you came this morning, albeit it was a bit of a shock. It is lovely to see you and maybe you can make amends after all.'

Her mother frowned.

'Maybe you'll get a second chance at all this. You are going to become a grandmother.'

CHAPTER ELEVEN

Amelia placed Reuben's supper in front of him in a stony silence. In fact she had not uttered a word all evening. Reuben scratched his head. He could not remember offending her but did not like to enquire the reasons for her distance. The return of Amelia's mother, Esme, had been quite a shock and Reuben was still sizing up the woman. He recognised where Amelia got her determined streak from and Esme was trying very hard to make amends. But there was a continual tension in the air. Reuben sighed, it didn't matter whether one was an aristocrat or a businessman; women would always be a bit of an enigma. Look at Lottie, how she now wanted to turn back the clock and forget Reuben had ever been created. As he had told her, firmly and without a doubt in his mind, it was much too late to go back.

Nevertheless, he worried about keeping his two identities separate, especially now he was married. Secrets were difficult enough without involving others in the deception. Sometimes, though, he thought he would burst with happiness and it was these moments which gave him the courage and the conviction.

When they retired to the sitting room, Reuben decided he must try harder to let Amelia know that he appreciated her.

'You have done a wonderful job at the Bazaar, my dear. I am most impressed with the organisation. It does help.'

Amelia tried to smile but the effort appeared too much and it slipped from her pale face.

'I do think you are fortunate,' Esme said positioning herself in Reuben's armchair next to the window. 'Having such a kind and supportive husband.'

Reuben frowned and sat opposite in the sofa, patting the place beside him as he beckoned his wife.

Amelia shook her head. 'I've forgotten to do something, I won't be long,' she said closing the door quietly behind her. Reuben stared at the empty space his wife had left. He turned his attention back to Esme.

'Indeed? I wondered how difficult it must have been for you raising Amelia on your own, without the aid of her father?'

'Well, that is a very forward question from a gentleman, might I be so bold to say, Mr Chambers?' Esme raised an eyebrow. But Reuben detected she was playing for time. She wasn't as open and as beguiling as her daughter, but no doubt they both had a mesmerising beauty.

Reuben allowed the silence to build a wall between them as he watched a small muscle in Esme's cheek twitch. She was not as handsome as her daughter but she had a strong chin and Reuben quite admired her in a way. Being a woman with a young child and no husband must have been extremely tough and not just financially.

'Of course, you are right, Mrs Gray, or is it Miss Gray? There is no need to answer. I have not asked Amelia, nor has she talked about her childhood. It is none of my business. As her husband, my curiosity is piqued that is all, especially when it is unusual for a woman of your standing to be in such a predicament.' He enjoyed her discomfort for a while. He wasn't sure why, but he didn't fully trust her intentions in reuniting with her daughter.

A long silence followed while she stirred her tea, the spoon clinking against the china like a shower of bells. Amelia returned to the room, her eyes fixed to the floor, her cheeks a little flushed. Reuben stood, offered his hand and invited her again to sit next to him.

'I was asking your mother how she provided for you,' Reuben sat and crossed his legs. Amelia nodded almost automatically and Reuben knew that she had not heard him.

'Amelia, my dear, are you feeling all right?' Reuben asked, ignoring the deep sigh from her mother.

'Oh, don't mind her, Mr Chambers, she's—'

'I'm just a little out of sorts,' Amelia snapped, stopping her mother with a hard stare. 'There is truly nothing to worry about, perhaps you wouldn't mind if I retire early. I don't want to spoil your evening.'

'No, not at all.' Reuben squeezed her hand. 'You do look awfully pale, maybe something you ate?'

Amelia shook her head. 'No. Maybe. Oh, I don't know, but please don't fuss.' She got up quickly and staggered against the chair. Reuben stood to steady her.

'Are you sure you are all right?'

'Yes, quite sure. I shall be as right as rain in the morning. A good night's sleep is probably what I need.'

'Certainly,' agreed Reuben. 'But if this persists, I insist we call the doctor.'

After Amelia had left the room, Reuben turned back to Esme.

'Is she really well? Is there anything I should know?'

'You're asking me?' Esme replied a surprised tone to her voice. 'I'm sure it is nothing for you to worry about. Not now at least.'

Reuben stared back at Esme, not believing her for a moment but neither could he push her any further.

'And your question regarding my abilities as a mother are not a matter of your concern. Although Amelia's father was absent – for reasons I shall not disclose – he was a generous benefactor.'

'Was?' Reuben asked. Who would be a generous benefactor to an illegitimate child he wondered.

'Well, yes, was. One of the reasons I had to leave Amelia, I knew she would do well without me.' At least she has shown some embarrassment, thought Reuben, as Esme flushed from the neck upwards. 'Now, Mr Chambers, if you've finished with your questioning, I really think it's time for me to go. Thank you for supper, a most pleasant evening. And I do hope Amelia tells you what is troubling her.'

Reuben frowned, insisting. 'Do you know what ails your daughter?'

'No of course not; I mean, why on earth would she confide in me? I'm afraid I have fractured the trust between a mother and a daughter and Amelia has never been one to forgive easily. However, I hope she feels better in the morning.' Esme Gray swallowed hard but Reuben had not missed her hesitation at replying. She knew more than she let on.

'Certainly, I'm sure she will – feel better – that is.' Something niggled at the back of his mind.

After Esme left, Reuben climbed the stairs with leaden legs. He reached their bedroom door and could hear a faint sobbing in the background. He tried the handle but it was locked. He knocked softly and whispered her name. The crying was replaced by a stony silence.

*

Amelia bit her lip as she heard Reuben's voice. Another soft knock.

'Amelia, I do hope you are all right.'

As she heard Reuben shuffle off in the direction of the spare room she resumed her sobbing into the pillow. Her terms had arrived that morning, heavier than usual and she was not pregnant as she'd thought. She had planned to make an announcement to Reuben and was anticipating his joy. Now she felt incredibly empty, like a desert devoid of water. She had gone over and over again in her head how she would break the happy news. But now, there was nothing to tell.

Since her mother's unexpected reappearance a fortnight earlier she had been hinting that she might have the spare room at 37 Queens Row. Every day she had visited Amelia, talking about how much she had sacrificed for her and how lonely she had been. She took to Amelia's challenge to make amends through her role as a grandmother with an enthusiasm that Amelia found hard to believe. She had told Reuben nothing of this and knew that he had been surprised by her mother's arrival, but much to her relief he had not asked any questions. He was intrigued and in his own quiet way he would seek further information. She was looking forward to their life together as a couple and had been waiting for the right moment to tell him of the addition to their family.

The doctor who had examined her the day before had confirmed the loss, told her that many first pregnancies ended this way, it was not unusual and that she was a young fit woman. He was not very sympathetic claiming that there were too many mouths to feed in his humble opinion and not enough to go round. Amelia had left his rooms feeling sullied and distressed and decided there and then not to tell Reuben of her failure.

When she rose the next morning, Reuben had already gone to the Bazaar. He had thoughtfully left the breakfast table laid and a single yellow chrysanthemum in a crystal vase that he must have picked from the garden. His act of endearment rendered her to tears, and they fell thick and fast onto the linen cloth in front of her. At that moment, Amelia sensed such an empty space within her, she wondered if she might disappear inside it.

Her mother arrived not long after and swept past her.

'Your husband has a lot of nerve, questioning me like some—'

'Mother,' Amelia sighed. 'I really don't feel like talking this morning. Please. Reuben is a very inquisitive man, I'm sure he didn't mean to offend you.'

Her mother's gaze fell on the table, the damp table cloth and the single flower.

'You've lost the child,' she said in a flat tone.

The tears pricked at the back of Amelia's eyes. 'I told you I didn't want to talk this morning.'

'Well, it was hardly a child, after all. These things happen. Probably happened lots of times to me, though thank goodness you were the only result.'

'Mother! How could you.' Amelia sobbed.

'I don't mean to upset you, but it is how it is. I wouldn't worry; you'll find yourself in the family way again, if that's what you want. You got caught pretty quick the first time and I'm sure Mr Chambers is more than—'

'Shut up!' She refused to discuss her marital relations with her mother. 'Reuben does not know about this, how I've failed him. And I would be very grateful if you would honour my position on that matter.'

Her mother's eyes widened in surprise and then her mouth set in a firm line.

'I'm only trying to help. I know where I'm not wanted. Don't worry, Amelia. I'll see myself out.'

Amelia knew she wouldn't give up that easily on lodging with them. Her mother had run out of other options and she wasn't getting any younger. But at that moment in time Amelia could not have cared less.

*

Edwin Hales arrived in Clomber on a fine spring Sunday morning. The daffodils swayed gently in the balmy breeze and small purple crocuses lifted their lazy heads towards the sun.

He spied the Abbey in the distance, casting shadows on the vast grounds, like a majestic keeper of the village. The money he had received from the Kenilworth family to keep quiet about his parentage had afforded him a new wardrobe and lodgings for six months. He meant to make good use of his time and his money, but the family were very naive if they thought they could buy him out. Although he had signed a contract, to a man of his upbringing, commitment meant nothing – he was, after all he thought bitterly, his father's son.

Edwin walked tall in his new breeches and leather boots, taking long strides on the sunlit cobbles. His jet black hair was thick and wavy and his smile confident and bright. He had none of the looks of his mother, he was tall and almost wraithlike, – and she had been small and rather rotund. He could see the vast grounds of Clomber Abbey from the village but had decided to bide his time. It was better to try and talk to the locals first, get prepared.

He ducked his head as he entered the Leg and Bell Inn, removing his hat as he did so and casting a gaze around the room – it was full but the chattering stopped as he entered. Edwin raised his hat and smiled. He was more like these people than they knew.

'A mug of ale, if I may.' He smiled at the barmaid, who scowled back.

'That will be thru 'pence,' she slammed the pewter mug on the wet counter.

Edwin produced his money pouch and deliberately counted out the money as the rest of the coins jingled and jangled together. He presumed that several pairs of eyes bored into his back.

'Thank you,' he said and gulped the yeasty liquid. He moved slowly without looking at anyone and stood beside a group of men, who were smoking pipes and playing dominoes. He turned his back on them and continued to sip his ale as he listened to the banter around him.

'I tell you, there's summat funny going on. The young William is always sneaking around, going off here and there, through those tunnels at goodness knows what time. Our Sarah says that Mabbot is always looking for him. And he only shows his face when there is something wrong. But his Lordship is a kind gent; I'll never forget how he saved our Sarah from drowning in that pond. And he did all that improvement work on our cottages, no more leaky roofs or whistling windows.'

'I hear your Sarah needs saving of a different sort.' Someone tittered in the background. Edwin couldn't resist turning towards the group.

'What do you mean by that?' A tired-looking, thin man stood up, pushing his chair behind him and throwing his dominoes on the table.

'Just that she's been seen with that young Bertie many a time.' A large fellow with a round belly and equally large red cheeks smiled benignly.

'I'll have her hide, that daughter of mine. She ain't got no business with courting, especially now she's got a job in the big house, we need the money with six young mouths to feed!'

'Don't fret, Tom Nuttall, your Sarah deserves a little bit of happiness, like us all,' replied the fat man as the group joined in his chuckles.

'Happiness is not what feeds the rest of the little'uns.' Tom Nuttall sat back down with a thud.

'Why don't you tell us more about the future Duke, the young Lord,' the fat man asked. 'Is it true that he's gone a bit mad? Shouldn't wonder with the Duchess on his back all the time. The Duke, his father, is never here since poor Master Henry died. I shouldn't be surprised if there isn't going to be some kind of showdown.'

'Oh, his lordship's all right, I shouldn't speak out of turn. He's been very good to me. Only he never seems to be here, even when he is. Ever since his brother died, things just haven't been right.' Tom Nuttall drained his mug and stood up again. 'Anyway, I best be off, they'll all be coming back from church soon and I have work to finish. And if you see that young Bertie—' Tom Nuttall grabbed the fat man by the shoulders. 'Tell him he'll have me to deal with if he don't leave my Sarah be.'

Edwin finished his drink and winked at the barmaid who returned a dark, sullen stare. Never mind, thought Edwin, plenty of time to charm the women, and followed Tom Nuttall out of the inn. He stayed a few feet behind until the thin man stopped and turned around.

'Are you followin' me?'

Edwin looked behind him. 'Who me?'

'You were in the inn just now. I saw you there. What you want?' Tom Nuttall narrowed his eyes. Strangers meant trouble in these parts. Everyone knew everyone.

'I'm sorry, I don't mean to alarm you, but I couldn't help overhearing your conversation.' Edwin smiled.

'Yeah and what?' Tom Nuttall began to walk away briskly, he favoured his right leg. 'I've got to get back to the Abbey, haven't time for chit chat.'

'Of course, I know you must be busy. I wondered if…well, my mother worked here a long time ago.' Edwin lowered his voice and looked towards the ground, grinding his toe into the soft earth.

Tom Nuttall stopped and turned back to Edwin. 'Lots of people worked here, the Kenilworth family provide us all with a job. So what was your mother's name?'

'Edith, Edith Price. She was a maid, over at the big house.' Edwin looked down at the floor again and sighed. 'She passed away last year and I didn't know until then that she'd worked here.' He held out his hand. 'I'm Edwin, Edwin Hales.'

Tom Nuttall did not take his hand. 'I'm sorry about the loss of your mother. But I don't know many who work up there, only my daughter of course.' Tom started to walk away again. Edwin ran to catch him up.

'Of course, it was some time ago, thirty years before I was born,' Edwin added. 'Maybe there are people here who might—'

'Have known her? Maybe, I dunno, but the family like to keep themselves to themselves. Apart from us workers on the estate and those of their own social standing.'

'Of course,' Edwin rubbed his face with his hands. 'I came here on a whim, wanting to find more about my background. You see my mother had been ill for some time, in a sanatorium. I wanted—'

'I can understand that, Mr Hales, sure I can. But I don't think I can help you. I'm sorry, now I really must go.'

Edwin nodded. 'Of course, I'm sorry to have troubled you, sir.'

Tom Nuttall raised a hand as he turned the corner and Edwin said, 'Did I hear you say your daughter worked up there at the big house?'

Tom stopped in his tracks and turned again 'You may have done, why?'

'Well, she may be able to introduce me to one of the older members of staff, one of the manservants perhaps?' Edwin raised an eyebrow – he needed access to the Abbey. 'I'll pay for an introduction.'

Tom Nuttall kicked at a spot on the ground. 'You'll pay just to talk to someone?'

Edwin rattled his money pouch, 'I have money and it's important to me and the memory of my mother,' he said with a solemn tone.

Tom fiddled with his pocket flaps and then shoved his hands deep inside.

'I'll see what I can do. I'm not promising anythin' and I don't want you telling people you spoke to me. You got that?'

Edwin nodded, trying to refrain from grinning. Money could usually buy you most things.

'I'll see you here tomorrow evening, if I have anything. Be here by seven. No later. I can't be out long.'

'Wonderful.' Edwin clapped his hands. 'I'll see you at seven, then.'

CHAPTER TWELVE

'I don't believe you Sarah Nuttall! You've always been one for telling fibs. Like that time about the fire, when there weren't one at all.'

Mabbot watched from the shadows as Sarah, one of the maids, put a hand on each hip and stared back at Bertie Ragg, the head gardener's son.

'I swear on my life, Bertie. I did see Lord William and he did speak to me, once. He told me it was our secret and I shouldn't tell anyone I'd seen him in the tunnels. He was dressed real differently, with a short jacket and very natty tie and those new style breeches. A real gentlemen he were too, not like you, you ruffian.' She shoved his chest playfully. 'And anyway, it would have turned into a fire if I hadn't told anyone you were playing with matches, I was only little at the time, how was I to know you were burning leaves on a bonfire?'

'You fancy yourself working up at the big house, don't you?' Bertie wrapped his arms around her and squeezed lightly.

Mabbot moved his weight from one foot to the other. The young pair were too engrossed in each other to notice him. He must have a word with the housekeeper about this Sarah and her fraternising but for the time being he had a feeling that she might prove very helpful to him.

'I'm surprised you still want to mix with the likes of us. I'm sure we're not good enough for you.' Bertie stuck his nose up in the air and sniffed haughtily. Sara laughed and spun around in his arms, kissing him lightly on his lips before pushing him away again. She checked her apron, replaced her cap, securing it firmly with a hairpin and smiled.

Mabbot knew that they met regularly in the tunnel which led from the big house to the main road. It wasn't hard to get information out of a recently appointed young scullery maid who was eager to please and wanted to keep her job. Mabbot liked to establish the lines of authority from day one and it appeared that Sarah trusted the newcomer with the tawdry details regarding her admirer. How naïve these people were, Mabbot thought as he shifted from one foot to another.

Bertie bent to retie his boot lace.

'Well I got to be getting back, or I'll be missed,' Sarah said. 'Poor Lord William looks worried all the time. No wonder he wants to come down here to escape.'

Bertie pulled her back towards him seeking a last kiss. She held onto her cap and obliged for a second.

'And how many times have you met your master down here? It makes me think you and 'im are up to no good. It 'appens you know, masters and servants. They don't care for you and he don't care for you no matter that he saved you from the pond. I was there, remember? I was the one who called the alarm, I was the one who really saved you. I'll fight him for your honour, I will.' He took a boxers pose, his fist clenched and Sarah giggled. Bertie was as thin as a plank of wood; he would be blown over with one wave of a hand.

'Oh, I've lost count, and it's not like that. I don't meet him. He don't see me hidin' in the shadows. Anyway, he did save me from drownin' in the damn lake that time. Mebbe he thinks I am special.'

Mabbot held his breath. So this is how William comes in and out without being seen. Why hadn't he thought of that before?

Sarah smoothed down her dress and picked under her fingernails. 'He always stops as if he's thinking, putting a finger to his lips like this,' said Sarah demonstrating. 'As I said he's always wearing different breeches and such, not at all like the clothes he wears around here, much more modern like the ones the visitors from London wear. His hat is much flatter and I swear he wears eyeglasses.'

'Eyeglasses?' echoed Bertie, 'but Lord William doesn't wear such a thing. Are you sure it's him?'

Mabbot stepped back behind a corner and breathed out. William had never worn spectacles. The damage to his eye was purely muscle related and he knew from his archery expertise that William had perfect vision. The Duke would never allow his son to bring attention to his physical defect, though it would make a good disguise. Now why would William want to do that? He stepped back into the shadows. The two had their backs to him now facing towards the exit.

'Of course I am, stupid. I'm not daft you know.' Sarah slapped his shoulders as he shrugged them. 'It is him; he looks really dashing and different. I wonder where on earth he's going to when he leaves the tunnel. I always see him on his way out, never coming back.' Sarah looked behind her for a moment but Mabbot didn't move.

'Well, he could easily get to the station unnoticed through these tunnels. No-one else goes in 'em as far as I know. And those new-fangled trains can take him to the big city in no time I heard one of the stable hands say the other day. How they can transport the horses to the races much faster.' Bertie scratched his chin. 'Hey, maybe he's got a secret woman like I have.' Sarah giggled and then went still.

'Does it feel like we're being watched?'

Mabbot had to strain to hear her.

'Nah,' said Bertie pulling on his jacket, the arms stopping inches above his wrists. 'Who wants to watch us? Maybe it's measly Mabbot spying on us!'

Sarah slapped his arm. 'Well, I wouldn't be surprised but you should see the look on the old toad's face when he's realised William has slipped out again right from under his nose!' She looked around again into the shadows and lowered her voice. 'His face swells up and turns red and I swear he is about to burst. And then he has the Duchess on his back all the time. Anyways, at least it keeps him out of our way. None of the girls like him, he snoops all the time.'

Bertie picked Sarah up and swung her around.

'Put me down, Albert Ragg, quick before I'm sick all over you!' He placed her gently on the floor and held onto her. 'God, me head is spinning! You're daft you are,' Sarah took a couple of wobbly steps.

'I know, daft on you. Are you a'right for tomorrow?'

'Of course I am, but we'll have to be quick, the old toad is watching me like a hawk at the moment, I'm sure he suspects something.'

She gave him a quick peck on the lips and then waved as Bertie left the tunnel. Sarah turned and walked around the corner, right into the fuming thunderous face of Mabbot.

*

Mabbot smiled, his senses had been right. Listening to this servant girl's chat with her companion had confirmed some of his suspicions. Old toad indeed, he would make her pay for that.

'Mister Mabbot, sir. I'm sorry, sir. I'm just on my way back now I…er…I got delayed. My mother – that's right, my mother, she's not well. I had to take her some broth, she can't eat nuthin' else, it was what Mrs Campbell gave to me. Leftovers, that's all it was, sir.'

The stupid girl couldn't even tell convincing lies, thought Mabbot. Did she think he was stupid? He grabbed her arm and was deliberately rough, feeling a heightened sense of frustration. One had to show these kinds of people who was in charge.

'You are a lying little hussy, and I've got a good mind to report you right now. You would be dismissed on the spot if it had anything to do with me and good riddance, I'd say. We don't need the likes of you around. And that wouldn't be very helpful to your poor ill mother, now would it?' He held his face inches away from her as the girl wriggled trying to get away, but Mabbot increased his grip a little more.

'Well, what have you to say for yourself?'

'Nothin', honest, I wasn't doing anything wrong, no harm to anyone, please let me go, Mister Mabbot, I have to get back. I swear I wasn't doing anything, just minding my own business. I'm telling the truth!'

She was a determined little creature, Mabbot would give her that, but she was going to be useful to him and she had given him an opportunity he could not waste.

'You think I'm stupid don't you?' Mabbot murmured in her ear. 'Well, I heard everything you said. I followed you here, you see. You've been disappearing at exactly the same time for days and I've heard complaints from the housekeeper that she can never find you around this time. How stupid. You didn't think anyone would notice? You are paid to work, not have illicit meetings with some riffraff from the grounds.'

The young girl stood her ground and tried her best to look defiant but a muscle twitched nervously in her cheek.

'I don't know what you are talking about.' She held his gaze, which angered him all the more.

'Yes, you damn well do, Sarah Nuttall. And I know all about you and your family.'

Sarah's eyes opened wide in surprise and Mabbot allowed himself a small sense of satisfaction. 'Oh yes, I know who you are and who Bertie Ragg is. I make it my business to know what is what around here. I have an important role in protecting this family.' Mabbot stuck out his chest with pride and released his grip knowing he now had her full attention. She rubbed at her arms vigorously and then wiped her nose with the back of her sleeve.

'And I could have you and your family banished from this estate with no references and no chance of work in these parts ever again. Do you understand?'

The girl shuffled uncomfortably from foot to foot. He hoped she wasn't going to start snivelling, that would really make him cross.

'Well do you? I don't have time to stand here gawping at your grubby little face all day. I've wasted enough time already and it seems you don't care about what you do, or your family.' Mabbot turned as if to go.

'Yes, yes, I understand. I'm sorry. Please don't go.'

'Sorry what?'

The girl looked defiant again for a moment and why not? Mabbot wasn't her direct superior but he had to demand her respect. He could do as he pleased – what would she know?

'Yes, sir,' the girl finally whispered back, her head hung low staring at the floor.

'That's better. I knew you would come round to my way of thinking. I'm sure you don't want your family involved in this, especially with all those mouths to feed.' Mabbot could not understand why her kind always had all these children and it vexed him they were allowed to live in relative comfort and freedom on the estate. Grubby little youngsters running around everywhere. He thought William too soft on them and this was a direct result.

'Now, tell me the truth. You see the young Master down here do you?' Mabbot circled around her like a lion.

The girl bit her bottom lip, reluctant to admit to what he already knew.

'It's all right; you won't get into any trouble, as long as you tell me and do as I ask. There shall be no repercussions.'

'You promise?' Her bright blue eyes pierced through him with a flash of bravery. Mabbot flinched at her insolence.

'You are not in a position to request assurances from me, young lady. I'm surprised you think you are or that you could be as bold.' He sighed heavily. 'I see I am wasting my time, I have lots of things to report, and it's a shame your actions are going to make your family suffer.' Mabbot turned to go again and had taken several steps.

'But it's supposed to be a secret,' Sarah blurted out. 'I promised not to tell anyone.'

Mabbot stopped and smiled again, then turned back towards her.

'Well, how strange, because you have already told someone have you not? That useless wretch, Bertie Ragg. You have already broken this so-called promise. I wonder what Lord William would think of you and your loyalty?'

Her face coloured and Mabbot had no doubt she would do as she was told to. Her kind could be bought very easily.

'Bertie's different,' she mumbled.

Mabbot stepped aside to let her pass and then grabbed her arm. 'Now be off with you. I'll think on what we've discussed tonight and we'll talk some more tomorrow.'

'Sarah, is that you in there?' A voice shouted from behind them. Mabbot turned still holding Sarah by the arm.

'And why have you got hold of my daughter?' A thin, tired man stared back and forth between them. Mabbot let go instantly, resisting the urge to brush at his hands.

'We were having a chat, weren't we, Miss Nuttall?'

Sarah nodded, tears formed at the corner of her eyes. Ah, she's scared of her father, Mabbot thought.

'Are you going to introduce us then?'

'Father, this is Ma… this is Mister Mabbot. He's very important in the big house, looks after Lord William, he does so.'

Sarah's father nodded. 'Does he now?' He raised his cap to Mabbot, at least he had some manners he thought. 'And what are you doing down here? Shouldn't you be up at the main house, doing your duties?' Her father shot the words out at his daughter.

'She was on an errand, weren't you Sarah?' Mabbot smiled at the girl's startled face, eyes wide, mouth open.

'Er… yes, well it must be time to get back.'

Mabbot waved a hand at her. 'Hurry now, and if the housekeeper asks where you've been tell her I'll vouch for you.' Sarah nodded, looked at her father for a fleeting second, and ran off.

'I'm Tom, Tom Nuttall.' Sarah's father had removed his cap and was twiddling with it in his hands.

'Yes, I know. Now I really should go,' said Mabbot.

'Wait! Just a minute. I met a man tonight, said his mother used to work here some years back. He's in the village. Looks trustworthy. But his mother died not long ago and he was after talking to someone who might have known her.'

'There are lots of servants who have been through employment here, I'm afraid.' Mabbot had no time for this. He wanted to think about how he could use Sarah.

'But you, you've been here a long time. I hear that the family consider you their most loyal servant.'

'I'm a valet, not a servant.' Mabbot sniffed.

'His name was Edwin now what was his surname? He did tell me now.' Tom scratched his head and then clicked his fingers. 'Hales, Edwin Hales, and his mother was Edith.'

Mabbot's ears pricked at the mention of a name no longer spoken at Clomber Abbey. A voice from the past. How things were turning out this evening, Mabbot thought narrowing his eyes.

'Indeed? It seems vaguely familiar—' Mabbot paused. 'I'll have a chat with the young man; see if he's the proper thing.'

'Thanks! I'll tell him tomorrow evening, he's staying at the Leg and Bell in the village. Shall I ask him to call?'

'Yes, but do be sure he knows to use the servants entrance, won't you?'

*

Edwin hadn't expected such quick progress. Last night in the inn, Tom Nuttall had earned his shilling with an introduction to the manservant, no less. Perhaps that morning he would find out a little more about where he had been conceived and the family who were desperate to keep him quiet.

He left his rooms at the Leg and Bell before breakfast, his stomach grumbled its loud complaint. As he passed the small railway station, he came across a large carriage pulled by two grand black stallions. Their coats shone in the early morning light and steam puffed through their nostrils as they kicked their hooves impatiently on the ground.

'The train is a little late, sir. But I'm told it won't be long.' The stationmaster stepped away from the door and Edwin spied a formidable figure dressed in a flat hat and glimpsed a pair of gold rimmed eyeglasses. Edwin raised his hat but no response was forthcoming.

He chose to walk the long driveway which eventually led to Clomber Abbey. He wanted time to think. He dawdled along the path which was skirted by a dense forest and formed the periphery of the estate. The birdsong appeared to be welcoming him along. He whistled softly as he dodged the dollops of fresh horse manure in his path.

As he turned a corner, he spied a figure ahead and stepped to one side of the path out of direct vision. It was a woman, an elegant woman dressed for riding in a long full skirt, with the right side much shorter than the left. She wore a peplum hemmed jacket which flattered the shape of her hips and on her head perched a black pork-pie velvet hat with a full pom-pom on top. Standing next to her, nuzzling into her hand was a beautiful black and white horse.

Edwin checked his cravat, adjusted his hat and stepped back out into view.

'Good morning, Miss. Can I possibly be of any help?'

The young woman turned sharply and snapped her riding whip. She took him in with a gaze that began at his feet and finished on his face. She did not return his friendly smile.

'I don't think so, sir. My horse is lame. My riding partner has gone ahead to alert the stable hand and I shall walk on slowly.'

'Oh dear, it doesn't hurt does it?'

'What doesn't hurt?'

Edwin noticed how her nose crinkled when she frowned, sending the tiny brown freckles that covered it into all directions. He watched the small bow-like lips upturn into a beguiling smile.

'Forgive me, I am not familiar with horses,' he lied. 'I mean being lame, does it hurt?'

The young woman laughed, the soft chuckles travelled through the air and fell sweetly on Edwin's ears.

'No, he's lost a shoe.' She lowered her head a little. 'Probably my fault, I love riding through the brush and it's full of brambles and things. He'll be all right when he's seen the farrier.'

The young woman tilted her head. 'I'm sorry, sir, I don't think you are from these parts, are you?'

Edwin laughed but quickly stopped when she arched an eyebrow and her smile slipped from her face.

'I'm sorry, I didn't mean to appear rude.' He took off his hat and bowed deeply. 'Edwin Hales, at your service, Miss.'

'I am quite sure you don't need to be at my service at all, there are plenty of people paid to do that here.' Edwin stepped closer and the horse whinnied a warning.

'Whoa, Gabriel, don't fret.' The young woman tugged firmly on the reins but her voice was soft.

'Gabriel, what a heavenly name, Miss?'

'I am Lady Charlotte, how do you do, Mr Hales. But why are you walking down the drive to Clomber Abbey? Do you have business here? Perhaps something to do with my brother, William? I do hope not, he is not here at the moment.'

Edwin narrowed his eyes. This was William's sister? He hadn't known that the family had a daughter. Edwin's earlier lightness greyed a little. She was most charming. Not what he expected from the family who had banished his mother from her friends without a thought. And he wasn't ready to meet William, yet. 'Well, not business, as such, I'm here to see an old friend of my mother's.'

'Oh, and who that might be?'

'Mabbot, I do believe he is a revered manservant here.'

Lady Charlotte's face hardened. 'Indeed he may be, Mr Hales. Perhaps you'd like to accompany me? I'm on my way back now.'

Edwin replaced his hat. 'I'd be delighted to, your Ladyship.'

'And I can show you where you can find Mabbot.'

'Oh, please don't go to any trouble, not on my account. Anyway, I'm told I must call at the servant's entrance.'

'Well, if you're with me, you can come through the main entrance. I have invited you, after all.'

'As you wish,' Edwin smiled. His day was beginning to get better and better.

CHAPTER THIRTEEN

Mabbot walked into the hallway as Lady Charlotte opened the front door.

'Your Ladyship.' He stopped in his tracks, his arms held straight by his side. 'I must apologise. If I had known earlier about your horse, I would have sent—'

'No matter,' Lady Charlotte interrupted. 'I enjoyed the walk on such a pleasant morning.'

Mabbot frowned at the gentleman behind her. A small grin twitched at the side of the visitor's mouth as he fell under Mabbot's scrutiny. The gentleman removed his hat. A white streak ran through his reddish hair and Mabbot started in surprise. He had only seen this unusual colouring in William and his father. Indeed, the portraits that hung around the Abbey of the Romsey men showed the same trait had existed for generations.

'I was unaware that you were expecting guests, your Ladyship?'

Lady Charlotte laughed and beckoned the gentlemen to step forward. 'Oh, Mr Hales is no guest of mine, Mabbot. But I must say he has made pleasant talk on our walk back, even Gabriel cheered up a little by the time we had returned him to the stables. Wouldn't you say so, Mr Hales?'

'Indeed, your Ladyship.' The colour rose from the base of the man's neck to the tips of his ears.

'Mr Hales?' Mabbot muttered. 'Did I not ask that you report to the servants' entrance?' His fingers fidgeted at his side.

'Yes, you did, Mabbot. However, I invited Mr Hales to accompany me. Now, I will let you get on with your business. I must go and change, I'm having lunch with the Duchess and I must rest before then.' Lady Charlotte turned to Edwin as she started to remove her hat. 'I do hope you find out more about your mother, Mr Hales. If you need any more help, please don't hesitate to ask.'

Edwin bowed deeply as Lady Charlotte swept up the stairs. Mabbot coughed and spoke from behind his hand. 'Come with me please, Mr Hales. I do not wish the Duchess to discover that you are here.'

Mabbot led him to his room at the end of the kitchen corridor. He spoke not a word until he had closed the door and turned the key in the lock.

'Now, I only agreed…'

'It is most kind of you to see me, Mr Mabbot. My mother, if she were here, would be very relieved that someone from her past has shown me such kindness.'

'Indeed, Mr Hales. Yes, I knew your mother. She was one of the kitchen maids and in those days this was a much busier household.' Mabbot raised his chin.

'I don't imagine you were employed as a valet at that time?' Edwin arched an eyebrow, his mouth curled up at the corners.

'What I was or was not is not your concern, young man. I only offered to see you as a favour. I am aware of the circumstances in which your mother left her employment here.'

'Ah, a favour…' The young man's eyes darkened.

'Yes a favour, but I don't think you should reveal yourself or your intentions too soon.'

'And why might that be?' Edwin scratched his chin.

'Well, you may be able to discover more if you retain your anonymity. After all, your mother left under difficult circumstances for the family.'

'I think it was much more difficult for my mother,' Edwin snapped. 'She never recovered from the shame, spent most of her life in a sanatorium and then died forgetting that I was her son. My mother suffered far more than this family ever did.'

'I'm sorry to hear that, Mr Hales. How dreadful for you.' Mabbot sniffed and tugged at his shirt cuffs but inside his heart ached. Poor Edith.

'Yes, well, the suffering was all my mother's. I didn't know anything about the origins of my father until after she died. She was too ashamed to tell me while she lived and by the end she had probably forgotten. I am sure it all contributed to her... to her state of mind.'

Mabbot sensed the bitterness in the young man's response, but felt little sympathy. If young maids played with fire, they would end up getting burnt. It had always been that way. The old Duke had an eye for the young ladies but they should resist such temptations. Unfortunately this encounter had been more tricky than most of the Duke's misdemeanours.

'Have you been in contact with the family before now?' Mabbot asked, suddenly wondering where this young man got the money to dress in the latest and most expensive fashion as well as travelling down from Scotland.

Edwin faltered, looking around the room and then striding over to Mabbot's only chair and sitting down heavily.

'Yes, I wrote to them, a couple of times. Soon after the death of Lord Henry.' He lowered his gaze. 'I finally received a response from the family's lawyer.'

'Ah, that was a dreadful time. The Duke... well no matter. Lord William is now the heir apparent.'

'Yes, I do know that, Mr Mabbot. The family were most generous. But it isn't only about the money, well, not then. I wanted more; to defend my mother and her reputation. What else should a son do? It angered me that they thought they could pay for my silence. To wash their hands of me, so to speak.' Edwin ran his fingers through his hair and sighed deeply. 'I don't really know what I'm doing here. I thought I did. Now, I'm not sure.'

'It's been a difficult time for you, Mr Hales. The family and you have suffered bereavement at the same time and perhaps you are feeling the same pain. The fact is your mother was not treated well.'

Edwin's forehead creased into a frown.

'Now, I'm not saying you have any legal rights…'

'You mean the Dukedom?' Edwin stood up quickly and paced the tiny room. 'It may have been read as such, but I wanted some justice for my mother.'

'Very admirable indeed I'm sure, and the money?'

'I used it to provide myself with some decent attire,' Edwin looked at his boots, covered in mud from the walk to the Abbey. 'And my travel and lodgings. I have enough for a month, maybe more. I'm at a bit of a loss if I were honest. Tell me, Lady Charlotte, is she betrothed?'

Mabbot fixed his gaze on the young man. 'I don't think I should be disclosing such personal information about Lady Charlotte with you, Mr Hales. It is enough that I have agreed to see you at all.'

'Yes, I know. I didn't realise there was a daughter. She is rather charming, and charismatic.' Edwin took his seat once more and crossed and uncrossed his legs. 'I suppose, given the circumstances, that she is my half-sister.'

'That may be the case, however, do not be distracted from your purpose. I do believe you may be able to assist me with a conundrum and in the meantime experience the family here a little more.'

'Oh, yes?'

'I must stress that nothing of what I say is to be repeated out of this room?'

Edwin nodded, and Mabbot paused wondering if he could trust this man. It was too good an opportunity to lose, after all, no-one else knew who he was.

'Lord William is having difficulty with his unexpected and important role as future Duke. His brother's death affected him the most and he is possibly still mourning. I've known his lordship since he was a young boy and obviously have his best interests at heart. He disappears for times on end and I worry about his safety. I understand that he has been using the underground tunnels that connect this abbey to the station, to move to and fro, unseen as it were.'

Edwin stared back, his pale face unreadable.

'I thought, given your anonymity, that you may be able to find out where Lord William is going and confirm that he is not getting into any activities that may appear undesirable for his status and that of his family name. Behaviour that would make the family's position very difficult.'

'You are asking me to spy on Lord William?'

Mabbot laughed nervously. 'Spy seems rather exaggerated don't you think? I merely wish to assure the family that their name and standing is not at risk by William's actions. I have been able to manage his absences in the past but they are becoming more frequent. His father has become rather frail of late and I fear sooner rather than later, William will be required to take the reins.'

'And why should I do anything to help the family who turned out my mother in her hour of greatest need?'

'Indeed,' agreed Mabbot. 'However, it would give you time to get to know the family a little more, and I'm sure a financial reward—'

'I'm not interested in finance, goddamit!'

Mabbot paused and his smile vanished. He hadn't wanted to resort to such measures. 'Well, the only other option I have is to disclose your true identity and your intentions to further blackmail this family.'

'But I'm not, I may have—'

'My word, a trusted employee, against yours I'm afraid, Mr Hales. And being as the family have already contributed to your loyalty, it would appear that you are attempting to exploit them.'

Edwin reddened. 'Exploit them! Hah!' His face crumpled. 'It appears I have very little choice, like my mother.'

After seeing Mr Hales out of the servants' entrance, Mabbot went in search of Sarah Nuttall. He couldn't help smiling to himself. How fortunate that things were all coming together. He needed to know what was going on, he felt powerless and his position continually undermined by the actions of the young master. After all, the Duchess expected him to know what was going on. But ultimately Mabbot longed for retribution for poor Edith Hales.

He found Sarah in the sitting room cleaning the grate. Mabbot checked his pocket watch; the fires should have been lit hours ago. She knelt back and yawned loudly. He coughed and Sarah let out a small gasp as she stood up to face him.

'Good morning, Sarah,' Mabbot said with a false smile.

'Good morning, Mister Mabbot.' Sarah whispered, her head bowed.

'I've been thinking about our little chat last night.' Mabbot circled around her, hands clasped behind his back. 'I think you and I will work together very well. It seems that Lord William trusts you – I heard it for myself.' He looked at her, half expecting some petulant remark but she kept her gaze fixed firmly at a place on the hearth.

'Therefore you will be my informer of his comings but more particularly his goings. Is that clear? You do understand the consequences if you fail me?'

Sarah now lifted her head to look at him. She swallowed hard. 'You want me to break my promise?'

'I fear that trust has already been broken.'

*

William was anxious to return to Amelia but also reluctant to leave the Abbey. His neck and shoulders ached and he longed for sleep. Living two lives had been exciting to begin with but the responsibilities now acted like a ball and chain around his feet. Amelia wasn't finding it easy having her mother around. Both women were independent minded and if he were honest, a little obstinate. A figure slammed into him tearing him away from his thoughts. He steadied himself on the wall of the corridor.

'I'm sorry...I didn't mean to, sir.'

William looked down at a young maid, her hands black and dusty. She wiped them down her apron.

'I hope I haven't marked your clothes, sir. I've been cleaning the fires in the sitting room.' Her gaze fell to the floor.

'Sarah, it is Sarah Nuttall isn't it?' William reached for her arm where a ring of purple bruises ran across the skin. Sarah flinched at his touch and stepped back.

'Whatever is the matter?' he asked.

Sarah shook her head, trying to step around him but he blocked her. Her face was streaked with tears.

'Something has upset you and I'd like to help if I can. But I certainly don't want to upset you any more.'

Sarah looked behind her as if expecting someone. 'I need to get back, sir, I shouldn't be away from my work, I'm going to get into awful trouble for being late and I've got the dining room to do, then the bedrooms. I'm sorry, sir.'

William laughed. 'No need to apologise to me, I know very well the feeling of wanting to get away.' Sarah was not listening she hopped from foot to foot, looking at him earnestly.

'Very well,' William conceded, 'but if there are repercussions you are to come to me at once. I promise I will do anything to help if I can.'

Sarah smiled weakly. 'Don't go making promises, sir. You may have to break 'em one day.'

William frowned. 'Really? I do hope I don't break my promises. Especially to you. Anyway, you hurry back, now. And be sure to wash your face before the housekeeper sees you!'

'Yes, sir of course. Now please, I really to have to go.' She slipped past him.

William watched as Sarah ran down the long corridor, until she disappeared. He wondered what she had meant about breaking promises and who or what had upset her. He sighed and turned towards the sitting room. He could make out a figure in the shadows of the dark corridor walking purposefully in the opposite direction. William frowned as he watched the unmistakable march-like swagger of his valet.

*

Amelia smiled weakly at Reuben. 'Are you not pleased?'

Reuben looked through her as if seeing someone else. His face was lined with tiredness, his skin pale. He forced a smile.

'Of course I'm pleased, it's a bit of a shock that's all. Becoming a father is a big responsibility.'

'Well, not sure why it's a shock. I rather thought it was expected.' Amelia swallowed the desire to cry.

Since the miscarriage twelve months past, her world had changed. She had become depressed and dark about everything and at first Reuben had tried hard to make her happy. She had pushed him away until the doctor said maybe she should try for another, it might help. Poor Reuben – how she had made him suffer.

'Are you sure everything is all right?' Reuben took her hand in his and brought it to his mouth kissing it as gently as he had the first day she'd met him. 'I mean for your health, Amelia.'

'Of course it is. The doctor gave me a thorough examination. Honestly I feel fine, a little tired and weary but fine. I'm rather further on than I thought.' Amelia lied – she hadn't been back to the doctor to confirm the pregnancy, feeling that it might tempt fate. She felt that if she kept it to herself and Reuben that it would all be safe, no harm done. And she had delayed telling Reuben until she was really sure. He had been away a lot in the past weeks that he hadn't noticed her expanding waistline.

'Well, I insist that we get someone else to help over at the Bazaar,' said Reuben, an authoritative note to his voice. 'And why don't you ask your mother to stay during the pregnancy and to help out a little. I'm going to be away on and off for some time.'

Amelia flinched at the mention of her mother. She had tried hard to make amends but her emotions about motherhood had been heightened with her pregnancies and she found it hard to forgive. What was worse, Reuben and her mother always appeared to know what was best for her.

'Dearest,' Reuben prompted, 'did you hear what I said?'

'Yes, but I think I'd prefer to be on my own. Mother fusses and gets in the way.'

'What are mothers supposed to do if not fuss and get in the way? And if I'm not here and something happens, I would never forgive myself. I won't take no for an answer.'

Amelia stared back at her husband. If she were honest with herself, she didn't want to be alone either. All she wanted was to have Reuben at her side. She chided herself for her sense of suspicion. But she couldn't help but wonder – with his air of distractedness and increasing number of absences – whether he'd taken on a mistress. It would be her fault alone if he did for her attention towards him had not been one of a doting wife. However, a ribbon of jealousy crept up from her toes and wrapped itself around her heart.

'There is someone at the Gentleman's Club who has recommended a chap that might be a good candidate for assistant. Apparently he's moved down here from the North and is looking for work. I'm meeting him in about...' he took out his pocket watch, '...half an hour.' He swung the watch back into its snug little pocket. 'I really should be getting ready too, as I've arranged to meet him at the club.'

'You mean you have been planning to replace me before I told you about the baby?'

A flush of pink spread up Reuben's neck from his collar to his face. He ran a finger around the starched neckline.

'Well, yes, my dear. I thought it was for the best. I've been extremely worried about your health and I don't wish you to worry. I discussed it with your mother – she is in full agreement.'

'You discussed it with my mother?' Amelia heard her voice high and strained. Although she knew it made perfect sense, she couldn't help herself. 'But we used to make these decisions together, Reuben, why is it different this time? Really, I don't know what's got into you lately, it's like you are a different man!'

She noticed a flash of pain cross Reuben's face at her accusation and immediately regretted her harsh words.

'Nothing has got into me at all; it is easier to make the decisions as and where required. I'm trying to help you and after all, I am your husband,' he snapped in a tone she had not been on the receiving end of before.

'I'm sorry, I do understand but I would have preferred if you had spoken with me first. I despair when you are away so often. I try to understand, truly I do. I only want us to have more time together.'

Reuben turned, his face flushed with frustration and brought out his watch again, fiddling with the cover.

'I will not discuss this any further. I must go now. I am only doing what is best and I'm very sorry I have to leave you on your own.' His face softened and Amelia saw the man she had first fallen in love with. 'Believe me, here is the only place I want to be. You don't understand. My intentions are only worthy towards you, my dear.'

Reuben stooped to kiss her but she turned away. He sighed deeply, collected his hat and coat and left. A single tear dripped down Amelia's cheek, which she wiped away with the back of her hand.

CHAPTER FOURTEEN

Edwin woke to the sound of banging on his door. He opened his eyes and tried to focus in the gloom. It wasn't even dawn, he fumed. Who the hell would be at his lodgings at this hour? The knocking continued, persistent and petulant like a young child who wants to get their own way. Edwin flung back the covers and grabbed a gown which he threw over his shoulders. In three long strides he stood at the door, yawning widely.

'I'm coming, this had better be good, interrupting a man's sleep with such a disturbance,' he muttered turning the key. As he opened the door, a young girl fell past him. She scrabbled to her feet, straightening her skirts and fixing her cap. Edwin realised that she must be employed at the Abbey, no-one dressed like that in the village. And she wasn't a girl, she was a young woman. A rather plain young woman on first sight, with her hair untidily tucked up under a cotton cap, displaying small ears. Her nose and cheeks were covered with freckles but her eyes were the most redeeming feature. Dark chestnut brown pools with long lashes.

'Well, being as it's a rather lovely young lass that has woken me, maybe I don't mind as much.' He stepped towards her and she stepped back, her eyes widening. 'Don't be afraid, after all it was you that woke me…' He watched her lips tremble. 'I'm not angry, I promise. Just don't like being woken with a start.' He combed his fingers through his wavy hair and ran his tongue along his teeth.

'I'm sorry, sir. Mr Hales, sir. I didn't mean to intrude. But M…Mab…Mister Mabbot said I had to tell you.' The young girl looked behind her towards the bed as Edwin took another step towards her.

'Mabbot?' Edwin frowned and placed his hands on his hips. 'And who is it that carries his message?' He wanted to remain as anonymous as possible, as Mabbot had first suggested.

'Me name's Nuttall, sir, Sarah Nuttall. I'm a maid at the big house, one of the servants.' She ducked to the left as Edwin neared and made back towards the door. 'I mustn't be long, Mr Hales, sir. I've ran all the way and I've got to get back to start lightin' the fires.'

'Ah, Tom Nuttall's daughter? Now what is that important to Mabbot that he should send you hurtling down here?'

The young girl's gaze fell and her face flushed, the freckles deepened in their definition. 'I've got to tell you, sir, not that I want to. I promised you see, but Mister Mabbot,' she wrung her hands. 'He says I 'ave to.'

'Did he now? Well don't be afraid, now spit it out. I can't stand here in my night attire with the door breezing a gale in! Either shut the door, take a seat and regain your composure or tell me what you have come to say.'

'Yes. Of course.' Sarah's voice fell to a whisper and Edwin could barely hear her. 'It's his lordship. Mister Mabbot said I had to tell you when he was leaving thru' the tunnel. He's on his way. Should be at the station very soon. He's in a black carriage driven by four black horses, one of them with a large diamond on its forehead. They come from the tunnels.'

Edwin stared for a moment and then realised that he had to move fast. Tom Nuttall had showed him the labyrinth and he had wondered why it was so large. To transport a carriage and horses, how clever! He grabbed his boots and started to pull them on, but lost his balance and stumbled. 'Dammit,' he swore as he hopped over to the bed. 'And what was he wearing? Can you give me a description?' Edwin raised his gaze towards the door but the girl had vanished.

Minutes later he was fully dressed and standing on the station platform. He blew on his hands, his fingers chilled with the early morning breeze. A carriage trundled onto the platform along a small ramp at the far end and the horses were led onto a flatbed carriage. Whistling softly Edwin strolled towards it, his hands clasped behind his back. He knew the train was going to London and was the only one that was leaving that morning and had purchased his ticket. He was sure that this must be William. The carriage was plain, buffed to a perfect ebony sheen and the horses were immaculately groomed. One of them lifted its huge head towards him and whinnied. A white diamond dominated its forehead. Edwin returned to the passenger carriages and made himself comfortable.

'Plenty of room.' Edwin stretched his legs and put his arms behind his head as the man checked his ticket.

'That is true, sir. People still very wary about these trains. Think they're creatures from medieval times or summat! Still that'll all change sooner than later. Enjoy your trip, sir.'

Edwin watched the rolling hills and green fields thinking about encountering William and discovering what he was hiding. His mind sped as fast as the train until, exhausted, he fell asleep.

The train jolted to a stop and shook Edwin awake. They had arrived in London. He checked his pocket watch, amazed at the speed before grabbing his hat and cloak and hopping down onto the platform. It took some time to offload the horse drawn carriage but Edwin had already secured a cab and followed it from a distance. Soon they had pulled up on the opposite side of the street. He paid the driver, leapt to the pavement and stood by a large street lamp.

The carriage had stopped outside a glass bow fronted shop with 'King Street Bazaar' painted in large gold letters. A tall gentleman stepped out onto the pavement and stood in front of the window, before opening the door.

Edwin had only seen a portrait of William but he'd spent some time in the Abbey grounds since his arrival and in the distance observed someone chatting with the estate workers. Tom Nuttall had pointed out William. Although the gentleman he had seen a moment ago was the same height and build as William, the clothes were of the highest fashion. The man wore bright mustard coloured trousers and a jacket, cut in the modern style, like Edwin's own clothes, and he wore a pair of gold rimmed eyeglasses, which gave him a mysterious but interesting edge. From the gossip mongers on the estate, Edwin had learnt that William dressed more conservatively, if not a little outdated. He also had a slight droop in one eye, an injury from birth, which he always tried to conceal with a large brimmed hat.

Edwin stood across the street for some time, not sure what he should do next. He ran a finger over his chin, it was rough and stubbly. He hadn't had time to shave before he'd left. He spied a barber's sign a few doors down from the Bazaar and decided to go and tidy himself up.

He left the barbers, feeling relaxed, and headed back to the Bazaar having decided he would go and look in the window. He checked his watch, two hours had passed since he had arrived and it was almost lunchtime. His stomach grumbled in agreement. As he approached the shop, he heard a familiar voice.

'Mr Hales? Is that you, Mr Hales?'

He turned to face Lady Charlotte in an elegant emerald green dress with matching dust coat and parasol. On her head perched a small hat with a cream veil. He removed his hat and bowed.

'Good morning, your Ladyship.' He raised his head, imagining the charming smile hidden behind the veil.

'How odd, running into you here? Do you come to London often. Are you on business?'

Edwin gaped as he searched for the most obvious lie.

'Oh, don't mind me. Blasting all these questions at you! What business is it of mine?' Lady Charlotte exclaimed, her hands fluttered around her neck. She looked behind Edwin, towards the Bazaar and took his arm guiding him in the opposite direction.

'No, not at all.' Edwin stammered, electrified by her touch. He had never found it easy to communicate with ladies, not that he had much opportunity. And Lady Charlotte was the most beautiful woman he had ever seen. He imagined stroking the pale skin on her neck and coughed with embarrassment. 'I... I was planning to surprise a colleague of mine but can't remember the address. How silly of me, never mind. But I mustn't keep you from your business.'

'Oh, how unfortunate,' exclaimed Lady Charlotte. 'And you are not keeping me at all. I was... ahem, visiting a family friend who lives near here. Listen, have you ever been to the park down the road. It is absolutely divine, and such a lovely day, come, I insist you accompany me. My carriage is here.' Lady Charlotte stopped by a small carriage, the green veneer almost a perfect match for her dress, and tapped the door with her parasol.

'Oh, I couldn't, my train leaves in a couple of hours and I—'

'I won't take no for an answer, Mr Hales, and my driver can take you directly to the station after our drive.' Lady Charlotte lifted her veil and her eyes burned with a fiery determination.

'Well, if you insist, how is a man to refuse?' replied Edwin forgetting all about William and King Street Bazaar.

*

Edwin pulled his hat further down on his head as he made his way to King Street. He had not returned to Clomber after meeting Lady Charlotte as he had intended. He needed time to think, and had taken a room at a small hotel within walking distance of the shop as it would be easier to come and go without being observed.

On four different occasions Edwin had watched William moving around the Bazaar with what Edwin presumed were customers. They moved from large artefacts to smaller ones displayed on a table. All the time William appeared to be providing the potential buyers with information. Edwin wouldn't have believed it if he hadn't seen it first-hand. William was leading a double life, working in a bazaar. And why would he want to go to the bother of performing such activities when he had everything that a man could ever want? Edwin hated standing around for day after day and did not wait around to find out where he went after closing. He reasoned that he must stay in lodgings nearby.

However, this morning Edwin had determined to go in rather than observe from across the street. He strode boldly up to the shop door ignoring the doubts that niggled at the back of his mind about confronting William. Perhaps it was best that he faced him without prepared speeches. His bravado popped like a punctured balloon when he found the Bazaar was closed. A handwritten notice on the door informed visitors that enquiries regarding the vacancy for assistant should be made to 37 Queens Row. He looked up at the black plaque above the door which read: *Sole Proprietor: Mr Reuben Chambers.*

Edwin scratched his chin, he couldn't fathom out why William wanted to work for someone else. It's not as if he needed the money. He walked along King Street until he reached a large haberdashery and went in to enquire the whereabouts of Queens Row. The assistant, a small man with a face like a mouse, was most helpful. He drew a neat little map, showing the shortcuts he should take. No more than thirty minutes on foot, the young man advised him in a nasally voice. Edwin smiled, refused the offer to be measured for a new hat and thanked the man before making his way.

After a few wrong turns, Edwin stared back at his reflection in a deep ebony glossed door. He walked up the three steps, banged the heavy ring of a brass knocker three times and turned back towards the street trying to compose himself.

'Yes, may I help you?'

Edwin turned to face a very heavily pregnant lady, she rested one hand on her back as if holding herself from falling forwards.

'Oh, I'm terribly sorry. I must have the wrong address. I went to the Bazaar—'

'Oh, no. You haven't got it wrong at all. Mr Chambers has been delayed, on business, hence the notice. I am his current assistant. Are you enquiring about the vacancy?'

Edwin's mind raced. 'Ahem… yes, indeed, the vacancy. Most intriguing, I thought I'd seen a male assistant there?' He faltered.

'Oh, no, that will be Mr Chambers; he is very involved in the business. But do forgive me, Mr…?'

'Oh, Hales, Edwin Hales. I don't mean to disturb you, I can always call at a time more convenient.'

'Indeed not, please do come in.'

Edwin followed the woman down the corridor, quietly shutting the door behind him. She led him to a bright sitting room where she invited him to sit. Tapestries like those he'd seen in the shop window that morning, hung on the walls.

'Some refreshments, Mr Hales?'

'Indeed no, my dear lady. I do believe you are in more need. I regret putting you to any trouble.'

'It's no trouble. I have been helping to run the Bazaar until…' she shifted in her seat, her distended belly cradled in her hands. 'Until recently.' She smiled brightly but Edwin noticed the dark rings around her eyes.

'It must be very tiring,' Edwin said. 'Still, no greater gift than that of a new life.'

'Oh, how I agree, though I think I shall be quite glad when I can move around again with more ease.' She averted her gaze, and Edwin realised he was staring.

'Do forgive me, ma'am. I really ought to be going.'

'Oh, not at all. The Bazaar is full of wonderful items, Mr Hales, and the customers are most faithful. I fear Mr Chambers loathes the attention. He is a modest man and takes his responsibilities seriously. But the work is far too much for him alone. And I'm afraid in my condition I can only manage the books.'

'I must admit that the window display pulls the eye in. The colourful shields and spears. I'm sure they must be the talk around the London dinner tables.' Edwin chattered on, as his mind raced.

'Thank you, the window display was my design, with Mr Chamber's approval of course.' The young woman flushed and held her head proudly, like a peacock. 'He has such an array of customers. Many of them ordinary people, with some spare money of course, living in London. But we are also visited by the aristocracy!' Her face flushed, and Edwin realised that she was doing her best to promote the business as a successful one. He smiled, encouraging her to continue. 'Well, I know one shouldn't boast, however, we should make the most of what we have. Don't you agree?'

'I do indeed and I'm sure you and Mr Chambers do a wonderful job. And attract the aristocracy, no less!'

'Yes, Lady Charlotte of Romsey has been a trusted benefactor.' Her hand flew to her mouth. 'Oh! I didn't mean to disclose the name, how boorish you must think I am.'

Edwin's heart beat in his rib cage. 'Lady Charlotte of Romsey?'

'Yes, you may have read about her, she is popular in London. Her family is well known I believe, though you mustn't think I listen to the town gossips. She visits the Bazaar from time to time, though I can't recall her buying anything... shouldn't imagine she is in need of such artefacts. Mr Chamber doesn't like to talk about it, I would be grateful if you would keep my indiscretion between ourselves?'

Edwin tried to find his voice and coughed loudly. 'Excuse me, and of course I shan't discuss anything you have disclosed. I shall call at the Bazaar on Mr Chambers' return.' His head spun with the fact that

Lady Charlotte must know what her brother was doing. But the reasons why seemed impossible to fathom.

'Certainly, Mr Hales, but I do hope you will apply for the post. Such a varied time you will have. Mr Chambers should be there on Wednesday if you wish to call and discuss the terms.'

'I most certainly will. Now I must go, I shall see myself out, if that is acceptable.' Edwin bowed. 'I'm sorry, thank you for your kindness, Mrs...?'

'How rude of me! I am Amelia, Amelia Chambers.'

'Ch...Chambers?' Edwin stuttered.

'Yes, Mr Chambers and I are married. In fact, Lady Charlotte was the first to know!'

*

A week later, Amelia gave birth to a healthy baby boy on a wet and damp Sunday afternoon. Reuben was at home when Amelia went into labour and was taken aback by her calm approach.

'Are you sure it's now?' he asked again. He had been due to leave to return to the Abbey that morning. He ran his fingers through his hair and loosened the tie at his neck. Through all these past months, this very moment had been very far from his mind. It was as if it were happening to someone else. His chest felt tight as if someone were squeezing him and he could hear his heart beating in his ears.

'Yes, my dear husband,' Amelia grimaced. 'Surely you cannot think of leaving me at this time?'

Reuben rubbed his hands together and forced a smile. 'Of course not, I just am not familiar with such matters.'

'Neither am I, Reuben. Now please, go and fetch the doctor.'

The doctor had returned with Reuben immediately and a nurse arrived not long after. Reuben had been ordered to stay out until they called for him. He paced their small drawing room, nervous by the lack of progress, taking his watch out from his top pocket every few minutes to check the time and then standing still, listening to the silence. Nothing. Not even a murmur. His temple throbbed and the skin around his fingers made sore by his picking. He was going to be a father very soon and he was not sure if he was ready. Yet at the same time he could not help the feeling of excitement at his role in creating a new life, someone who would look up to him, seek his advice. He made a promise there and then to always be there for his child, no matter what.

'Reuben, do please stop fussing so – you are making me feel dizzy!' Amelia's mother got up and straightened her skirt. 'I'll go and make us some fresh tea.' Reuben nodded, looking for something to distract him other than wait, it was more than unbearable.

Amelia had agreed for her mother to stay during her pregnancy and it afforded Reuben a great peace of mind. Amelia was more settled when she had company and less tearful when he had to go away. He realised it was difficult for her and wished that it could be different but that was a stupid wish and not worth wasting his thoughts on. He was aware that Amelia's mother was restless and bored and he wasn't convinced that the role of grandmother would be enough to satisfy her. He'd tried to talk to her about her plans but when he did she became withdrawn and distant. Reuben prayed that Esme would not abandon her daughter for the second time just when she needed her the most. He sat down, his feet aching from his pacing and closed his eyes. A few moments later he heard footsteps coming down the stairs and rushed out of the door, bumping straight into the doctor – a grave and sickly looking man wearing round spectacles with thick lenses that wobbled on the end of his bony nose as he spoke.

'Aah, Mr Chambers. It has been long and hard. Mrs Chambers is extremely tired but you do have a healthy baby son. Marvellous job. Well done.'

Reuben shook his hand vigorously, 'A son? Thank you, doctor, and thank you.'

'You don't need to thank me, sir, Mrs Chambers did all the work I can assure you. The nurse will call you when she has finished—'

But Reuben had already raced up the stairs, taking two at a time. He hovered outside the bedroom door for a second wondering if he should knock but then burst in unable to contain himself a moment longer. Amelia lay back against the pillows, her hair in two braids, a few damp locks stuck to her forehead. Her dark eyelashes trembled against her pale skin and she looked like an angel. Reuben's heart hammered in his chest. He stood stock still not daring to disturb her but longing to gather her up in his arms. The nurse fussed over a cradle in the corner of the room, then looked up at him and smiled.

'Reuben, is that you?' A weak faint voice came from the bed. Amelia opened her eyes and held out a shaky arm to him.

'Amelia, my love. How are you feeling? The doctor said you had a difficult time. Can I get you anything?' Reuben sat gingerly on the edge of the bed scared that he might hurt her and then leaned forward and kissed her damp forehead.

'I'm fine and all the pain was worth it. Have you seen him yet, our son?'

Reuben shook his head as the nurse came over and placed a small bundle in his arms. He swallowed as he took the child in the crook of his arm as though handling broken glass. He had never held such a tiny person before. All his previous anxieties dissipated like melting snowflakes as he rocked back and forth.

'Don't worry, he won't break,' Amelia laughed weakly. 'He is quite adorable isn't he?'

Reuben teased the pale blue blanket away from the tiny face and said hello to his son for the first time. The child's eyes were tight shut as if he didn't want anyone to look at him, and his button nose was the image of Amelia's. Small cherub pink lips pursed together and wobbled gently as he slept. Reuben held out his little finger to the tiny perfect hand and the fingers wrapped around his, like a cocoon. His hair was dark and shiny and like his mothers, stuck damply to his head. Reuben rubbed the soft downy lobe of his son's ear and his heart filled with love.

'Well done, darling, I've been annoying your mother with my worry and thank goodness all is well.' Reuben turned to Amelia who had fallen asleep again.

'It's probably best if she rests now, sir,' said the nurse taking the baby and replacing him in his cradle, tucking the sheets and blankets in around him.

'Yes, yes of course,' whispered Reuben, then kissed his fingers and placed them lightly on Amelia's cheek. 'I love you.' She grabbed his arm as he rose to leave the bed.

'Reuben, a name, we haven't named him.'

'Oh, but there is plenty of time for that, my dear one. You must rest. We can talk about it later.'

'No, we must name him now. He has to have a name. I would like to call him—' Amelia stopped to cough and the nurse offered her a glass of water.

'You really need to rest, Mrs Chambers.'

'Whatever you wish, dear Amelia, I am happy to agree with a name of your choosing.'

Amelia smiled and lay back against the pillows, her eyelids fluttering with sleep. 'Then he shall be called Henry.'

CHAPTER FIFTEEN

After Henry's christening four weeks later, Reuben returned to Clomber Abbey more with a heart as heavy as a stone. Leaving Amelia and his adorable son had torn him apart. It had taken him sometime to call his son, Henry. The name caught on the edge of his tongue. Amelia cannot have known the name of William's elder brother, how could she? Now, it seemed appropriate, a fitting name for his son in honour of a lost brother.

He hadn't slept properly for the past few nights, wandering in and out of the nursery, trying not to wake either his wife or child and wishing that time could stop still. He was more than surprised by his reaction to fatherhood. He had naively thought that Amelia's life would change, not his, after all, child rearing was the role of women. Since the day he'd held Henry in his arms he had felt a change, a deepening somewhere inside his core.

But he knew he couldn't stay away from William's duties any longer. The reasons for his continued absences would always be harder to explain away and he had tired of the charade. Mabbot was waiting for him in the hallway and William's jaw tightened. How did the man know when he was going to arrive?

'The Duchess has been enquiring about your whereabouts, sir,' said Mabbot, taking his coat, hat and gloves from him, his tone pious.

'Really?' replied William, matching Mabbot's bored tone. 'Can't a man have a few days peace now and again?' Mabbot raised his eyebrows a little, his gaze moving over William's right shoulder.

'Not when he is preparing to be the future Duke.' His mother spoke from behind him. 'Really, William, this can't continue, disappearing for days on end when no-one knows where you are!'

William thrust his arms behind his back, turned and raised his chin in defiance.

'I can't imagine that you are that worried about my absences, Mother. As a child I used to disappear all the time and I wager you never noticed nor cared.'

The Duchess shot him a short sharp look, her gaze fleetingly landing on Mabbot. 'This is neither the time nor place to discuss the matter.'

William turned to Mabbot and watched him slide a finger along the dado rail and scowl, but he knew Mabbot always listened, whatever he may be doing.

'Indeed not, shall we retire to the library? Mabbot, do be a good man and run and tell the stables that I will be riding later this morning and to saddle up.'

'Run, sir?'

'Oh, Mabbot! It's just a figure of speech for heaven's sake. What I mean is don't waste time hanging around asking stupid questions. You could be halfway there by now.'

Mabbot's shoulders dipped for a second at the slight but he straightened his back and clicked his heels. 'Certainly, sir.'

'You do put that man in the most difficult position,' muttered his mother as he opened the library door. 'How is he supposed to do his job properly if you continually undermine—'

'Oh, Mother, don't we have enough to talk about other than the way I treat my manservant?' William closed the door behind him. 'What was it you wanted to talk to me with such urgency?'

William ignored the indignant look on his mother's face and she pursed her lips in refusal to answer. William shrugged his shoulders and turned to go. He would rather be out riding, with his thoughts of Amelia and Henry. The birth of his son had brought such unexpected emotions, at once a ferocity to protect yet filled with a sense of sadness that he could not provide that every minute of every day.

'It's regarding your sister,' his mother blurted out as his hand lingered on the door handle.

William stopped and closed the door again.

'What about Lottie?' he asked with a concerned tone.

'Oh nothing much, being her usual stubborn self. I really don't know what I've done to deserve such wayward children.'

Her words jarred. She always spoke about them as if they were such a nuisance. And now as a father himself, he could not bring himself to accept his mother's cool attitude. He was sure that Amelia would be a fine loving mother despite how Henry behaved. For a fleeting second he wondered if his mother would act differently towards a grandson, be more connected.

'Well, if she is in good health, then there is nothing to discuss. Look, Mother, will you please get to the point.'

'I will if you allow me to. Don't rush me.'

He watched as his mother crossed the room, past the ceiling to floor shelves, leather spines with embossed gold lettering gleaming in the dusty air. She sat down on a large leather chesterfield which stood in the curve of a long bay window. Despite the expanse of glass, the library emitted a sense of gloominess. William stood, trying hard not to tap his foot.

'I believe you are aware we have had a new visitor to the Abbey?' She clasped her hands tight in her lap.

William had not, should he know every coming and going at the Abbey?

'I'm not sure I do, no.'

His mother's gaze darted around the library, as if she wanted to look anywhere but him.

'Well, that's not surprising seeing that you come and go as you please.'

William bit back a retort. He could not explain his absences and he hated having to conceal the bursting sense of happiness inside him. One of the biggest disadvantages to his dual life were the lies that he had to weave constantly and the physical effort of dodging questions about his truancies.

He focused on the view from the window; he loved this time of the year when the leaves were beginning to turn from green, to the pleasing red and oranges. Such a fantastic splash of colour to mark the end of a season yet promises of new beginnings. Although the familiar view did little to soothe the discomfort in the pit of his stomach as he struggled with the different lives of Reuben and William. Both always trying to do their best and the best not being quite good enough. For Reuben a child had entered his world and the responsibilities lay heavy and for William at Clomber, the renovations were coming along well, but it needed constant attention and management.

'It is very difficult, you see… of such a delicate nature.' His mother twisted the gold wedding band on her finger. 'Not something I find easy to talk to you about and the last thing I wanted was to burden you.' William looked at her shrewdly. She looked worried and tired, her heavy brow furrowed and her chin trembled. This was something a little more than her usual meddling, he was sure, and she didn't think that he could handle it.

'Well, whatever it is I'm sure together we can find a solution. We've got through before, I can't see how different or more difficult this matter can be.'

His mother bit her bottom lip; her fingers lingered over the bright sapphire and diamond necklace that lay at her throat. Whatever could be the matter?

'You don't know what you are talking about,' she continued. 'I do wish I didn't need to tell you, your father has become ill with the worry of it all. Pah! He should have thought of that before—'

'Mother, this mysterious talk is not getting us anywhere. Father is ill? Again? I thought he had recovered from that bout of gout? Now I do have a lot of pressing matters, and I'm desperate for a ride around the estate, to see how things are going. I thought that is what you wanted.'

'Well, it would help if you were around more,' snapped the Duchess. 'Sneaking off to wherever it is you go and when you return it is as if you're not here at all. You've always been a bit of a day dreamer, William, but I swear some days I think you are someone entirely different.'

William shot a glance at his mother, was he really blending his two lives? He must be letting his guard down. He ran his fingers through his hair and then around his collar. His head spun and his face flushed hot and sticky.

'You won't like what I have to say, you may even refuse to believe it, but I have no reason to lie to you.' His mother glanced at him, hesitating yet again. He shrugged and said nothing. 'Your father, before you were born... he... he had a minor indiscretion with one of the servants.'

'A minor indiscretion?' William arched an eyebrow. 'What kind of 'indiscretion'?'

'Yes, we were having a difficult time, I was having a difficult time... these things do happen between and man and wife as you will no doubt find out, one day. Anyway, I refuse to go into the details. Usually we can sweep them under the carpet, forget about them and – oh damn your father! I do wish he was here to explain his foolish wrongdoings.

Dr Murray visited this morning and says I must not upset him!' She spoke through tight lips.

'And this definitely can't be swept under the carpet?' He reeled from her unusual openness regarding her relationship with his father. At the same time he had little doubt about his father's behaviour. He had overheard the gossip from the servants in dark corridors when they were unaware of his presence.

'There was a… a consequence.' His mother eyed him shrewdly. 'Yes, a consequence in the form of a child. And more to the point – a boy.'

The silence swallowed the air like a deep well. William stared at his mother unblinking while his mind fluttered and flustered over the information that she had imparted.

'If it, sorry – he – was born before me, that would make him—' He swallowed an urgency to laugh at the absurdity of the implication. His mother swooped up to him and grabbed his arms.

'Well, his birthright certainly cannot be proved, of course! I would not tolerate it. I won't tolerate it. I have to protect the legacy of this family at all costs and this dilemma now proves exactly why I need you to take it seriously.'

William slumped in the chair as the realisation began to dawn. 'So this 'child' could effectively claim—'

'Edwin Hales cannot claim anything. His mother was sent to Scotland as soon as the misdemeanour became evident. Apparently she became ill, was put in a sanatorium where she died. He was taken in by a respected, local family.' She spoke with control, her words measured and her shoulders and chin held high.

'He wouldn't stand a chance on any claim, it has been tried before and it is impossible. However, that is not the problem here.' The Duchess drained her glass and sat it deliberately on the table next to her. She looked back at William as if waiting for the penny to drop. His eyes widened in alarm and disbelief as it fell into place. Lottie.

'What you are really telling me,' William said slowly hoping that he may, perhaps, have got it wrong. 'Is that Lottie has become friendly with—'

'Yes,' said the Duchess nodding. 'Yes, your sister has been seeing your bastard half-brother.'

*

Three days had passed since the conversation with his mother and William still searched for the answers. He made very general enquiries with the estate workers about any strangers on the Abbey estate and Tom Nuttall told him that Edwin Hales had stayed at the inn but had not been seen for a month. Tom wouldn't be drawn any further but William sensed that he wasn't telling him everything.

William hesitated outside his father's bedroom door, unsure about his feelings. His father had not risen from his bed for more than a week and Dr Murray came and went with various potions and prescriptions. This morning he and Lottie were summoned by their mother to attend. The unspoken understanding hung in the air, was that the old Duke was not going to recover.

William tapped on the door before entering the spacious bedroom. He had only ventured once into his father's room as a young child. He'd discovered that it wasn't only one room but a suite of three, entered through a small hallway of its own where he stood now. As well as a bedroom, there was a small sitting room scattered with newspapers and journals and a dressing room. Fortunately his little adventure was interrupted by Nanny Simkins as he'd wandered around touching his father's things wanting to feel some sort of closeness. She'd scolded him and said that he was never, ever to enter his father's room without being asked first. And he'd never been asked. Until now.

As he peered into the gloomy darkness, he saw his mother and Lottie sitting at either side of a large bed. The large ornately carved head and footboards stood tall, hiding the occupant, and navy blue silk bed curtains hung neatly around four posts. The heavy damask curtains at the long windows were pulled closed and not a chink of daylight found its way through. Candles burned and flickered on the wall sconces throwing off slow shadows which moved around the bed, as if waiting. William stood transfixed for a moment, the silence and fetid smell of impending death caught in his throat and he fought his desire to run back out. No Nanny Simkins to whisk him away now.

It was his mother who stood first, smoothed down the creases from her dress and walked over to William. She smiled weakly as she took his hand, it felt cool and unfamiliar, her bony fingers folding around his and he allowed himself to be led.

'Don't be frightened, William. Dr Murray says he is in no pain and Father John has been and prayed with us all. It won't be long until he goes to our Lord.'

William looked into the deathly pale face of his father, once so large and intimidating. His eyes and cheeks now sunken, the large moustache clipped short and showing his broad mouth that struggled to take in air. Lottie stared across the bed at him, as if in a trance, her eyes glistened with unshed tears.

'Sit,' his mother ordered. 'I need to update the servants. I shan't be a while. They need to start the preparations.'

'But I can go—'

'No, William, you need to be here. You need to say goodbye to your father. I have already made my peace.' His mother turned and slowly walked out of the room.

William sat gingerly on the chair his mother vacated, as if it might break, and swallowed hard. What could he say to the man that had no faith in him neither as a son nor as an heir? What words would convey his disappointment to the man who betrayed his mother and his family? The giant of a man, who had spoken forcibly about family honour and obligations. William thought bitterly about Edwin Hales and that he was welcome to everything he possessed, the title, the responsibility, the guilt.

The old man spluttered and coughed, fighting for his breath as he tried to sit up. William stared at the faint white streak that went through the centre of his father's hair. The only trait they shared he thought bitterly.

'Papa, it's me, Lottie.' She stood and supported her father as he leaned forward a little still coughing and spluttering. 'And William is here too.' The old Duke turned towards William and moved his hand towards him. His father's lips, dry and cracked, mimed the words, but no sounds uttered. 'Don't exert yourself so, please.' Lottie implored, looking between her father and William.

His father's hand, skin as thin as silk, with bloated blue veins, crept further toward William. The Duke grabbed his wrist, almost pulling him onto the bed with a sudden burst of strength. He fixed his gaze on William.

'Sorry,' the Duke grunted heavily as he released his grip and fell back against the bank of feather pillows. William looked over at Lottie, who sobbed silently into a lace handkerchief. William searched for some kind of reaction but could find nothing but a cold stone in his heart.

'It's too late, Father.' William whispered. The Duke sighed as if in acceptance before closing his eyes for the last time.

*

Edwin arrived back in Clomber on the day of the Duke's funeral. He stood at the station as a large black hearse with a glass carriage passed by pulled by six black horses. Behind the coffin a line of estate workers followed, caps in hands, heads bowed, dressed in the darkest clothes they possessed. Edwin stepped back into the shadows as he spied Mabbot who led the procession through the village. The Duchess, William and Charlotte, he presumed, were locked away with their grief inside the glass carriage. The entourage turned left into the road which led to the Abbey and Edwin made his way to the inn. It was empty of customers. The innkeeper stood behind his oak bar and polished glasses, setting them in neat rows on the counter.

'Mr Hales, 'tis a sombre day. But God rest his eternal soul, the old Duke has kept this village going. Let's hope that his shadow of a son can do the same.'

'Indeed,' murmured Edwin, rubbing his chin. 'Had he been ill for long? I've only been gone a few weeks, maybe more and all told he was as robust as you and me before I left. The Duke, I mean.'

The innkeeper looked about him 'He took ill very quickly. Apparently he's been under some strain, so I've heard from them up at the big house. Summat that happened years ago, but I don't know what. Shame that the action a man takes when he's young ends up killing him, but I'm sure that he made his peace. He was a one for the ladies; especially when he was young.' The innkeeper chuckled then checked himself, his ruddy complexion deepening in colour. 'I don't mean to sound disrespectful or nothin'.'

Edwin shuffled uncomfortably. 'No, no of course not. I did not know the man. Never met him.' He struggled to contain an overwhelming sense of loss. 'Look, I'm tired, do you think I could have supper brought to my room? That is if you still have the room?' Edwin had paid to keep the room available and a handsome sum at that, more than he could afford.

'Of course, yes of course, Mr Hales.' The innkeeper twiddled his moustache. 'Nothin' has been touched. I promise you. And supper, yes, the wife will be back shortly. She's hoping to get some of the funeral flowers. Brighten the place up a bit.'

'That would be grand. Thank you. A light salad and a jug of wine will do.' Edwin turned to go and then stopped. 'Oh, and I'd be very grateful if you could keep my return to yourself.' He fished in his pocket for a crown and flipped it over the counter. 'I'd rather not be disturbed.'

The innkeeper caught the coin and his wrinkled brow smoothed out with his broad smile. 'Of course, Mr Hales. Anything you say.'

Edwin climbed the stairs to his room, his legs like lead. He lay on his bed, but sleep evaded him. It was eerily quiet, almost as if time stopped still. The past month he had followed Reuben Chambers to and from London all the time planning his future. A future that he could now secure. After all, why did he need to include Mabbot? He was a snotty little servant, a man whom, if life had been different, would have been taking his orders, not the other way around. And now, with the death of the Duke, the stakes were even higher for Lord William. There was more to lose and he had his family to consider. He didn't want recognition, he wasn't stupid enough to believe that he could threaten the legality of his position, but such a thought could be used to his financial advantage and why not?

The anger that had risen in his gut on the day his mother died rose once more and he tasted the bitter bile in his throat. William was making a mockery out of people who had nothing, people like him, people who didn't have the choice about their life and how it unfolded. It was his position that allowed him to have it all, dammit, and fool everyone. Or that is what he thought. How arrogant of his kind.

What burned at his heart was that Lady Charlotte seemed to be somehow involved. It cannot have been a coincidence that he saw her near to King Street and Amelia Chambers had offered the fact that she had been to the Bazaar. Edwin tried to rid the image of her from his mind. He had seen her regularly over the last few weeks in London. She was fun to be with, light and gay and despite her privileged background, did not treat him with distaste or indifference. He had begun to fall in love with her but it was useless, she was his half-sister.

He found solace in the taverns where he searched for the courage in the bottom of a tankard or two instead of furthering his negotiations with William, or Reuben, which one he didn't care. And that meant that his funds were running short. He needed to secure more money and very soon.

*

Reuben kissed Amelia's head and then that of Henry sleeping in her arms. He was in London sorting out the Duke's legal matters following the funeral a week earlier. It was easier to stay at Kenilworth House. The Dowager Duchess and Lottie were invited to the coast to stay with relatives for a short while. His mother objected at first, but he convinced her that it was not frowned upon to mourn with family and he would be too busy sorting things out. He was surprised that she had not needed more persuasion.

He had not given much thought to the other problem of his bastard half-brother, but with his mother and sister out of harm's way for a while there was space to think. And he had taken the opportunity of being in London, to become his other half; he was desperate to see his wife and son.

'And your mother?' Reuben enquired as he sat opposite his wife and poured himself some tea. 'Has she been much help while I've been away?' He noticed the set features of her face, which a moment ago had been soft and full of joy.

'No, I'm afraid she has done her vanishing trick again. Competition for attention from a small baby must have proved to be too much. She said she was going to visit some old friends, but I'm not aware she has any. The money you generously loaned her has given her the opportunity to run, Reuben. She will never be any different.' Amelia sighed with resignation.

'What a pity. I do hate leaving you alone. And I will have to go away again pretty soon, the orders are flying in and I have to secure the goods.' Reuben pushed down the anger that rose in his chest about Esme. Amelia appeared to accept her waywardness, what could he do about it? He put his hands on hers as Henry blew tiny little bubbles in his slumber. 'He is rather wonderful, isn't he? I would like to shut up the Bazaar and spend all the time with you two.'

'But, Reuben, you can't. What about the customers? And now with Henry, we can't—'

'I was only teasing, my dear. I do know that I must provide for you both. Thank goodness for the new assistant. Mr James seems to be grasping things very well, though he is no replacement for you, my dear.'

Amelia's smile turned into a frown. 'Oh, I've just remembered. I swear my head was in the clouds in those final weeks of my confinement. I forgot to tell you, before little Henry arrived a gentleman called. It was when you went away unexpectedly. He'd seen the sign in the shop, and came here as it directed. I completely forgot all about him. How stupid of me. He said he was going to visit you. Did he ever enquire? Such a nice gentleman, I thought he would fit in very well.'

'I only received a few enquiries and all at the shop. Mr James was the last. I had all but given up hope. What was his name? I'm sure I would remember.'

Amelia shifted Henry in the crook of her arm. 'Now, what was it? He was a handsome chap, red hair, with a kind of stripe I remember. Very polite, from Scotland but he didn't have an accent... now... Edward. No Edwin, that's right. Edwin Hales.'

Reuben sat still in his chair not daring to breath. His bastard half-brother had been following him.

CHAPTER SIXTEEN

Edwin refused breakfast, deciding to keep what little money he had, but his stomach objected with a loud growl. A good walk would take his mind off food, he decided as he strode through the village. Since the funeral four weeks ago, he'd been kicking his heels. The discomfort of intruding on the grief that hung in the air like a heavy curtain.

However, the delay had meant he was low on funds and he had pawned his mother's sapphire necklace. It was the only thing of value she possessed when she died. But he had no choice, apart from returning to Scotland, and he wasn't ready, he wanted more time here in Clomber. He had been surprised to discover that she owned such a piece of jewellery. He could never remember seeing it. The blue stones were as vivid as her eyes and the gold gleamed like new. He simply needed more time and the means to pay for board and lodgings. He had managed to secure a reasonable sum of money, but ever since the exchange, he had felt dirty and sullied. As if he had trampled on his mother's memory.

Edwin swallowed back the bile that rose from his empty stomach and increased his pace. He came upon a kissing gate on the edge of the village. Walking always helped him to sort things out and he followed the winding path; the morning dew caught the sunlight and shone like strings of pearls on the tips of the long grass. The path led to the small village church, which four weeks ago overflowed with estate workers paying their last respects to the old Duke.

Edwin stood still and soaked up the peace and tranquillity that surrounded him. Several large plane trees stood like soldiers guarding those in eternal sleep. He wandered around the headstones, trailing his fingers across the rough tops. He heard a faint rustling and came upon an old lady, replacing some flowers at a grave dedicated to a Harold Black, who had died some twelve years before. Edwin stopped and removed his hat.

'Good morning,' she said, brushing away the dead leaves with the back of her hand. Her wrinkled skin was covered with liver spots. She stood with difficulty, but even then her back didn't straighten fully.

'I like to keep it tidy,' she said wistfully looking at the stone. 'My husband demanded tidiness, even in death.' She smiled, rheumy tears filled her eyes.

'Yes, I'm sure,' stuttered Edwin, a little embarrassed. 'I'm sorry to interrupt you, I—'

'Don't mind me, young man. It's not often I get out, only once a month to come up here. I live a quiet life now, but I used to work up at the big house, with my husband.' Her trembling fingers pointed back towards the grave. 'Oooh,' she gasped clutching her chest. 'This damn pain…'

As the old woman toppled slightly Edwin stepped forward and caught her arm.

'Here, there's a seat nearby.' Edwin held her lightly, afraid that she might break. 'Will you allow me to help you? I think you need to sit down a while.'

The old woman nodded, unable to catch her breath and they took small steps to the wooden seat, where Edwin helped her to sit. She closed her eyes and steadied her breathing. Edwin stood over her and hoped that she wouldn't expire in the churchyard. Eventually the old woman patted the seat beside her. 'Sit here, next to me. It'll pass, it always does. Do not worry, it is not my time. Not yet.'

Edwin did as she bid and sat next to her.

'Did I hear you say you worked up at the Abbey?' Edwin said to fill the silence that had once soothed him but now hovered like a menace.

'Yes, I was housekeeper, long time ago now. And my husband was the head butler. We made a good team.' The old lady turned toward him, the colour returned to her cheeks as two red spots. 'You look vaguely familiar…' She screwed up her eyes and peered at him. 'Do I know you?'

'No, I don't think so. Though you may have known my mother. She must have been at the house when you were there. Edith, Edith Hales.'

The old woman glanced at him and then turned her head. 'Ah, yes, Edith. It's the eyes, you know. You have the same blue eyes. Like cornflowers.'

Edwin blushed. 'Yes, she did have pretty eyes.' He sensed her hesitation. 'She left under a bit of a cloud.'

'I know all about Edith, your mother.' She took his hand and squeezed it, the grip loose and cold. He smiled tightly at her wondering if he should have started this conversation. 'She wrote to me a few times after she left.'

'I didn't know my mother could write,' Edwin responded a little harshly. The hair on the back of his neck bristled. There was a lot he didn't know. Sometimes he wished he could let things be. What could he hope to change?

'Well, when I say that, a friend wrote on her behalf. Never knew who but I was very grateful for the contact. I replied regularly until my sight started to go. It is Edwin isn't it? If my mind serves me correctly, though God forbid, it regularly lets me down.'

'Yes, that's right, Edwin.' He swallowed hard, regretting his waspishness. His mother had left no correspondence, though the organisation at the sanatorium was not the best, her things had probably been lost ages ago. The necklace she'd had the sense to put in safekeeping before – well before she could no longer think for herself – he supposed.

'I haven't heard from her in a long—'

Edwin drew in a short breath. 'I'm sorry, I should have said. My mother died, last year.'

The old woman took her hand away, her eyes round and wide. 'Oh, I'm sorry. I didn't know.'

'No, don't apologise. She—'

'Your mother was a good girl at heart.' The old woman spoke over him as if he wasn't there. 'She was young and impressionable, but aren't we all?' She stared at something in the distance. 'She worked hard, didn't deserve what happened, but there you go. She couldn't turn the clocks back and God has his harsh way of making us pay for our sins.' She turned to him. 'She loved you very much. But always said she wasn't good enough for you. That you deserved better.'

Edwin bristled, his skin tingling as if he'd been stung.

'But she never blamed…' her voice dropped to a conspiratorial whisper. 'Well, you know who. In fact I think that he cared for her in his own way. He was a hard man on the outside, but it was all bluff. They have it drilled into them. These people in high places, silver spoons an' all - they can't help themselves. He'll be paying for it now.' She raised her eyebrows heavenwards. 'He gave her a beautiful necklace, I remember. Your mother showed it to me before she left. It had sapphires of pure blue, like her eyes.'

Edwin jumped up and wrung his hands. The necklace had been given to her by the Duke, of course! But such a treasure. His despair returned at the thought of what he had done.

He started as the old woman tapped his back. 'I'm sorry; I didn't mean to upset you. I often think aloud without a mind about what I'm saying. Been on my own too long.'

Edwin looked into her cloudy eyes and swallowed hard. 'She died in a sanatorium. She didn't know who I was at the time.'

'Oh dear, that is sad.' She patted his arm. 'But know this, Mr Hales. She did love you and you were born out of love, never mind the rights and wrongs. Now, I must be on my way, I fear I've said enough.' The old lady shuffled off without a backward glance.

Edwin brushed at his hat in irritation, he wanted someone to pay for his suffering, and his mother's suffering. He didn't want to know the Duke had cared for her. He continued around the back of the church but stopped at the sight of a man and a woman, standing at a large family tomb. William and Charlotte. Edwin crouched down behind a large mossy gravestone, the lettering barely legible, hoping he wouldn't be spotted.

'It doesn't seem like a month has passed, William.' Lottie's voice sounded strained and worn. 'I tried to talk to Mother whilst we were away, but you know what she's like.' Lottie attempted to laugh, but her voice cracked. 'I heard rumours.'

'Rumours?' William repeated, his hands twitching behind his back. 'I hope you haven't been listening to tittle-tattle again. It's human nature to gossip but you have to be careful what you listen to.'

'Well, it seems that's the only way to find out things around this place!' Lottie exclaimed turning towards where Edwin hid. He ducked quickly. 'You are absent half the time, and when you are here it seems like you are somewhere else and mother speaks in riddles. Yet I know something bothered Papa before he died.'

'Lottie, don't torture yourself. Papa had a weak chest. He couldn't shake off the pneumonia this time.'

'I know all that, but I heard, well that someone is trying blackmail us! Surely that can't be true? Something Papa did, years ago. Who would be so cruel? And what on earth could Papa have done that was dreadful enough to want to damage our family and our reputation? I know some thought him a harsh man, but he did provide employment for many people. Oh, I'm tired of all this suffering, it's all just too much, William.'

Edwin's heart beat like a trapped bird. He peered over the top. Charlotte wept silently into a handkerchief and William rested a hand on her shoulder. Edwin ducked back down.

'Come, Charlotte, let me take you home. Please don't upset yourself with listening to wicked talk, it won't bring Father back.'

Edwin lay with his back against the headstone until the light began to fade some hours later. His knees stiff with crouching and his heart empty of tears.

*

William took hold of Lottie's arm but she turned back towards the cemetery. 'Did you hear something? I feel sure we are being watched.' She spoke in a low whisper and William scanned the ground.

'There's no-one here. You are full of conspiracies! Come on, I think you have worn yourself out.'

Lottie allowed him to lead her to the labyrinth. William relaxed his shoulders, the familiarity of the low tunnels, the earthy smell and the natural light which led their way.

'I can't believe it, William. He didn't appear unwell, though he'd never recovered from Henry's death.' Lottie held a hanky to her nose but no more tears flowed.

'At least it was pain free,' William mused aloud, not sure what to say. He had dreaded this very moment. The death of his father ensured he had no choice in his future. He was expected to step up to the challenge and take on his duties. At one time the very thought of becoming head of the Kenilworth family would have filled his head with darkness. Now he sensed a kind of freedom. From what, he wasn't sure but he knew that whatever it was he would cause hurt and shame. He straightened his shoulders. And then he realised. He needed to claim his future and ensure that his wife and his son were not tainted by his actions.

'Mother said he always suffered from a weak chest. But I'm sure he'd given up. There is something they are not telling us. I'm sure about it.' Lottie stopped and grabbed his arm, searching his face. 'And it's not just rumours. Mother muttered something about a threat to the family and that Father was responsible. That she had to tell him. Do you know anything, William?'

William turned away from her penetrating gaze and shook his head. 'No, Lottie, I don't and Mother has been very anxious. I'm sure she has not known what she has been saying. They had been married for over forty years, this must be terrible for her.'

'But no loss to you, William?' Lottie sniffed. 'Not that I blame you, at all. He treated you abominably. I used to wish and pray that he would at least mellow with age and yet he was kind and gentle to me. But that's all too late now.'

'Things have never been any different. What matter does it make? Father is dead and now one thing has become clear – I have to take up my responsibilities.' William had never experienced the pain that gripped at his heart at this very moment. It was as if his whole world was collapsing around him and all brought to a head by the death of his father. And it wasn't he that William mourned, it was the life he had yearned for and lived. A life that he now had to sacrifice, a wife that he had deceived and a son that he had to leave. He could see no other way to protect them any longer.

'Oh.' Lottie stopped and stood in front of him. Her nose was red from crying and her lips trembled. 'But of course you have to. Things are going to get much more difficult for you.'

'I must do the right thing,' William muttered half to himself than in response to Lottie. The sense of loss almost took his breath away and he stopped to lean on the wall of the labyrinth. It felt cold, like his heart at the thought of life without Amelia and Henry. But they were the innocent ones. 'I can't go on like this. You were right. I should have been satisfied with creating a second identity. But no, I insisted on living two lives in two different worlds and playing with the happiness of others. It has all become so complicated, yet being Reuben has given me some of the greatest joys I have ever experienced. But it can't go on; I can't do this to Amelia any longer.'

'But what will you do? How—'

'I'm not sure. Reuben has to go, Lottie. Much as I regret to say, but he can't just disappear. It has be more permanent. It is the only way. The only way I can do this to Amelia. The only way she will accept it and get on with her life. I can set up some kind of financial support, something to keep her and Henry…' William faltered as the image of his baby son filled his vision and he swallowed back the tears. 'They will be better off without me.'

*

Amelia prepared lunch whilst Henry gurgled happily in his pram. She told him stories as she worked and sang nursery rhymes. She couldn't bear to be far from him, unless he was sleeping. Then the door opened and in burst Reuben. He almost fell through into the kitchen, his hair in disarray, a thick stubble on his chin and a dark ring under his eye. It was as if he hadn't slept in days. He picked at his clothes which were creased and dusty.

'Reuben, what on earth is going on? Is everything in order? I thought you were away on business.' Amelia held out her hand to him. Reuben brushed past her without saying a word and strode over to Henry, gathering him up in his arms and holding him tight, cradling him into his neck. Large tears fell onto the child's head and Amelia gasped at the sorrowful sight.

'Reuben, what is the matter? Please, you are scaring him. And me for that matter too, you are holding him too tight. Please.' Henry's face crumpled and his bottom lip quivered and he began to wail in protest. Amelia put her hand firmly on Reuben's arm, not wanting to make a scene and make the boy even more frightened than he was. 'Reuben, let me take him. I know you didn't mean to upset him.'

Reuben gently lowered Henry into her arms. Amelia stroked his sandy brown soft curls, and tickled his chin as the crying subsided. She put a hand on Reuben's cheek, it felt hot and sticky.

'Look, why don't you go and wash, maybe change? We can talk over lunch. It's such a surprise to see you.' Amelia tried to hide her concern. 'I'll put Henry down in the nursery. He's due a nap. Probably why he cried.' She swallowed, not wanting to show her alarm at Reuben's behaviour.

Reuben stared through her as if she wasn't there. Could this stranger really be her husband? He looked like Reuben, but something was missing, though she wasn't sure what. Then as if nothing had happened at all in the last five minutes he smiled briefly, like the old Reuben. Somehow though she knew it was false. It was as if he'd just snapped out of a trance.

'Of course, I'm sorry I didn't mean to scare the boy, nor you for that matter.' Reuben ran his fingers through his hair then bent down and touched Henry's head softly. 'I'm sorry. Sorry for everything.' He turned and kissed Amelia. 'I'll wash and change whilst you take him for his nap. Everything will be well.'

Amelia put Henry in his cradle, humming his favourite lullaby. He struggled to keep his eyes open, his gaze fixed on her face, until tiredness overtook him and his eyelids fluttered shut like a resting butterfly. He wouldn't sleep for long but Amelia knew he was ready for it. She sighed as she sat in her nursing chair in the corner of the room, rocking backwards and forwards. She searched for explanations of Reuben's odd behaviour. Things were different but she could not describe exactly what had changed. She tried her best to support and encourage him but it was as if he was distancing himself from her and Henry yet on the other hand, she knew that he loved their son as much as she. Her mind turned constantly to his loyalty. She woke several times during the night when she was alone, startled awake by dreams about Reuben and a woman without a face, always with their backs turned to her. She had put it down to her overactive imagination, but could she really trust Reuben? Her past experiences with the people who were supposed to love her unconditionally, like her mother, made her naturally distrustful of anyone. But she truly thought that Reuben was different and up to a short while ago, he had never given her any reason to doubt his love and his commitment.

Henry stirred a little, rolled over and curled himself into a tiny ball, his bottom stuck into the air. Amelia sighed; Reuben and her son were the best things in her life. She had everything she dreamed of. But this underlying tension, wrestled inside. She wanted to find out what was wrong for it was no use believing that this would resolve itself. Perhaps Reuben was ill, with all this travelling who knows what he may have picked up?

She stood up and smoothed the wrinkles out of her dress, re-pinned her hair and took a deep breath. No, it was better to face these things, and deal with them head on even if it was another woman. She wasn't quite sure how she would deal with it, but she knew that she could not go on like this much longer. She owed it to herself and she owed it to Henry. She tiptoed out of the nursery and returned to the kitchen.

As she came down the stairs, she noticed the front door was wide open; the breeze had blown in a small carpet of dry leaves.

'Reuben?' Amelia called out looking in each room before looking out into the street. She shut the door. It appeared Reuben had left.

CHAPTER SEVENTEEN

Reuben slept in the Bazaar for two nights after he left 37 Queens Row. He dismissed the assistant with a full month's stipend and a glowing reference. Slumped behind the large totem pole at the back of the shop where he had first seen Amelia, he rested his head on his hands. Damn the Duke and damn Edwin Hales! Shame filled his empty gut. What a fool he had been to believe he could have everything he wanted. Reuben had played with the lives of others, those who trusted him and depended on him. And now he was going to turn their lives upside down, cause them great pain. The responsibilities of becoming a father and the love that filled his heart for his son encompassed him like a heavy cloak. He had to do the right thing for Henry. For the memory of his brother and now for that of his son.

A loud banging from the doorway caused Reuben to lift his head. He covered his ears, he wanted to block everything and everyone out. As the door opened he jumped to his feet. He must have forgotten to lock it after the assistant left. Reuben ran his fingers through his untidy hair and straightened his jacket.

'Sorry, we're closed.' Reuben spoke the words with force. A man, a little older than himself stood in the doorway as his gaze flittered around the shop. Something familiar about the visitor tugged at the dark corners of Reuben's memory but he couldn't place it.

'Did you hear me? I said we are closed. The notice on the window is quite clear.' Reuben thrust his thumbs into the collar of his jacket. The man turned and faced him, his ruddy complexion covered with tiny beads of perspiration. Finally, he removed his hat revealing a faint white streak running through the russet coloured hair. Reuben held his breath. He had seen this man before and he was sure it had been at the Abbey with some of the estate workers.

'Have we met?' Reuben asked with a building sense of doom.

'No, no, not formally. But I do know who you are, Mr Chambers.' His tone was clipped.

A pulse throbbed in Reuben's neck and he rubbed at his aching temple.

'Now, are you going to tell me what you want? I don't believe you're here to buy anything.' Reuben straightened his back to stand at full height and fixed his gaze on him.

'No, you are correct. I am not looking to buy.' The man paused as if waiting for Reuben to say something else. 'I know all about your double life. And I think you know who I am. No doubt your mother, the Duchess, has provided the background to… to my arrival.' The man returned Reuben's stare. 'My name is Edwin Hales.'

The words hung in the air between them like a dense fog. A muscle twitched in Reuben's cheek and he clenched his fists. This was the bastard son of his father. This was his half-brother.

'I'm not sure what you mean?' Reuben snapped, moving away. It was a futile gesture, this man had obviously been following him. 'What is it you want?'

Edwin laughed, a short sharp laugh, and then paused for a moment. 'Please, Lord William. Don't insult my intelligence any further by denying that you don't know who I am. I had wanted recognition from your family about my existence, an apology, perhaps regarding my mother's treatment. And yes, I admit, maybe more money.'

Reuben raised his eyebrows and watched the colour rise in Edwin's face.

'My mother died a pauper,' Edwin spoke through gritted teeth and a spray of spittle showered Reuben's face. He stepped backwards. 'I pawned the only possession she had, a beautiful necklace given by your – or should I say, our – father, so that I could stand face to face with you today. I'm sure that your mother would not want—'

'Enough!' Reuben made to grab Edwin but he was too slow. Edwin bunched his fists and hit Reuben square on the nose. He staggered back, his vision blurred. Reuben wiped his nose and stared at the crimson streak across the back of his hand. The sight inflamed him and he charged at Edwin, keeping his head low like an angry bull.

Edwin stumbled and lost his footing. He fell and hit his head hard on the totem pole, which wobbled menacingly. Edwin slid to the floor in a heap, his head resting on his chest.

Reuben's heart raced as he watched for signs of recovery but Edwin was still and silent. Was he dead? Had he killed him? Reuben took a step towards the inert figure as Edwin groaned and rubbed at the back of his head. He looked at Reuben and scrabbled onto his knees. Reuben offered his hand, but Edwin shook his head, blinked and stood up, his arms held outward as he tried to maintain his balance. Edwin straightened, fixed an angry glare at Reuben and brushed the dust from his clothes.

Reuben chewed at his bottom lip as he walked over to the entrance and turned the key in the lock.

'Come through and take a seat, Mr Hales. It seems we have much to talk about.'

Edwin's gaze flicked towards the door.

'I'm not normally a violent man, Mr Hales. However,' Reuben dabbed at his nose with a handkerchief, 'it was you who threw the first blow. You are free to leave at any time.' Reuben gestured towards the entrance. 'But I do think we need to talk?' Edwin scowled and followed Reuben into the back room, flopped into a chair and sighed.

'You visited my home, my wife?' Reuben tried to control the tremor in his voice.

Edwin kneaded his neck. 'Yes, yes I did. I didn't realise how far your existence had extended at that time. It was more than a shock that you had gone to such extremes. Up until then I thought…' Edwin tapped his finger on the table next to him. 'Well, I thought it was a game played by a rich man. A rich man with lots of opportunities and a privileged life. But seeing Mrs Chambers, in her condition, I realised that this was more than that. She is well, Mrs Chambers?'

'I don't think that is any business of yours,' said Reuben. 'Why don't we just get to the point?' He sat down opposite him, crossed his legs and put his palms together. 'What is it exactly that you want from me?'

'Well, I've made it my business.' Edwin squinted at Reuben. 'What I don't understand is why you married her in the first place? You must have known that it would be hard to continue with the lies. Unless she was a damsel in distress, and you were her dashing knight?' Reuben's face flushed at the mocking tone of Edwin's voice. 'Ah, I made the right assumption.' Edwin tapped at his chin and then snapped his fingers. 'She was underage wasn't she? The marriage is a sham. And another bastard son fathered from your stock. Quite a family trait isn't it?'

His bastard half-brother stared back at Reuben with familiar features. His father's deep set eyes, a strong nose, the pointed chin and the white streak of hair. The man was right of course, he was repeating his father's history, the very core of which he found despicable. Reuben searched for a response but anything he said could never make it right. He had wanted to help Amelia, save her from a life of ruin. What he hadn't expected was the depth of feeling that she aroused in him, and now Henry. Reuben wondered if things had been different whether he and Edwin would have been close as brothers.

Edwin coughed and spoke in a low, deliberate voice. 'My mother died around the same time as your brother – or should that be our brother – Lord Henry. She left me a letter telling me who my father was. I had no idea until then. She never talked about it. I was angry. I wanted revenge. My mother died in a sanatorium and had lived a life of shame. She never forgave herself. And I suppose what I wanted then was revenge.'

Reuben lifted a match from a small pot next to the gas lamp and turned it round in his fingers. 'Revenge?'

Edwin paused, and his eyes softened. 'I hadn't anticipated meeting Lady Charlotte or your wife. Until then it was all so anonymous. You were all figures to blame in the distance. A privileged life, full of opportunities that I never had. A family who presents on the exterior as one to look up to, but a family with its secrets and its pain. Really no different from any other ordinary life, like mine.'

'Yes, but I do understand that very same family paid you a handsome sum, for your…' Reuben rested his chin on his hand which smelt of sulphur, '…how shall we say? Your loyalty.'

'Yes, a handsome sum.' Edwin leaned forward. 'But I was paid for my silence, not my loyalty. Your family has done nothing to earn my trust. The money allowed me to travel to Clomber and see for myself where my mother suffered such shame. Banished from everything and everyone she knew. My intentions, I admit, were fuelled by anger, hatred even, call it what you will. And the only thing she treasured was this necklace, a necklace I had never seen before. She should have sold it, to help with…' His shoulders slumped like a deflated balloon. 'But now I am weary. I've betrayed my mother's memory and she would not want this. The revenge and anger have eaten away at my soul and I shall pay for my deeds. Nothing you possess can change any of that.'

Reuben understood the anger and the hatred, but could he trust him? Was this all a cover, to lure him into a sense of security? 'Are you saying that you no longer wish to blackmail my family? To expose the misdemeanours of my father?'

'But now it's not only the misdemeanours of your father is it?'

Reuben dropped the match and dabbed at his nose with a clammy hand.

Edwin sighed and shook his head. 'Your father is dead; there is no harm I could wish upon him now. I yearned for a father all my life.' Edwin pressed his lips together. 'I thought having a father might make everything right, heal my mother's pain, but when I found out that he had not wanted to know me, something snapped inside of me. I wanted someone to pay.'

'It seems to me that both of us acted in ways we might wish we hadn't.' Reuben mused. 'Both of us have desired a different life for whatever reason.'

'Yes, perhaps you're right. I don't believe you are a bad man, not here.' Edwin put his fist to his chest. 'I don't think you will allow your son to be tainted with the label of a bastard. I trust you have more backbone than our father?'

'At this precise moment, I'm not sure. I fear I have let everyone down, everyone who depends on me, who trusts me.' Reuben swallowed hard. 'I do not deserve any loyalty, as you say. I am in no position to make demands.'

The atmosphere between them changed. It was as if the cobwebs had been brushed away and the tension that had charged the air, evaporated.

'I am intrigued though. How did you manage to find out? About my life as Reuben Chambers?' He leaned forward and rested his arms on his knees.

Edwin smiled, a short smile that evaporated quickly. 'I fear that some of your closest staff think they have your best intentions at heart.'

Reuben nodded. 'Ah, Mabbot.' Of course, the man is like a terrier. 'But not alone surely?'

Edwin hesitated. 'No, a maid. But I'm sure she does not mean to betray you.'

Sarah. So that's what she meant by breaking promises when William had found her in tears.

'Please, I do not wish to cause Miss Nuttall any consequences from our conversation. I'm convinced she acts only under extreme duress.

And her employment at the Abbey is essential for her family.' Edwin rubbed the back of his head again.

'Do not concern yourself, Mr Hales. Sarah would never be disloyal willingly. I know that. But you, are you going to betray me?' Reuben waited. He would not be surprised, the man had admitted he wanted revenge after all.

The silence lasted for an age and Reuben stood and paced the room. There was nothing he could do and why should he not be punished for his crimes of deception? He had to make retribution somehow out of this mess.

'No.' Edwin's voice was strong and determined. 'No. I am returning home, to Scotland, at the end of the week. I have thought long and hard, but I wish you no harm. What kind of man would that make me? God forbid me, but I did want you to hurt, I wanted you to feel my pain. But I see you have enough of your own. It is not a life I wish for.'

'You surely don't expect me to believe you have compassion for me?'

'No, but only you can put things right, make some kind of amends. However, your sister, Lady Charlotte…' Edwin's voice cracked with emotion. 'My feelings for her can never be realised and I cannot act in any way that brings her harm, or to those she holds dear. She is a loyal sister and I know that she has a part to play in this charade. To expose you would involve Lottie and I will not be part of that. She does not know of my background? I pray you will be as loyal to me and not betray my identity. I don't think I could bear it.'

Reuben swallowed hard. 'No, but my mother is aware. I have not found the opportunity to talk with Lottie and you are right, it is best that she does not know. It would upset her; despite her very independent exterior, she would be devastated. Without her I would never have…' he faltered as the image of Amelia and Henry filled his vision. He pushed them away. 'But that was before. I take you at your word, Mr Hales. I suppose we have to trust each other?'

Edwin stood, replaced his hat, and held out his hand. Remaining seated, Reuben's mind raced. Edwin withdrew his hand slowly, and a veil of sadness fell over his face.

'Of course.' Reuben rose from his chair, took his hand in his and shook it. He watched Edwin leave, twirling the match around in his fingers until he realised what he must do. It was the only way.

*

That night, the flames that had started at the base of the totem pole ripped through the King Street Bazaar, the shop window cracked and shattered. The sign above the door caught light and the letters spelling '*Sole Proprietor: Mr Reuben Chambers*' melted away in the fierce heat.

*

Amelia put her embroidery on the table, got up from the chair and peered out of the window for the seventh time since lunch. Reuben had not returned in the three days since he had acted like a mad man. He had never gone away without telling her when he would return. The sky was grey and she could make out a light drizzle. The gloominess enhanced her state of depression. Even Henry grizzled in his sleep, unusually fitful and difficult to settle. Amelia sat down and picked up her embroidery, then sighed and dropped it into her lap. As she closed her eyes, a loud, urgent knocking came from the hallway. Reuben! Amelia gathered her skirts with one hand and rearranged her hair with the other. He must have forgotten his key. Her hopes soared as she approached the door. She must be calm. She took a deep breath, put on a smile and opened the door.

A tall policeman stood in front of her.

'Mrs Chambers?'

'Yes.' Amelia's heart slowed to a pace that made her breathless. 'Can I be of any help? Is there some trouble?'

'Best if I come in, ma'am. Is anyone else here with you?'

Amelia stepped aside as the large man removed his helmet and passed through. 'No, just my baby son. My husband…' her voice trailed off. A sickly taste like metal gathered in her throat. She showed him through to the sitting room, where Henry lay asleep in his cot under the window. The man coughed loudly, holding up a fat fingered hand to his mouth.

'I'm afraid I bring some bad news regarding the King Street Bazaar.' He coughed again as if the words irritated him.

'Would you like a glass of water, Constable?' Amelia asked turning to the kitchen.

'No, ma'am. Thank you. There has been a fire, at the shop. The Bazaar on King Street?'

Amelia gasped and held the back of a chair. 'Oh, my goodness. My husband. Does he know? He had such a lot of expensive stock. Items for customers all paid for in advance. Oh my, what a terrible shock. Mr Chambers will be devastated.'

'Perhaps you should sit down, ma'am.' The policeman offered his hand but she shook her head. 'The joint owner of the shop…' the policeman took out his notebook as he paused. '…a Lady Charlotte Kenilworth, has been informed and is on her way here now.'

'Lady Charlotte?' Amelia frowned. Joint owner? That was the connection between her and Reuben, why hadn't he told her? Lady Charlotte must have helped to finance the Bazaar. Oh my goodness, what trouble for her on top of the sudden death of her father? Poor Lady Charlotte.

'But, Mrs Chambers, the shop was burnt to a cinder, the heat was very fierce. And your husband, when was the last time you saw him?'

Amelia stared at the man's face until her vision blurred.

'Ma'am?'

'Three days ago,' she whispered. 'But I'm sure he's away on business.'

'I'm sorry, but we have reports that your husband was in the shop shortly before the fire began.'

Amelia let out a moan.

'But we, well, they haven't found any evidence of anyone who may have… ahem… perished.' He reached into his pocket and then held out his hand. 'Apart from this, do you recognise it?'

Amelia stared at Reuben's pocket watch; it was black and charred but it was Reuben's, a gift from her after their wedding and he never went anywhere without it.

'Ma'am?'

Amelia tried to move but her legs wouldn't support her. She saw Reuben's face smiling at her beckoning to her and she reached out for him but he vanished as the room spun and her world turned black.

*

Amelia saw only darkness where she sought freedom from the pain that tore through her heart. But the stifled cries from her son somewhere in the distance tugged at her senses. She heard the faint sounds of someone else moving around her, touching her shoulder and the muffled sound of a voice. Her mind snapped into action. It must be Reuben! She forced her eyes open and tried to sit up but her arms were not strong enough. The brightness blinded her for a second and she fell back against the pillows. Again she felt a hand on her shoulder, a light touch.

'Amelia, thank goodness you are awake. It's me, Lady Charlotte—'

'No,' Amelia groaned. Oh, no, it must be true, Reuben was really gone. She had hoped it had all been a bad dream. She sobbed, wanting to return to her dark world.

'Amelia, you have been sleeping for days now. I arrived moments after you fainted. It was a good job, because the policeman was in a frightful state. Please, I know this is difficult for you, but I'm here to help.' Amelia heard a small sigh. 'I cannot tell you how worried I have been for you. And for your child.'

Amelia opened her eyes again, slowly this time, until her vision adjusted to the light. Lady Charlotte sat on her bed and tilted her head to one side, a sad smile crept to her lips. 'I am so glad you are back with us.'

'Henry?' Amelia whispered. 'Is Henry well?' The stifled cries that had woken her were now silent.

'Yes, he's fine. The doctor has visited you every day and the nurse has been here all the time. They said it would be a matter of time. That the shock had been too much. You blocked us all out, and I must say quite terrifying it was too.'

'I can't believe he's gone.' Amelia sobbed, the tears flowed down her cheeks and chin. Lady Charlotte dabbed at her face with a damp cloth.

'Amelia, the policeman told you they didn't find any...' Lady Charlotte's voice trembled. 'They don't think Reuben was in the shop, but he hasn't turned up. It seems to all intents and purposes he's disappeared. Can you cast any light on things? Has he been well?'

Amelia scrabbled to sit up, the mist started to clear from her head. 'You mean he isn't dead?' she whispered.

Lady Charlotte paced the floor, wringing her hands together and creasing her brow. 'They don't know, Amelia, my poor dear. It looks like he may have started the fire; the business it seems was struggling.'

'Struggling? Surely not? Though he was not himself the last time I saw him.' Amelia admitted. 'I was worried about his health, but I haven't seen him since. Oh, my word. Reuben. He wouldn't leave me and Henry like this, I'm sure!'

'I don't think so either, but perhaps things got too much for him.' Lady Charlotte lowered her voice. 'He may have done it for insurance purposes, in order that you would get the money.'

Amelia gasped and clamped her hand to her mouth. 'No, Reuben could not do such a thing. I know he couldn't.'

'But I've looked through the papers and Amelia, I found your birth certificate.'

Amelia shook her head distractedly. Lady Charlotte sat on the bed and took her hand. It felt warm and soft. 'I know this is the most difficult time for you, but I don't think we're going to get any answers regarding Reuben. Henry needs you right now. He's been fine, with the nurse feeding and changing him, keeping him clean. But he needs his mother's love now more than anything and you need the comfort of your and Reuben's son, especially right now.'

The coldness in Amelia's chest thawed a little. 'Can you bring him to me?'

Lady Charlotte smiled and nodded to the nurse. Amelia took her son in her arms, breathing in his fresh baby smell as large teardrops fell again, soaking his dark hair. His fingers reached up to her face and caressed her chin. She drew him near and vowed never to leave him again.

'I'm afraid you will have to sell 37 Queens Row.' Lady Charlotte got up and bustled around the room nervously. 'The customers will need to be reimbursed and the insurance Reuben arranged for you, Henry and the shop is made null and void because, well because you were underage when you married—'

'Sell our home?' Amelia hugged Henry tightly to her chest. 'But where can we go?' The darkness returned as thoughts of the poor house returned. She would not allow that to happen to Henry. Amelia's senses were numb but all around were reminders of Reuben. Everywhere. Where was he? She searched her soul for some understanding, for some reasons. It was as if she were in a big black hole. An emptiness crept over her.

She wanted to run away, get away from all that they had shared. She tried to answer but her dry lips stuck together, and she reached for a glass of water on her bedside table, nestling Henry in her lap as she drank.

'Well, I may have just the solution.' Lady Charlotte tickled Henry under the chin. 'I need to talk to my brother, the Duke, but I'm sure he would agree. We've been talking about educating the children on the estate for some time.'

Amelia frowned. 'I'm not sure what you mean.'

'Oh, I'm sorry, I was thinking aloud. But we need a governess, a young, bright woman to teach the children to read and write. You are perfect.'

'I am?'

'And the job comes with a small but very comfortable lodge in the grounds, plenty of room for little Henry to run around in. And of course we would pay you.'

Amelia searched for the words to respond. She could not fathom why this woman was going out of her way to help her and Henry?

'I feel responsible, you understand,' Lady Charlotte said, as if reading her mind. 'I helped Mr Chambers to set up his business, and his life here in London. I really would like to help you out and in return you will be offering such a valuable opportunity to the children on our estate. We value our workers very highly.'

Amelia found herself nodding, fast and furious. She would agree to anything, to get away from the despair she felt at this moment.

*

William sat in the small family chapel at Clomber Abbey. He didn't know why he was there; he never attended service. He took a taper and lit two candles, one for Reuben and one for his father. In the ten days since the fire at the Bazaar there had been a hundred times he yearned to see Amelia and Henry, to tell them everything was all right. Today he had woken early, listening to the bird song wishing he had found the strength to forgive his father. What harm could it have done? To say sorry to a dying man whose weakness had ruined lives? How was Reuben any different and would Henry find the strength to forgive him? He worried about his father never finding peace, drifting in the hinterland of the afterlife.

William wanted some escape from all the turmoil but wasn't that where all this had started? He hadn't bargained on meeting Amelia in such a vulnerable position with no home and had thought that marrying her would give her some security but more so because he had fallen in love with her. Now that act had turned around and bitten him. His heart ached with regret and remorse yet at the same time he thought that he had done the right thing. How he longed to feel the comfort of her arms and the scent of her skin. He slumped into a pew and rested his aching head in his hands.

William heard a soft swishing along the stone floor and wiped his face, hoping whoever it was would not disturb him. The swishing stopped and he held his breath.

'William? Is that you?' His mother's voice was weak and reedy. He turned to see her standing in the doorway, her hands fidgeting in front of her.

'Yes, Mother. It's me.' He rose and walked towards her holding out his hand. She took it as he led her to the candles and she lit one from his taper. In the flickering light he noted the sallow colour of her skin, the dullness in her eyes.

'Two candles? God forbid someone else has left us?' She gazed up at him with fear in her dull grey eyes.

'No, of course not.' His mother lowered her head, and she trembled. 'Come, come and sit down for a while.' William stepped aside.

'Thank you. I'm surprised to find you here, though it does comfort me. The sense of serenity helps to ease the pain. Forgive me.'

William helped her to the pew and sat down beside her. 'There is nothing to forgive you for. It is I who should apologise. I have not been the son you deserve.'

They sat in silence for a few moments watching the flickering of the shadows that leapt from the burning candles.

'Saying sorry is all well and good,' said his mother, the strength returning to her voice. 'But at the end of the day, we must get on with our lives. But with all the scandal that a certain person could bring on our family, it's hard to imagine.'

William turned towards his mother and took her hands in his. He ran his thumb gently over the papery skin, dotted with liver spots. 'You do not need to worry about that anymore. Mr Hales is no longer a threat to our family. In fact I found the man, my half-brother, had a very moral side.' His mother bristled beside him. 'Oh, I don't doubt that his first intentions were less than honourable. But he has given me his word.'

'And you trust him?'

'I have to; we don't have any other option. He admitted to blackmail; he has as much, if not more, to lose.'

'But if—'

'Please, let me take the burden. It is my responsibility now, as Duke.' William spoke with authority.

His mother arched an eyebrow. 'Are you back with us now for some time, William? No more absences? If I didn't know any better I would swear that there has been the influence of a woman on your recent behaviour.'

William swallowed, he could not confide in his mother. She placed a hand on his arm. 'You know, things change as we get older and we lose the people that are closer to us. I know that I have been rather hard on you particularly and for that I have no regrets. However, we all mellow, things that once appeared to be important lose their colour, fade with time. Unlike this family, I hope. And if the cause for your, how shall we say – change of heart – is a woman then she has my approval.'

William looked away from his mother, afraid that his face might betray him. 'Mother, I'm sorry, I misunderstood the reasons for your actions. I know that I have let you down, and I cannot explain. I only know that now, from this moment on, I vow to serve this family and this seat of Romsey. I will endeavour to do all I can to ensure that I fulfil my responsibilities.'

His mother stood and squeezed his shoulder. 'All will be well, William. I believe all will be well.'

After his mother left, William stared into the candlelight, mesmerised by the flames until he pulled his gaze away. How he wished that her words were true, how he wished he deserved her support. But now he had other issues on his mind. Time to confront Mabbot.

CHAPTER EIGHTEEN

Mabbot paced the corridor. 'Damn that servant girl,' he muttered under his breath. He had told her to be here promptly and she'd kept him waiting. He prowled like a guard dog, growling at anyone who had the nerve to pass by. Servants scurried past like mice chancing the path of a hungry cat. Mabbot's pulse raced in his neck.

'Ah, Mabbot, I was hoping to catch you.' It was William. Mabbot counted to five under his breath.

'Right now, sir?' Mabbot asked.

'You have other things to do?' William arched an eyebrow.

'No, of course not, sir. I am at your service.' Mabbot eyed his master. There was something different about him. His nose looked slightly swollen and misshapen and his droopy eye seemed more pronounced. And no disappearances for a week or more. What was going on?

Mabbot tried some delaying tactics. Maybe Sarah would show. 'Have you eaten, sir? Your mother has retired to her quarters for a rest. She ate very little lunch, had a headache. I do believe she is not well, sir. Shall I send for Dr Murray?'

William's stomach grumbled loudly and he put his hand on his belly. 'Ah lunch, of course, I missed that and breakfast.' He looked at a spot on the floor. 'Can't remember when I last ate actually. No, don't send for Dr Murray at the moment, I'll check with the Duchess later. Be a good chap and ask cook to prepare me lunch?'

'Certainly, sir, though cook has left on an errand for Lady Charlotte, I believe.' Mabbot paused. 'I can rustle up a plate for you, I'm sure.' Mabbot counted again under his breath and his fingers twitched in his white glove.

'I thought that preparing a meal was a little below you, Mabbot.' William tucked his hands behind his back. 'But, things do indeed change. Thank you, Mabbot, now do be quick about it, my stomach thinks my throat has been cut.'

Mabbot frowned at William's teasing, of course preparing meals was below his status. He needed to see the girl first. Before retreating, Mabbot bowed his head and then turned on his heel. The kitchen was not organised to his particular standards, he fumed to himself. It was shoddy and mishap. A woman's place indeed! Eventually he located a large piece of ham, a few tomatoes and a slab of freshly baked bread. Tearing a small corner off the doughy loaf, Mabbot chewed thoughtfully. He worked like an automaton as he filtered through his thoughts; folding a napkin with precise sharp edges, rubbing at a knife and fork that were already highly polished and arranging the food on the plate. Then he filled a small decanter of red wine and checked a crystal glass for smudges.

The kitchen door creaked open and Mabbot made a mental note to tell the housekeeper, it was most annoying when one was deep in thought. He turned his head as Sarah Nuttall peered in, and on seeing Mabbot disappeared quickly.

Mabbot dashed to the door and grabbed her arm. 'Miss Nuttall, do please join me if you don't mind. We need to prepare lunch for the Duke.' He released his grip a little and stared at the two servant girls who were polishing and dusting in the hallway. Mabbot allowed a small thin smile, knowing that she had little choice but to obey his command. She reddened, then retraced her steps back into the kitchen. Mabbot shut the door firmly behind him, as Sarah stood head bowed, fiddling with the ends of her apron.

'I was expecting to see you this morning as arranged,' said Mabbot, his voice controlled and unkindly. He marched past her and began to set the lunch items on a silver tray.

'Oh I was, I couldn't get away without seeming suspicious.'

Mabbot observed the girl's pale face. Lying wench. She knew something but didn't want to tell him. 'Oh really? Well you don't usually have any problems getting away do you? Not when Bertie Ragg is involved. What was different this time?' Mabbot continued to set the tray. Sarah shuffled from foot to foot and bit on her bottom lip. 'And you decided to ignore my request? And don't have any reasonable explanation for it? There is a price to pay for such insubordination. I really advise against any rash behaviour you may be planning.'

'I'm not, honest, Mister Mabbot.' Sarah blurted out. 'I couldn't get away, it's the honest truth. You have to believe me.' She stared at Mabbot earnestly but her defiant attitude made his head ache.

'Tell me what you know and I will forgive your tardiness.' He walked over and stood beside her, she was tiny and his shadow engulfed her body. The girl shook her head. 'You must tell me. Where is Mr Hales?'

'I don't know,' Sarah insisted. 'I don't know nothin'. He's gone. From the inn. But I swear, I don't know where!' She moved away from him and Mabbot grabbed her arm. 'You will tell me you disgusting little wench or I'll—'

'Tell you what exactly, Mabbot?' boomed William's voice from the doorway.

*

William glared at Mabbot and the struggling Sarah.

'Unhand the girl right now,' he demanded. Mabbot flushed red, did as he was bade and stepped back. Sarah stood still, her eyes wide with fear and embarrassment.

'Are you all right?' William asked. Sarah rubbed at her arm unconsciously. 'Yes sir, I'm fine. No harm done honest. It was just a misunderstandin'.' She stepped away from Mabbot looking up at him from under her eyelashes.

'Very well then.' William's voice was cold and harsh but that was for Mabbot's benefit. 'Please wait for me in the drawing room, Sarah. I shan't be long.'

'But, sir, it was just—'

'Please, do as I ask, Sarah.' William wiped his hand across his brow, suddenly very weary, but also he was damn hungry. He needed to eat. His stomach rumbled loudly in agreement.

'Yes, sir, of course.' Sarah dipped into a curtsy and left the kitchen without a second glance.

The silence filled the room. William's gaze fell upon the tray in front of Mabbot. 'I presume that is my lunch? Where did you say cook was?' William had hoped for something more warming and comforting, Mabbot's idea of lunch looked like a summer's picnic.

'She's gone into town. Lady Charlotte has asked her to secure some provisions for the new governess.' Mabbot bustled about with the plates and cutlery.

William's heart skipped a beat. 'Ah, yes of course.' He had not forgotten that Lottie had offered Amelia the job of governess at the Abbey. A row had ensued from which his sister had reigned victorious, claiming that he had relinquished his responsibilities with the fire. And furthermore when Lottie had told him Amelia had been under the age of consent and therefore all the financial arrangements he had made as Reuben were useless, he had to agree that it was the only way forward. He had saved her from the poor house once and he wasn't going to go back on a promise. He resigned himself to the torture of knowing she and Henry would be close but there was no need for their paths to cross, that there was plenty to keep himself busy.

'Shall I take it to the dining room, sir?' Mabbot stood in front of him with the tray of food.

'No,' said William walking over the large pine table, which dominated the room. He pulled out a carver chair and sat down, his fingers tapped at the large wooden arms. 'I'll eat here.' Mabbot's jaw dropped. 'If it's good enough for the servants, it should be good enough for me.'

'But, sir, wouldn't you be more comfortable in your quarters?'

'No.'

Mabbot bowed slightly and turned to leave the kitchen.

'I'd like you to remain here while I eat. We can talk at the same time.' William popped a tomato into his mouth and allowed the soft fruit to burst over his taste buds.

'As you wish, sir,' Mabbot replied a little too quickly, his face contorting as he struggled to maintain his composure. William quite enjoyed seeing the man squirm for once. As he chewed he considered his next move. He knew that Mabbot had asked after Edwin Hales.

'Now, what was it with the girl, then?' asked William with a mouth full of bread and feigned disinterest.

Mabbot moved around in his usual ghostly manner, his face now stone like.

'Oh nothing for you to worry yourself with, sir, some silly indiscretions.'

'Indiscretions?' William probed, sipped at the wine and refilled his glass.

'Yes, insubordination and gossip, that kind of thing. I will make the housekeeper aware of it. She deals with the maids and she won't take kindly to any messing around.'

'Indeed, Mabbot,' said William not believing a word. 'But it is most unusual, is it not, for one servant to manhandle another particularly when one of them is a young girl?'

Mabbot stiffened and William realised he had touched a raw nerve.

'Well, yes,' Mabbot blustered on, 'you only saw the moment when you entered.' Mabbot spoke slowly, obviously trying to concoct an explanation. He removed William's empty plate. 'I believe we have a walnut cake, sir, if you are still hungry.'

William shook his head. 'No, that will suffice, thank you, but I would like to hear what went on before I entered the room. Just in time, it appeared to me.'

Mabbot stared back at him and a small muscle twitched in the corner of his mouth. 'The girl was spreading malicious gossip about the family, sir. I saw it as my duty to determine what it was and to insist that she stop doing so.'

William arched an eyebrow. 'Malicious gossip, eh? And what are the details of this slander on my name?'

Mabbot lowered his head. 'I'd rather not repeat what is spurious and evil chit chat. I'm a firm believer in the less said of certain things, the better.'

'Indeed, Mabbot.' William smiled; the man must think him a fool. 'But that still doesn't explain why you had a grip on the girl and why she was struggling to get away? Surely that is not considered acceptable behaviour?'

Mabbot blinked and without further effort declared, 'The girl kicked me, sir. I was merely trying to defend myself. I am afraid she is nothing but trouble. The housekeeper only confided in me the other day, but she has been troubled lately by her absences and time keeping and was considering letting her go.'

William sat thoughtfully for a while, allowing Mabbot to go over his cover story. His respect for his faithful manservant was fading fast.

'Well, if she did indeed kick you, Mabbot, you have every right to defend yourself. Of course. As to absences and time keeping that is not my concern. However…' Mabbot stiffened again. 'However, I will listen to what young Sarah has got to say. Her father is one of our finest stable workers. I would hate to see her getting into trouble. Leave it with me, Mabbot.'

William watched the small muscle in Mabbot's cheek twitch again.

'As you wish, sir.'

William stood as Mabbot approached the door to leave. 'And, Mabbot. I don't expect to hear the name of Edwin Hales in this house ever again. He has left Clomber and that is the end of that. Do you understand?'

Mabbot's head nodded a short nod, his face as unreadable as a wooden mask. The swing door creaked angrily as he left.

William made his way to the dining room.

'Sorry to keep you waiting, Sarah,' William said as he strode in.

'No, it's me that's sorry, sir. I didn't mean no 'arm. Mister Mabbot—'

'Don't worry, you are not in trouble. I know that you think you have betrayed me…'

Sarah wrung her hands, tears forming in the corner of her eyes. 'I'm sorry, sir, but I need me job. Me father'll kill me if I don't bring the wage in…'

'I don't need your explanations, your position here is safe, I promise. But I have to ask one last favour from you.'

Sarah looked back at him and wiped at the tears with her sleeve.

'You are to mention nothing of this incident with Mabbot, or Mr Hales, to anyone. Not even Bertie.'

Sarah nodded frantically. 'I swear I will never tell, ever again.'

William smiled. 'I'm pleased and you may have done more good than harm. Now go, quickly and get on with your chores.'

*

Mabbot returned to his room and sat heavily on his single bed. He had gone too far, and now what? Where would he go? He was sure that Lord William would not give him a reference. A person of Mabbot's standing was supposed to be trustworthy and loyal. What had started off as a mild irritation of not knowing where his master was, turned into an obsession and one which was going to cost him dear. But he had one last card up his sleeve.

Mabbot looked around the room. It was very sparse and simple but to him it was where he'd called home since before he could remember. A home once too to his father and his grandfather before him. He reached into his bedside drawer and pulled out a small cameo. It pictured two faces in profile; his mother who died following his birth and his father who worked proudly for this family for all his life and then passed away peacefully in his sleep on the second day of his 'retirement'. Mabbot ran a finger over the glass, his memories of them faint and distant. Not only was this home but it was his family too. Damn that girl, Sarah, he was sure that she would be bleating to William about his harsh treatment of her.

Mabbot put the cameo on the bed and took a small suitcase down from the top of the wardrobe. He unlocked the lid and fumbled in the side pocket and withdrew a necklace, with a central blue sapphire, the colour of Mr Hale's eyes. Edwin Hales was not the only one who could snoop around. The local pawnbroker was easily persuaded that his business would be at risk if he was found to be in possession of this precious piece of jewellery. Mabbot informed him that the family heirloom went missing several years before. Around the same time as poor Edith was seduced by that lustful old Duke.

Mabbot fingered the sharp edges of the stone. He had been in love with Edith but never found the courage to tell her. And he had not wanted to take advantage of his position. He knew many servants who managed to keep their personal relationships and their duty to their employers separate but he'd wanted to take her away from the drudgery and began to save every penny he earned. When he discovered that the Duke had taken advantage of her, the Duke who possessed everything possible he could ever want, his anger bubbled over like a boiling pot. Why mess with a young servant girl? And the damn man had dangled this necklace in front of Mabbot's face. 'Be sure this gets to the girl, before she leaves,' he demanded. And Mabbot with a heavy heart wrapped up the necklace and presented it to a tearful

Edith. And the poor girl had never thought to sell it to help ease her life.

A light knocking interrupted the memory. 'Who is it?' he snapped.

'It is I,' William strode through the door without waiting. Mabbot stood up and straightened his jacket sleeves, showing an inch of white shirt cuff.

'I'm so sorry, sir, I didn't mean to—'

William waved a hand. 'No matter, even you can't see through doors, Mabbot.' William's smile slipped as his gaze fell to the necklace that Mabbot still held in his hand. He turned and closed the door behind him and leaned his forehead against it. Then William indicated to Mabbot's chair. 'May I?'

Mabbot nodded.

'Can I ask where you got hold of that necklace?'

'I think you know that, sir.' Mabbot's voice trembled. He'd wanted to watch from the periphery, while Edwin Hales made his demands on this family and he remained the faithful servant. But he couldn't wait; now he had no other choice. William would not give him a reference and he had nowhere to go.

'Look, Mabbot. I understand things, not to mention myself, have been difficult of late. I have not been here as much as I should and I have made your job difficult.'

Too late for apologies, thought Mabbot.

'That necklace belonged to Mr Hales. Well, his mother, Edith.'

Mabbot frowned. 'But... you can't have known—'

'Mr Hales has been to see me. He has told me everything.'

Mabbot shifted his feet and wriggled his toes, which tingled as if they'd been stood on. 'Everything, sir?' He gripped his hands, the sapphire stone bit into his palm.

'Yes, everything.'

'But—'

William raised his hand again to silence him. 'Do you want to tell me how that necklace is in your possession? Mr Hales told me he pawned the item.'

Mabbot's head bubbled with anger. 'He was going to expose you, and your father. He wanted to have his revenge. He told me!' His voice no longer trembled. He held the necklace up in front of William's face. 'This was your father's pay off; this was how he valued the life of a young woman.'

William squinted. 'Mr Hales has returned to Scotland, Mabbot.'

'But you have to pay!' Mabbot shouted. 'Your father ruined everything.'

'Indeed, but I cannot be held responsible for my father's misdemeanours. I can only put my own wrongs right, or attempt to.' William's face crumpled for a second. 'I am sorry, I did not know that you were involved in the unfortunate circumstances.'

'I cared for Edith Hales, I planned to,' Mabbot's throat tightened. 'Well, it matters no longer what I planned.' 'But when Mr Hales turned up, it seemed to be that some kind of justice might be served.'

William nodded and lowered his gaze. 'I'm sorry, Mabbot. I had no idea—'

'No, I do not expect you did.' Mabbot sighed almost resigned. He was a servant, not one with the authority to question the odd behaviour and eccentricities of his employer, despite his desire.

'I cannot provide you with full explanations, and anyway that would compromise your position more. I thought that we could work our way through this. But now I realise that your position is untenable.' William stood. 'I ask that the necklace be returned to my family. I will pay a handsome sum.'

'Will you?' Mabbot sneered but his courage was fading. 'And a reference? I would need a reference.'

William coughed. 'Of course, I will provide a reference, on one condition.'

'Condition?'

'I've promised to put things right, Mabbot. I would ask your assurance that you will not use the information you have against this family. In writing.'

Mabbot snorted. 'You are not in a position to demand conditions.'

'Indeed,' agreed William running a finger around his collar. 'But I still like to think that you are essentially a man of honour.'

'Unlike some,' Mabbot retorted. 'Perhaps after I have been able to review the…' Mabbot shrugged his shoulders, '…the severance pay and my reference I will consider doing what you ask.' He gathered the necklace up into his hands. 'Until then, the necklace remains in my possession.'

William stared at Mabbot's stony face before smiling tightly and walking out of the room.

CHAPTER NINETEEN

William looked upwards to the huge domed ceiling of the new ballroom. He could almost hear the tinkling of ivory keys, the rhythmic beat of the drum and the laughter of the dancers spinning around the room. It was quite huge, in fact far too huge, thought William as he strode around the highly varnished floor. But it was in memory of Henry, his brother. His last gift to the estate, and William wasn't going to change a thing.

'William, here you are! I've been looking all over for you.' Lottie swept across the ballroom floor, dressed in a slate grey gown, edged in magenta. She fought hard to honour the severe black required for mourning but she needed some colour. It was in her nature. 'I have a quarrel to pick with you.'

'Oh, yes?' William tucked his hands behind his back and walked forward to meet her. She reached up on her tiptoes and kissed each cheek. He could smell the lavender water she and Amelia favoured and his heart ached.

'Mabbot.' Lottie looked sternly at him, like a stern school mistress. He straightened the smile that had begun to form.

'Oh, Mabbot.' He waved his hand. 'What's there to quarrel about? You didn't like the man and now he's gone.'

'Well, yes, but he stole away in the middle of the night! One day he's here stalking around like the resident ghost, next thing he's disappeared like the flame of a candle puffed out by the wind.'

'You are so fanciful, my dear sister. He wanted to take up another position.' William started to walk and Lottie picked up her skirt to follow him. 'I don't remember where and I'm not sure why. I haven't been altogether the best of masters.'

'Pah,' snorted Lottie. 'Mabbot enjoyed his status here. I cannot believe he could find better. The servants are gossiping you know, some mischief or another.'

William stopped and turned to face her. 'Mischief? You've been listening to too much gossip. You know what it's like, the story becomes distorted by the time it reaches our ears.'

Lottie pouted. 'I don't listen to gossip. It's just that everyone seems to be disappearing…' her voice trailed off and William realised she must be thinking about Edwin.

'And there will be new people in their place, Lottie. It's not like you to be wistful.'

'I am not wistful. It's…' She fiddled with the lace on her cuff. 'Oh, it doesn't matter. I am being silly.' She beamed a broad smile that did not reach her eyes. 'Amelia arrives this morning. She is a very strong and determined young woman.'

The silence echoed around the empty space. William closed his eyes and let out a long sigh.

'And Henry?'

'Oh, he's adorable! He has the most engaging smile. Just like his father.'

Hot tears stung William's eyes. 'I cannot wish he never existed. Whatever I have done, I know it was selfish but Henry is—'

Lottie took his hand and squeezed tight. 'Of course, and I know that this is difficult but you are doing the right thing. I share the blame. I should never have encouraged you—'

'Oh, Lottie. You cannot blame yourself. This was totally my doing. After all, it was a bit of fun to begin with. Then it escalated and the more I lived as Reuben, the more comfortable I felt. Now I realise that it was a sham life, I already had a life that I should have been content with. I was selfish and arrogant, exactly the opposite of the character I hoped I was. I am a fool.' William put his head in his hands. 'But it is impossible, Lottie. How do I explain about the upheaval and the lies I told, I'm not sure I can face her.'

'Excuses, William. These are hurdles to overcome. I'm not saying it will be easy. Don't rush into things. I think Amelia's love for Reuben is encompassing. In fact, I know it.' Lottie fixed him with a determined stare.

'Indeed, I hope so. I do swear, Lottie that you have some of mother's traits.' He smiled as he held out his arm. She faltered for a heartbeat, her eyes wide, and her mouth half open in retort.

'Perhaps,' she admitted as they walked out of the ballroom. 'But I don't believe you about Mabbot's disappearance, there is something you are not telling me. I won't give up, you know.' William had no doubt about his sister's last remark.

*

Amelia stepped down onto the platform with Henry in her arms, grateful that he had slept most of the way. She'd spent the journey wondering if she had made the right decision. When Lady Charlotte offered her the post of governess to the children on the estate, it was as if she had been given a lifeline.

The porter collected their luggage. 'The coach from the Abbey is ready for you ma'am.' He lifted his hat a little and tickled Henry under the chin. 'And aren't you a handsome young man if ever I've seen one?' Henry turned away and buried his face into Amelia's chest. He had been a little withdrawn since the fire. It had been almost eight months and every day Amelia had expected Reuben to reappear with some kind of explanation. She could not believe that he would leave her and Henry in this darkness, like a shadow that always followed her. With all her heart she hoped that here at Clomber Henry would have a rich childhood full of opportunities not to be found in the city.

'Thank you,' Amelia said as he loaded their cases. She scrabbled in her purse and thrust a shilling into his hand. 'No, ma'am it's what I do – I'm just doing my job. Save that for the little 'un here.' Amelia smiled and climbed into the carriage.

The driveway to the Abbey was long and winding and she sat with Henry on her knee as they both looked out of the window. At the edge of the woodland, rabbits with their tiny young hopped and tripped, nervously looking out for predators and under a large oak tree, a peacock of vivid blues and greens charmed its mate, extending its vast tail. Amelia pointed these all out to Henry, his bright eyes blinking in amazement.

'Oh, Henry. I do hope you will be happy here.' Amelia kissed the soft hair on her son's head, a faint white streak ran through the chestnut locks. The carriage pulled up outside a large set of stone stairs, which led to a huge covered veranda and the biggest front door Amelia had ever seen. The Abbey was vast and sprawling; an imposing edifice that loomed down on them. Amelia shuddered, it gave her the impression of being alone despite its vastness. The windows were too numerous to count, the lower ones framed by climbing roses in dusky pink and lemon yellow. A young woman dressed in grey skipped down the stairs towards them. It was Lady Charlotte.

'No, stay in the carriage, I will take you straight to your lodgings. You must be tired after your journey! Plenty of time to explore this old mausoleum later.' Lady Charlotte stepped up and sat next to Amelia. 'How lovely to see you, my dear, and Henry! My, how you have grown?'

'I can't thank you enough,' began Amelia. 'It really is most kind of you when you have gone out of your way for us already.' Her young son stared blankly at Lady Charlotte. She pulled Henry towards her.

'He's a bit tired, too young to take it all in but I'm sure given a little time he'll come round.'

'Oh, I'm sure he will. And there is nothing to thank me for, it is you who is doing me a favour. I have so long wanted to provide the children on the estate with some sort of education. It only seems right and proper. They are all excited at the prospect. I expect their mothers are busy scrubbing in places that have never seen soap and water. You're going to be the talk of the town, my dear Amelia!'

Amelia winced. 'I do hope not. I don't want any fuss. But I must admit I am looking forward to meeting the children. It feels a privilege to be able to participate in helping others.'

'Look, we're here!' exclaimed Lady Charlotte as they stopped outside a small cottage with a thatched roof, its overhang casting a shadow around the walls. A small wooden fence and archway led to the front door and a white jasmine curled itself around the wood, its aroma bursting from the delicate star-like flowers.

'But this is beautiful, more than I ever imagined.' It was as if she was in a dream and soon she would wake to the doom and gloom of London.

'The estate workers cottages are along that path.' Lady Charlotte pointed to a stone walkway, 'and of course the abbey is not far.' They turned to see the huge mansion that sat on a small mound surrounded by a perfect green lawn. In the shadows of a huge oak tree, stood a man, tall and straight backed, holding the reins of a large horse.

'Come on, I will show you inside…' Lottie followed her gaze. 'Oh, and that is the Duke, my brother. He has inherited the title and responsibilities since my father died. He wasn't born to be a Duke. That was a place reserved for our older brother, Henry. But you don't want to hear about all that! You will meet him some time.'

Amelia listened and shaded her face with one hand as she continued to stare towards the oak tree.

'He is an extremely shy man,' Lottie continued, taking her hand and pulling her gently into the cottage. 'I am sure he will pluck up enough courage to introduce himself when he's ready. You must excuse our family.' Lottie lowered her head towards Amelia's ear. 'We can be a little eccentric, I'm afraid.'

*

The following week sped by as Amelia made the cottage her own. Everything was very understated and simple yet created a sense of homeliness. It was as if the place had been built for her. The main bedroom overlooked the duck pond and she loved to show Henry the tiny ducklings swimming in a line behind their mother. His room was next door and large enough to sleep at least three children. Steep stairs led straight into the living room where a small writing desk, full of ink, paper and quills sat in once corner. However, her favourite place was the bright, small kitchen with a stone floor and a door that led into a garden planted with a small selection of vegetables.

Every day since she had arrived, she observed the tall Duke, standing in the same spot in the shadows under the oak tree. They had not yet met and Amelia was intrigued by the figure who appeared to be interested in her arrival. She squinted her eyes trying to bring his face into focus without success. The young girl, Sarah Nuttall, whom Lady Charlotte suggested could mind Henry when she started teaching the children, only had good words to say about him but would reveal very little. Henry took to her without a fuss holding out his chubby arms whenever she arrived with a broad smile on her face. 'I'm used to youngsters,' Sarah had explained as she picked Henry up. 'Havin' seven little brothers and sisters!'

Amelia was looking forward to starting her role as governess. Lady Charlotte had made sure that there were plenty of slates, chalk and a globe. And one of the old stables had been cleared and cleaned and furnished with two large tables and chairs. Not that Henry did not fill her waking day, but he was a constant reminder of his father, which could at once bring her into memories of great joy and then a torrent of tears. She truly believed that Reuben would return to her one day. She had to believe, for Henry's sake.

She heard Sarah's footsteps running down the path. She came every day after lunch when her duties at the big house were finished and Amelia welcomed her arrival.

'Afternoon, Miss Amelia.' Sarah's voice fell to a whisper as Amelia pointed to the sleeping Henry. The young girl grinned and put a hand to her mouth.

'I'm going to take a walk to the duck pond, I won't be long. You will be all right here, won't you?'

'Course I will. Your Henry's as good a gold. Better than my ma's brood. They pinch and scream all the time.' Sarah tickled Henry's chin causing two large dimples to appear in his smiling cheeks. 'Be careful out at the pond. I don't like water. I was saved once from drownin' in that pond. I was going under all the time, thought I was goin' to die I did. I don't go near now, it scares me rotten. But he saved me.'

'Oh, how dreadful. Who saved you?' Amelia asked tying a bonnet under her chin.

'Young Lord William as he was then, before he was Duke. He jumped in and saved me. If it hadn't been for him, I wouldn't be here.' Amelia listened as Sarah recounted the day she had fallen into the pond and her curiosity regarding the young Duke increased.

When Amelia returned from her walk, the huge horse she had seen standing under the oak tree every day with its master, munched away at the grass by the gate. She stopped in her tracks and held her breath. She had never met a Duke before. How should she behave? Should she curtsy? Amelia heard the gurgled chuckling of her son through an open window and all intrigue about meeting the Duke disappeared. As she closed the door, she pulled at the ribbons from the bonnet and automatically adjusted her hair.

'Sarah!' she called. 'I'm back.'

There was no reply and she followed the gurgling sounds through to the living room. A tall gentleman dressed in a long voluminous riding coat stood at the window where she had paused outside. His back faced her and from over his shoulder, Henry beamed a smile and held out chubby fingers.

'Oh, my word. I'm sorry, Sarah should be—'

'I sent her home.' The deep voice had a familiar richness and for a second she almost thought it could be…no. Her heart fluttered and then paused. Of course, it could not.

'Right, I'm sorry. I'm Amelia, Amelia Chambers and this is my son, Henry.' The man continued looking out of the window. 'My Lord,' she added as an afterthought.

'Please call me William. I am most pleased to meet you.' The voice shook a little as the man turned round, holding Henry out in front of him. Amelia took him in her arms and hugged him tight. 'I hope he hasn't been a nuisance,' she said and stepped aside to face the Duke. She gasped and held a hand up to her mouth. The man had a silver white streak through his hair similar to Henry's but more defined, and his right eye drooped slightly. He did not have sideburns or a moustache but if she had a bible at that moment she would have sworn on it that he was Reuben.

*

The urge to turn and run was most intense and William gripped the back of a chair. She looked beautiful even with the dark rings under her eyes, and the pale skin. She had lost some weight also, the dress around her shoulders hung in folds. He swallowed hard.

'Amelia, I am sorry. I have some explaining to do. I regret, more than you can ever know, hurting you. It was never my intention.'

Amelia shook her head, as if she did not want to hear what he had to say. 'I'm sorry it's just that you look like…' She faltered. 'What happened to your eye?' Her gaze fell to the floor. 'Forgive me, for being so forward. It is very rude of me to ask such a personal question.' Henry struggled in her arms and she walked over to the pram and sat him in it. She spoke in a singsong voice and placed a rattle in his hand, which he shook excitedly.

'No, it is not rude.' William ran a hand through his hair. 'I … I am aw-aw-aware this is all going to sound rather out of s-s-sorts.' William cursed his stammer and wished he had not walked into the cottage that afternoon. He was not prepared. But he had been unable to keep away, so drawn at the thought of seeing her. His heart still ached with the sense of emptiness without her in his life. When he had seen Henry out in the garden with Sarah, he had acted without thinking. Now he was stumbling through an explanation that would shock Amelia. His finger lingered over his eye. 'It was an injury at birth, apparently a difficult birth. My mother, the Dowager Duchess, suffered far more than I did.'

'And the streak through your hair?' Amelia ran her fingers along the white strip of hair on her sons head.

'A family trait. Quite unusual. It has been in the family for generations.' William longed to gather her up in his arms.

Amelia was not listening. She grasped the pram handle. 'I don't, I don't understand.'

'I need to explain myself properly. I have to tell you all about Reuben Chambers and most of all I want to tell you that I am sorry and that I love you with every part of my heart. I need to ask you to listen to me. Then you can do whatever you want. Throw me out if you wish. I have to explain.'

'You love me?' Amelia let out a small laugh. 'But how silly, we've only just met.' Her face flushed and she looked away from him. William wanted to kick himself for making such a mess of it.

'And how do you know – did you know – my husband?' Amelia asked in a small voice as he took her hand and led her to the sofa. She sat down and he pulled up the chair from the writing desk.

'No, I didn't know Reuben. I was Reuben. I was Reuben Chambers and I was your husband. I am Henry's father.'

*

The light had faded by the time William had finished his story. Amelia sat and listened as he requested, watching his face contort with the pain of his confession, seeing the familiar tiny mannerisms that she had observed in Reuben.

'But how could you betray me?' Amelia twisted her hands in her lap. 'I was distraught when I first heard about the fire, but then, when Lady Charlotte told me you might be missing and not dead after all, well then a flicker of hope remained in my heart.' She banged at her chest with a fist.

'I am sorry, I cannot explain myself any better, but you took my heart and held it in your hands, Amelia. At first I admit, I married you because I wanted to protect you from a bleak future. I wanted to save you, to have a purpose for my deception rather than admit it was a sham. But then I found myself deeply in love with you, in fact I suspect I had been since the day you walked into the shop. But with the arrival of Edwin, well that changed everything.' William took her hands in his. 'I can only ask for your forgiveness, Amelia. I do not expect it, nor think that I deserve it, not for one moment.'

'But, how did you expect to keep your two lives separate? How did you think you could continue with all the responsibilities here and that as a father...?' Amelia sobbed and put her head on William's shoulder. It felt like Reuben's had, strong and protective.

'I know, it was stupid of me. You and little Henry are the most precious things in my life and always will be. I didn't agree with Charlotte's plans to bring you here at first. I wanted to keep running away. But now, I am glad. Please, Amelia I want to watch my son, our son grow, I want to make things right.'

As she listened she heard Reuben, she heard the confession of the man she loved and still loved. The father of her son and the man who had saved her from a life of ruin in the poor house. She listened to him torture himself for his misdemeanours and although she could never understand why he had done what he did, she knew she would forgive him.

'Edwin Hales was your brother?' she asked, pulling herself away from him, trying to create a distance. William lit some candles and went to stand by the small fireplace, one foot resting on the grate.

'Edwin is my half-brother and I can fully understand why he wanted to make my family pay. Unfortunately he wasn't the only victim to suffer from my father's actions.'

Amelia frowned. 'There were others?'

'No, but some of my staff remember Edwin's mother. You see, at a place like Clomber Abbey the servants are like a family. They look out for one another, sometimes they are cruel, but like any other group of people they have to learn how to live together. Sometimes they fall in love.' Williams's voice dropped to a low tone, his gaze fixed on her from under his eyelashes. The stammer that had peppered his confession at first had evaporated, now replaced by a determined delivery, measured yet thick with emotion.

'And your mother, the Duchess – sorry, the Dowager Duchess – she knows all about his existence?' Amelia shifted her position; her back ached with sitting stiffly and the effort of putting all the pieces together, rather like completing a large complex jigsaw.

'Yes, she does, but she will never be able to accept Edwin's identity. It hurt her that Papa could betray her in such a public and unforgivable way.' The word 'betray' seemed to bounce around the room and William clenched his fists. 'And I have done no better. I have betrayed you, Amelia, and our son. I shall never forgive myself.'

'But, William, I too have deceived you. How could you have known when you made those arrangements that our marriage was not legal because of my age? We have both kept secrets from one another. Not the solid foundations for an honest relationship between man and wife?' She smiled wryly. 'And for that I too am sorry, but at the same time my heart is lighter without the deception.'

Amelia walked over to the window. Many of the mullions at the Abbey shone with the warm glow of gaslights. They lit up one by one, like square beacons leading the way. As the birds twittered their goodnights, Amelia rubbed at her throbbing temple yet her heart was light. William's footsteps stole up behind her and his warm breath stroked her neck. Amelia shivered and turned. William's head bent towards her and she stepped to the side, unable to trust her reaction and her overwhelming desire to kiss him.

'The evening is cool. I must go and fetch a shawl. Can I bring you any refreshments?'

William ran a finger over his droopy eye. 'No, I couldn't eat. I feel exhausted, as I'm sure you must.'

When Amelia returned, William stood in the dusky candlelight clasping his hands together in front of him. Amelia lit the gas lamp in the window and watched the light come to life, throwing shapes on the walls and floors. As she stepped back, she almost fell over William's feet and he put out his arm to steady her. Amelia gasped as he took her hand in his; his touch reminded her of the embraces on the day of her marriage to Reuben. A marriage not recognised in the eyes of the law. She had accepted his offer in full knowledge that she was underage. And she knew that should she bear a child that it would be born out of wedlock. But she ignored all her head had told her and blindly followed her heart. She squeezed William's hand; she had no regrets about that.

'I am sorry, Amelia. I have been an arrogant and selfish man and I don't deserve your forgiveness. However, as I think you know, I do love you, I have always loved you and I would honour my proposal to make you my wife. My legal wife.'

Amelia searched his face. 'I don't need any charity, Reub… I mean, Lord William. I accepted a job here as governess. And anyway, I don't think your mother would approve.'

'Things and people change,' William replied. A small smile formed at his lips. 'And as Duke am I not allowed to choose my own wife?'

Amelia wanted to laugh but she straightened her back. 'From what you tell me, no. William, I am serious. So much has happened. We need time to think about things. I cannot take it all in at once.'

'Tell me you don't care for me,' William insisted.

'I do care, more than you will ever imagine possible. Oh, William, my heart is bursting with happiness that Reuben is not dead, yet at the same time, he will never return. And as for you, as for William, his life is as far from mine as the stars in the sky.' Amelia could not stop the tears from falling. 'You say you do not deserve my forgiveness, but what else is left if not? I am not sure you want a Duke's life for your son, do you? It is not what you desired. How can we place that responsibility on Henry, who like you wasn't born to inherit the title?' William increased his hold on Amelia's hand until she pulled away.

'You cannot begin to imagine how my mind is spinning at the moment, it has made me all a bit faint. You must understand that?' She rubbed at her wrist.

'I'm sorry; I didn't mean to hurt you.'

Amelia shook her head. 'You cannot hurt me, William.'

'I do not want our son to be a bastard. I do not want him punished for my mistakes, my indulgences. And I do want to honour my vows to you, Amelia.'

Amelia gazed out of the window at the Abbey, now twinkling with light. Did she really belong here? At this moment, she did not know what she thought.

'It's late, William. We are both tired and I have to be ready for the estate children. Let us bide our time. Let the dust settle before we make any decisions.'

William nodded and released a large sob, burying his face in his hands. Amelia rushed to him, took him in her arms and together they stood united until the candle light expired.

CHAPTER TWENTY

Four Years Later

William's gaze followed Lottie as she spun around the ballroom with her future husband. Lottie's forthcoming marriage to Alasdair Forsyth was to take place the following week in London and promised to be a huge affair. But she had insisted that they host a celebration in advance where everyone on the estate could attend. All the workers wore their Sunday best and were in high spirits; merry with the effects of rum punch and their bellies full with game pie, roast partridge and fresh fruit. The family planned leave after this dance, allowing the staff and their families to relax in their own company.

William spied Amelia in the far corner with Henry. He wore a navy blue sailor's suit and his brown hair, which reached the lobes of his ears, was brushed to a bright sheen. Amelia held his hands and took him through the dance steps. Henry focused his gaze on his feet, the tip of his tongue protruding through his lips as he concentrated on copying his mother. She clapped enthusiastically as he came to a stop and his son turned and beamed a bright smile in his direction. William waved.

'Your sister dances well considering she always complained about her tutor.'

William had not seen his mother come to stand beside him.

'I know, but you know that's Lottie. She does everything well when she puts her mind to it.'

'Indeed.' The Duchess sniffed. 'Including her choice of husband. Mr Forsyth will be of great use to you in parliament.'

William glanced at his mother. He still loathed some of the duties that came with his role as Duke, but with someone like Alasdair, a gifted and intelligent politician, it would certainly make his role easier. It never harmed to have friends in the right places. Lottie had already immersed herself in several of her fiancé's commitments to charitable organisations and was making an impression.

'He already is, I assure you. Alasdair is well respected, even by the more senior members.' William's focused once again on Henry and Amelia at the other side of the room.

'And the governess, Mrs Chambers? I understand her work with the estate children has produced astounding results?'

William tore his gaze away from Henry to look at his mother. The corners of her mouth upturned into a small smile and her eyes twinkled in the gaslight.

'Yes, most of them can now read and complete simple mathematical problems.'

'Including the girls?' His mother arched an eyebrow.

William coughed to hide his amusement. 'Yes, including the girls. It will offer them more opportunity when they are older.'

'I suppose so,' sighed his mother. 'I do hope that the opportunities are there for them when they are ready to enter the world. It would be disappointing if not.'

William nodded his agreement. His father had been scornful of educating the children, stating that they would be frustrated with the knowledge they couldn't possibly hope to use. William hoped he would never become so short sighted.

'She is very charming, isn't she?' His mother continued. 'She would make someone an excellent wife.' William stared at the polished toes of his boots. 'I understand that there is some question regarding the legality of her first marriage which makes her an eligible wife to be?' The Duchess scanned the room, raising her parasol to Lottie who still whirled around the floor.

'Eligible for whom, Mother?' William asked raising his head.

'Let us not play games. That boy needs a father, and I am no fool, William. There has been enough fuel for gossip within this family for far too long. And a mother can tell when her son is in love.' She took a sharp intake of breath. 'Though in my time, love had very little to do with a marriage prospect.'

William stepped back, surprised by his mother's openness and unsure of what to say. Since his father's death, his mother and her actions surprised him on a regular basis. Lottie suggested that she was making up for times lost. William wanted to believe that and they had all changed since those hard days.

'Well, William?' She took his arm as the music came to a finish and they went to greet Lottie and Alasdair.

'I've already asked, a long time ago but—'

'Ask again. Some women have a habit of changing their minds.' Indeed, thought William, shocked at her change of heart. But she had mellowed since the death of his father, as she had told him in the chapel. He smiled as she squeezed his hand and then turned to greet Lottie.

*

A week after Lottie's celebration, Amelia watched Henry running around with the other estate children, happy and content. Today was his fifth birthday and she was pleased that he had the company of those his own age. He had taken some time to come out of his shell, but then he was like his father. Amelia had not seen William since the party and she realised that she missed him.

The truth about Reuben had been very hard to comprehend at the time. A small part of her had wished that there had been another woman; it would have somehow made things easier. With each passing year her life at 37 Queens Row and the King Street Bazaar with those ornaments and figurines was as distant as the faraway lands from which they had come. At the end of the day, her love for William was stronger than it had been for Reuben. The two men's lives had blended and her devotion for them both alongside.

She held her breath as Henry tried to follow the older boys and climb the tree. His little feet slipping as he scrambled to find a grip. One of the taller boys took his foot and hoisted him onto the lowest branch of the old fir.

'Look at me, Mama! Look!'

Amelia waved. 'Don't go any higher, Henry, and do keep still! We don't want you falling out of a tree on your birthday.'

Amelia began to lay out the picnic, throwing a huge chequered rug onto the floor. It was a lovely early summer's day, the egg yolk-coloured sun, round and warm, and a gentle breeze rustled through the leaves. She turned her face to the warmth from the sky, leaned back on both arms and closed her eyes.

'Mama, Mama I won the race!' panted Henry plonking himself down beside her and breathing noisily through his nose.

'Well done.' She hugged him tight to her, his heart beating against her chest. Henry struggled to be set free. 'I bet you are thirsty from all that running.'

He drained the beaker she offered and then ran back to the small group of boys. 'Let's have another race and I have to win, because it's my birthday!' he shouted bossily.

Amelia's thought turned to her mother who had not been in touch since the day she left Queens Row. How could she reject her only daughter and grandson? Long ago, she had accepted that her mother was much too selfish to change now. Amelia vowed not be like that with Henry. He was the first thing she thought of when she awoke and the last before sleep claimed her. Since she had become a mother herself, she saw things differently. She was no longer the young girl with nowhere to go and no-one who cared enough. There was nothing she would not do or sacrifice for Henry.

She shielded her eyes from the sun with one hand and watched Henry as he prepared himself for the next race. He kept darting off too early and the other children protested loudly. 'Cheat' they shouted with voices full of laughter. Amelia waited, they would sort themselves out and Henry would have to play by the rules. Being an only child had not gifted him with the concept of sharing, but he would soon learn, one way or another.

Behind the children, she saw a figure approach leading a small horse. She peered through the sunshine, she could not make them out. But when they walked into the shade offered by the huge oak trees, she recognised William. A warm glow settled in her chest. She stood up and walked to greet him.

*

William collected the pony from the stables, gave it a final brush and added a tiny saddle and reins. She nuzzled at his pocket smelling the sugar cubes he had collected from the kitchen.

'What is it, what do you want?' he teased and then dipped a hand and offered it, her soft velvety nose stroking his palm. 'Come on then, we have to go and find your new master. I do hope you like him!' He clicked his tongue and the young mare obediently followed as he walked out of the stables and along the path that ran past the underground tunnels.

In the years that had passed since the disappearance of Reuben, William had thrown himself into his role as Duke, determined to prove to himself, as well as his family, that he was worthy of the position. His reputation as a good employer ensured that the estate workers were loyal and hardworking and in return, he ensured that the pay was fair and their accommodation developed and maintained to good standards. After all, happy workers ensured that the Abbey and the grounds were kept in good condition.

The families had, at first, viewed the appointment of Amelia to educate the children with some suspicion. But she had soon won them over, with her pleasant approach and natural way in engaging boys and girls in wanting to learn. Sarah Nuttall was one of her finest achievements. In return for looking after Henry, Amelia had given her private tuition and had discovered that she had a natural talent for numbers. Sarah had shown such ability that she soon outgrew the lessons and Lottie had taken her on to help her with the charitable accounts she would be responsible for as Alasdair's wife.

William sighed and made his way through the meadow, the shouts of excited children becoming louder and louder. Since the night of Lottie's celebration, he had thought of nothing else but the conversation with his mother. Every night, whilst trying to seek solace in sleep, he practised proposing marriage again to Amelia. Each time he dreamt of being rejected and now wondered if he could cope with her refusal.

He climbed up the bank to see Amelia sitting on a picnic rug, laughing at Henry. He brought the pony to a stop, taking advantage of the moment. She looked as beautiful as she had done the first time he saw her. His heart ached with longing. But he had to respect her wishes, even his mother could not change that.

Henry spotted him and ran towards him, long arms and legs whirling like a windmill. 'William, it's my birthday!' he shouted at the top of his voice.

William laughed, 'I know it is, young Henry. Happy birthday!' He bent down and swept him up and onto the pony. Henry's eyes were wide with anticipation and excitement – not a sign of fear. That was a good start. Amelia walked up to join them.

'And it's Lord William, Henry. Even on your birthday.' William glanced at her. 'It's only fair to the other children; they call you Lord William.'

William shrugged as he shortened the stirrups and adjusted the reins. 'Hold the straps like this.' William demonstrated to Henry. 'Yes, that's good.'

'Is this mine, Lord William?' Henry asked, stroking the silky mane and looking from William and back to his mother. William smiled at Amelia. 'Well, if your mother agrees you can keep her, then yes, she is yours!'

Henry looked pleadingly at his mother who frowned and then broke into a huge smile. 'Of course, darling. But, on one condition.' Henry nodded and squirmed in the saddle. 'As long as you share her with your friends.' Henry continued to nod and pulled at the reins gently.

The group of boys stood around Henry. William knelt down to the tallest, oldest looking one. 'Would you take him round the field very slowly?' He handed him the guide rope. 'Then I'm sure Henry will let you all have a go.' The boy took the rope and the group of children walked off, Henry chattering away.

William took Amelia's hand and kissed it. She blushed and shivered.

'You look tired,' she said as they walked back to the picnic rug. 'Is there something bothering you?'

William sat down, crossed his legs and picked up a sandwich. 'Well, yes and no. But it doesn't matter. It's Henry's birthday, everyone has to be happy. He is a delight to be with, Amelia.' William tried to keep his tone light.

'He is and we are happy and settled here. I couldn't imagine bringing him up anywhere else.'

William chewed on the sandwich and went through his proposal again in his head. But all he heard was his stammer.

'I had a visitor yesterday,' Amelia said, sitting next to him, tucking her legs underneath her.

'Oh, yes?' mumbled William as he swallowed.

'Your mother.'

William licked the crumbs from his lips. 'My mother?' he repeated. 'And what did she want?' His heart fluttered inside his chest like the first time he asked Amelia to marry him.

'Oh, this and that. She was most gracious about my success with the children.'

'You have done a wonderful job,' William agreed. But his mother could have told her that at any time.

'And she mentioned that you might…' William took her hands and pulled her to her feet. Amelia looked up into his eyes, her face flushed. 'Oh, that you would… make a proposal?' She turned away, trying to hide a smile that formed.

'Amelia, you are torturing me!' William groaned as he pulled her back to face him.

'William, please don't fret. I cannot tease you any longer, as much as you deserve it. The answer is yes.'

'Yes?' whispered William. 'You mean, yes you will marry me?'

'There is no greater honour.' Amelia smiled as William picked her up at the waist and spun her round and round.

'Mama! William! I've ridden all way around the lake!' Henry shouted as the horse and her followers stopped in front of them, their gaze focused on William and Amelia.

'Well done.' Amelia clapped as William placed her gently on the ground.

'Hurrah!' Henry shouted. 'And one day I shall be a Duke riding around here, just like William!'

*

'You are a hard man to track down.' William sat in the chair the waiter pulled out for him.

'I didn't expect you to want to see me again. I kept my word, as promised.' Edwin Hales pretended to scan the menu but William sensed his gaze cast over him.

'Yes, I know you kept your word and for that I thank you. Now I know my way around Edinburgh as well as I do London, scouring the place for you. But no matter, here we are.'

Edwin nodded. 'This is the finest restaurant, as you requested, and of course that is reflected in the prices.' He tapped at the leather bound folder.

'Do not worry about that. Please allow me to take care of the bill.'

Edwin placed his menu on the table and made a cradle with his fingers. 'I read in the paper that Lady Charlotte is married?' He shifted his gaze around the room before returning to face William. Hot tears pricked at the distant memories. Edwin swallowed. 'I presume he is a good man?'

William raised his glass. 'Yes, Lottie is happy. Alasdair Forsyth is one of the finest men I know. He has a great future in front of him, and with Lottie as his wife, he will be well supported. She busies herself with his charitable obligations and is becoming very good at wheedling money out of local businesses.'

Edwin tried to smile but could not quite manage it. 'I am very pleased for her,' his voice was thick with emotion. 'Truly, I am.'

William nodded and replaced his glass. 'And you, Edwin. Have you—'

'No. There is no-one. I am afraid that I have set my sights too high.' He straightened his back and made a show of inspecting the cutlery. 'And Mrs Chambers?' Edwin hesitated. 'I am sorry, I shouldn't ask so many questions, I have a curious nature.'

William shuffled in his seat. 'Of course, not at all. Amelia has agreed to become my wife. It will come of no surprise to you that her first marriage is not recognised in law. We shall be married in the spring. She and Henry, her—' William let out a deep breath. 'Our son. They live on the estate. She teaches the estate children to read and write and very good at it she is.'

This time Edwin beamed broadly. 'Congratulations, Lord William. I am most pleased that you worked things out, I toast your future happiness.' He raised his glass and took a small sip.

They ate lunch in a contemplative mood, stopping only to compliment the food. William wiped his mouth with the napkin and leaned back, satisfied.

'I'm sure you are wondering why I wanted to see you,' he said.

Edwin nodded as the waiter cleared their plates.

William waited until the crumbs had been swept from the cloth and two brandies set in front of them. 'I have a business proposition I would like to discuss with you.'

'A business proposition? With me?' Edwin frowned.

'Yes. My brother, Henry, and I ran a successful riding partnership up until his death. Since then, for various reasons – as you know – it has limped along. However, it is time to revitalise it in his honour. That is what he would have wanted.'

Edwin stared at William waiting for him to continue.

'I would like to offer you Henry's stake in the partnership.'

Edwin sat back as if the breath had been taken from him.

'There is no cost to you,' William hastened to add, worried that Edwin might think he was trying to sell him the share.

'You want to give me the share in your successful racing partnership?' Edwin asked in a voice that trembled. 'But why?'

William closed his eyes for a second. 'I cannot change my mother's stance in denying your existence. At least not whilst she is living. That does not mean I agree with her – we see things from different perspectives. For the Duchess, you are a reminder of the betrayal by my father, which hurt her deeply, more than she would ever admit.' William paused and played with the folds of his napkin. 'For me, you are the half-brother I never knew. Well, not until now, and I'd like to share this partnership with you, as I did with Henry.'

Edwin nodded, but William saw that he had yet to gain his trust. 'I understand that this must seem rather odd to you.' He reached inside his waistcoat pocket and withdrew a document, tied with a red ribbon. 'Therefore, I have taken the liberty of having a draft contract drawn up which guarantees your share in the partnership. I ask you to give it your serious consideration.'

Edwin took the paper from his hands and read it carefully. 'I don't know what to say—'

'There is nothing to say, Edwin. It can hardly put right anything that my father did to your mother and consequently to you. I would like you to join this partnership and help keep my...' William pondered. 'Or rather, our brother's spirit alive.' William checked his pocket watch. 'Is that the time? I must get to the station. My train leaves in an hour.' He turned to gain the waiter's attention.

Edwin hesitated and then put the contract in his pocket. 'My carriage is waiting,' his face coloured slightly. 'I must admit I wasn't going to stay and have lunch but it has been a most interesting time. I would like the opportunity to offer you my hospitality and a lift.'

By the time they arrived at the station, the light was beginning to fade. William and Edwin stood on the pavement, both lost for words.

'You will give it your consideration?' William asked, holding out his hand.

Edwin shook it and nodded. 'Yes, and I have. I would be delighted to join the partnership. I do not doubt that the contract is honour bound. It is a great opportunity.'

William patted Edwin on the shoulder. 'I can't tell you how much that means to me.' William fumbled in his cloak pocket. 'Oh, and one more thing before I go. This, I believe, belongs to you.' He thrust a box into Edwin's hand. 'I will be in touch soon about the partnership.'

Edwin squinted in the dim light as he opened the lid. Inside, resting on a black cushion of satin was the sapphire necklace. He looked up but William had disappeared into the shadows.

About The Author

Louise Charles is an accomplished author and has had stories and articles published in print and online.

Louise moved to rural Italy in 2007 to live 'the good life'. She founded the online writing group for expats, Writers Abroad, which has contributed to and published four anthologies, comprising short stories, essays and poetry, the profits of which are donated to book charities.

She is surrounded by her myriad characters from a rich genre who infiltrate her thoughts at all times of the night and day. Also keeping her company is her soul mate, Simon and their family of rescued pets, including: dogs, cats, kittens and chickens. She is a terminal people watcher on the rare occasions that she ventures from her desk.

The Duke's Shadow is her debut novel and the first chapter was long listed in the Flash 500 Novel Opening competition in 2013

Printed in Great Britain
by Amazon